Dark Isle:
The Final Battle

DarkIsle:
The Final Battle

D A Nelson

Published by
Strident Publishing Ltd
22 Strathwhillan Drive
The Orchard
Hairmyres
East Kilbride
G75 8GT

Tel: +44 (0)1355 220588
info@stridentpublishing.co.uk
www.stridentpublishing.co.uk

Published by Strident Publishing Limited, 2014
Text © D A Nelson, 2014
Cover art and design by Shona Grant

ISBN 978-1-905537-95-2

Typeset in Lucida by Andrew Forteath | Printed by CPI Books

The publisher acknowledges support from Creative Scotland towards the publication of this title.

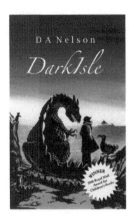

DarkIsle

Ten-year-old Morag is being held prisoner until a resourceful dodo and a talking rat accidentally rescue her. She jumps at the chance to join them on a dangerous mission to retrieve an ancient stone that protects their northern homeland.

The stone's thief is hiding off the west coast of Scotland. And only a stone dragon knows how to find him. Together, these four friends journey to a mysterious island beyond the horizon, where danger and glory await. Along the way she finds clues to the disappearance of her parents ten years before.

ISBN 978-1-905537-05-1
hardback, RRP £12.99
ISBN 978-1-905537-04-4
paperback, RRP £6.99
ISBN 978-1-905537-47-1
ebook

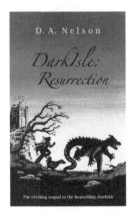

DarkIsle: Resurrection

Two months after saving The Eye of Lornish, Morag is adjusting to life in the secret northern kingdom of Marnoch Mor.

But dark dreams are troubling her and a spate of unexplained events prove that even with the protection of her friends—Shona the dragon, Bertie the dodo and Aldiss the rat— Morag is still not safe from harm...

ISBN 978-1-905537-18-1
paperback, RRP £6.99
ISBN 978-1-905537-49-5
ebook

For Mum and Dad

Chapter 1

The red witch hurried along the cold corridor of the castle, a nasty smile playing about her lips. She had stayed up late doing a bit of research in the library and had come across something she thought would interest her father, Devlish; something to help him wreak his revenge on that little upstart Morag MacTavish. Mephista pursed her lips as she thought of the girl who had once again escaped her clutches — the girl she had recently found out was a princess of Marnoch Mor.

"Princess! That's a laugh," Mephista muttered to herself as she hurried up to the wooden doorway that led into her father's chamber. "*I* should have become a princess of Marnoch Mor, not Morag. And certainly not her mother!"

She clutched the spellbook tightly to her chest. The book had been hidden in a crumbling box in the darkest part of the extensive library, but Mephista had found it all the same. Beneath its flaking, fragile cover were spells of such power and evil that the witch could hardly believe their strength. She inhaled deeply, enjoying its musty dusty smell. *I'll get you back, Morag MacTavish*, she thought as she shifted the book into one arm and lifted the other to knock on the bedroom door. *You see if I don't.*

Mephista's knuckle was a hair's width from the dark wood of the door when she paused it in mid-air. Something about the tone of the conversation inside made her want to listen.

Her father was deep in discussion with Kang, a huge four-armed creature known as a Girallon. And, going by his angry outburst, it was clear to Mephista that her father was displeased with whatever Kang was telling him. Before she could stop herself, Mephista's natural nosiness took over. She stood at the door, which was slightly ajar, and listened, ears straining to hear what was being said.

"Why didn't you find me someone young and strong, Kang?" she heard her father snarl. Why did you give me *this* body? It's...it's getting worse, look at it? It's decaying far quicker than we expected."

"I'm sorry, your liege, it was the best I could do in the circumstances. I thought you would appreciate being in the body of a man who held such magical power in life...I...I thought..." Kang said in a low voice.

"You thought? You *thought*? You thought nothing!" snapped the wizard. "Look at it! It's melting! Great clods of skin come off every time I move. You should have got me someone younger! Get me someone younger! Stronger! And better looking!"

"We need to wait until the next full moon before you can body shift, you know that, my liege. Until then...we'll make sure you look all right before you go out in public."

"Hmph," said the wizard patting his own cheeks as if trying to bring a bit of colour into them. "When I think of the bodies I've inhabited in the past...the strong warriors... and now I am reduced to this skinny weak man...!"

"It's not so bad my liege. A little make-up might help, or some plastic surgery..."

At the door, Mephista wondered. And the more she wondered the more she wanted to see what they were talking about, so she crept closer and put a curious eye to the gap.

At first all she could make out was the back of Kang, his four hairy arms folded in front of him, an ancient claymore dangling from his sword belt. He was wearing a bright blue velvet tunic decorated with silver embroidery in a swirling design, and black leather trousers. His ape-like feet were unshod. When he finally stepped out of the way she was able to get a view of her father, who was robed in scarlet and gold.

Devlish was standing in front of a tall mirror, scowling at his reflection. He turned this way and that as he adjusted his outfit, picking off pieces of fluff and adjusting the long coat and trousers that identified him as a warlock. He raised a thin white hand and combed his fingers through his blazing red hair, dislodging several strands.

"Do you see what I mean?" he snapped at the ape. He threw the hairs at him and scowled. "I'll be bald before the day is out."

"It's not that bad, my liege," the Girallon said. "There are just a few minor changes. No-one will notice if you don't tell them."

"Hmph," retorted the warlock.

He drew his hands over the angular shape of his cheekbones and a little skin peeled off. He leant forward and peered more closely at himself. As he did so, Mephista noticed something odd. Every time her father's face drew closer to the mirror, his reflection seemed to boil and contort. When he drew back, the reflection returned to normal. As she watched, and as Devlish remained ever more static, the reflection contorted some more and then settled into something so horrible it made the witch recoil in horror. It was the most hideous face she had ever seen: a grotesque mask of red leathery skin and the most evil yellow eyes. Its equally yellow teeth looked as if they had never been cleaned. The creature had two tusks protruding from its lips and wore heavy gold rings in its large ears.

That didn't look like her father! What *was* that thing? Was there something wrong with the mirror?

She looked again and saw the same thing happening. Her hand went to her mouth as she tried to make sense of it. Morag had claimed that Devlish's body had been taken over by a Mitlock Demon and she, Mephista, had laughed at the audacity of such a claim. But what if...? *No, it can't be*, the witch thought. *He's my father. I'm sure he is.*

However, although she thought the words, deep down the witch did not truly believe them. Indeed she had not believed them for some time now. She couldn't put her finger on when the little doubts had crept in, but crept in they had, like a sickness spreading over her. It could have been her father's new-found love of meat — Devlish had been a lifetime vegetarian. Perhaps it was the way he seemed not to recognise his courtiers. Or was it the sly looks he gave her — looks that made her flesh creep with disgust. And then there were the rumours. She couldn't believe them, but people were saying servants had gone missing and someone had even suggested they had ended up on Devlish's plate. She shuddered. No, not that. Surely he wasn't *eating* them?

She stepped back from the door and opened the ancient spellbook. She was sure there was something in there about old world creatures. She flicked through the pages and came across a passage about Mitlock Demons. She gasped. The ink drawing, carefully coloured in red, depicted exactly what she had seen in the mirror. *Oh my!* She felt sick. Her knees began to buckle. It pained her to admit it, but Morag had been right all along. This *was* a Mitlock Demon! *In her father's body!* She let out a small whimper.

"What was that?" the creature in her father's body snarled as he spun round to look at the door. Mephista drew back and pressed herself into the stone wall. She held her breath as she waited to be discovered.

***

That same night a few hundred miles away in a palace in the middle of Marnoch Mor, a young girl was trying to rest.

Sleep did not come easy to Morag at the best of times.

Every night, she tossed and turned as she worried about her future as the princess of Marnoch Mor and how she was going to free her parents from their painting prisons. This night was no different and Morag sighed in frustration as the midnight bell tolled on the palace clock. She kept her eyes closed and prayed for sleep. One o'clock came and went. Two o'clock. Finally, sometime before 3am, tiredness overcame her and she fell asleep.

However, it was a slumber of horror and fear. Lying in her huge four poster bed on the first floor of the palace, Morag was again visited by the ghastly vision of a white-faced warlock full of accusations and revenge. Since her battle with Devlish some months before, Morag's sleep had been haunted by him. Sometimes her dreams re-ran her skirmish with him on the slippery pier at Murst's cold beach. There the Eye of Lornish, the magical stone that protected Marnoch Mor, had overcome her, forcing her to say the words that had brought about the evil warlock's end. Occasionally, they involved Devlish chasing her through Murst Castle intent on taking her life. But more recently the warlock had come to her only as a kind of floating head and he was back again tonight, his eyes wild and full of passion. He seemed to be shouting abuse at her, a tirade of foul words meant to distress and disarm. Except that no words came.

"What?" Morag muttered in her sleep. "What are you saying? I can't hear you."

Devlish's mouth opened and shut as he ranted. But there was only silence and Morag could not read his tortured lips.

"What? What is it?"

Again, the warlock shouted, but no sound came.

"I don't know what you're saying!"

With a look of sheer frustration, the spirit gave up and faded from view, leaving the disturbed girl to her broken sleep.

5

***

Mephista was still pinned to the wall outside her father's bedroom, listening to the conversation beyond the door.

"What was what?" Kang asked, burnishing the hilt of his sword with his hand. "I didn't hear anything."

"I thought I heard something at the door," the thing in Devlish's body said.

"Do you want me to go and check?"

Mephista readied herself to flee but held on long enough to hear the response.

"No, I was probably just hearing things. I'm still not quite used to this body and its odd ears."

Mephista let out a sigh of relief. *That was close!* She toyed with returning to her own room, but couldn't tear herself away.

"Is everything ready for the 'festival'?" the Mitlock Demon asked.

"Nearly sire, we just need to recruit a few more soldiers."

"What's stopping you?" he snapped.

"We don't have enough villagers or castle staff to make an army."

"Then get more!"

"Already in hand. A scouting party departs this very hour for the mainland. By tomorrow, we should have a few more fresh bodies for our little Marnoch Mor party!" At this the ape snorted with laughter. "They won't know what's hit them. While they are tucking into their turkey, we'll be taking over."

The pair laughed together and then the creature said: "And then there will be no-one to stop us from attacking the humans."

There was more laughter.

"Your plans are well executed, master," she heard Kang say. "It won't be long now until you rule not only Murst, but Marnoch Mor as well!"

"Why stop there?" sneered the warlock. "There's a whole world out there ripe for the picking!" They both enjoyed the joke, cackling away like it was the funniest thing. Then the Mitlock Demon said: "I'm hungry, Kang. I need a bit of fresh meat. Go and rustle up something for me, will you? I need to bolster my strength before addressing the courtiers later. Make it a fresh kill!"

"Sire!"

"And prepare the ritual so that it is ready. But be careful, she must not suspect."

"Are you sure she is the right one?"

"Of course I'm sure. Do you think me stupid?"

"No, Sire. It is just that she has..."

"...A woman's body? Yes, she does. That is because she is a woman! But more importantly, she has a *royal* body, Kang. That is what matters. A royal body will increase my power. Or don't you think I deserve the very best?"

Mephista didn't wait around to hear Kang's answer. Fearful of being caught and terrified of what she had just learned, the red witch withdrew from the door and hurried down the corridor to the sanctuary of her own room. She reached the door, carefully shut it and bolted it. Leaning against the wooden frame, heart stuttering with fright, Mephista closed her eyes. What was she going to do now?

"Compose yourself, Witch!" she whispered to herself. "You are the daughter of the great Devlish of Murst. You must not be weak. You must be strong."

She took a deep breath and raised herself to her full height. Head back, she walked to her four poster bed and placed the spellbook on top of the fine silk covers.

Once again, her hand went to her mouth as she tried to make sense of what had happened. Like a caged animal she paced around the room, her mind a maelstrom as she mulled over what she had seen and heard. The thing in her

7

father's body...it was horrible. And she had no doubt now; it was as Morag had warned her — a Mitlock Demon.

Should she try and make a deal with it? Try and get some of the spoils for herself? No, as her spellbook made clear, Mitlock Demons were tricky. In her heart of hearts she knew the only reason this one was keeping her alive was because it wanted to take over *her* body?

Mephista suddenly felt faint. This was all too much to take in. She slumped against her bed. What was she going to do?

It was in this state that her chief maid, Madam Lewis, found her some moments later.

"Is something the matter, my Lady?" Madam Lewis asked as she bustled in. She took up a metal poker to stoke the fire in the carved stone fireplace of the bedroom. The tiny flames flickered and danced as she pushed the firewood around the hearth. "Shall I get one of the maids to re-lay this fire for you, ma'am? It seems to be dying."

"What?" Mephista responded absently. Her father was dead. Her beloved father was *really* gone. And she was alone...to face that *thing* that was living in her dead father's body. She felt as if she was going to be sick. Her stomach retched, but nothing came. She sighed, strode to her window and peered through its multiple diamond-shaped panes to the grey sea and sky beyond. Snow fell like confetti in front of her, but Mephista seemed not to notice.

"The fire, your Ladyship? Do you want me to have it re-laid? It's getting cold in here," her maid said as she busied about sorting out discarded clothes and searching for a shawl to put round her Ladyship's thin shoulders.

"No, no, I'm fine...it's fine," the witch said.

"Are you all right, ma'am? It's just that you seem a bit... well, funny," Madam Lewis asked.

Mephista turned and revealed such a look of utter

dejection that Madam Lewis feared for her mistress's mental health.

"It's not him," the witch said, her voice barely even a whisper. "He's not my father. They warned me, they said so, but I thought they were lying — I didn't want them to be right. I thought...Oh *what* am I going to *do* Lewis? This is all my fault."

"What's your fault, ma'am? What is it? Who are you talking about?"

Mephista breathed deeply before speaking.

"My father, Lewis...my father..."

"What about his Lordship?"

"He's...he's...not my father. He's something else, something evil."

"My Lord Devlish was always evil, ma'am. He's known for it," Lewis replied, puzzled at this outburst.

"No, you don't understand, Lewis," said Mephista grabbing her maid by both arms and shaking her. "The body is my father's, but the person inside...the soul or whatever you want to call it...is *not* my father. It's a creature, a Mitlock Demon. I've never seen anything like it."

She closed her eyes, trying to blank out the truly awful memory, and before Lewis could stop her Mephista collapsed with a sigh to the floor. The last the witch knew of anything was Lewis calling her name in a voice that sounded far, far away.

***

Morag woke the next morning feeling battle weary, as if she had not slept in several days. Heavy-eyed and exhausted, she dressed and descended to breakfast.

The oil paintings containing her parents were propped up on chairs when she entered the private dining room she had asked the servants to set up for them. Although they could not eat, Nathan and Isabella still liked to attend meals with their daughter to make up for their many years apart from her. They both greeted Morag as she took her usual place at the table.

"What's the matter?" Isabella asked, her voice soothing and gentle.

Morag took a piece of toast from the rack and placed it on her plate.

"Nothing, mum," she replied as she began to carefully butter the cooling morsel.

"You look so tired. You have dark circles under your eyes. Didn't you sleep well last night?" her mother continued.

"I'm fine," muttered the girl.

"Is something bothering you, my dear," Nathan asked. "Are you sickening for something?"

Morag looked at the paintings and tried her best to act normal. She did not want to burden her parents with her problems, not so soon after they had all been reunited. She wanted to maintain the happy atmosphere surrounding them, to lap up the sheer joy of just being with them and to keep all her worries at bay so they did not intrude into this new family life. So she didn't tell them.

"I'm fine, dad, honestly," she answered, hoping they wouldn't detect the lie. "I was kept awake last night by the sound of an owl outside my window."

"Well, if there is anything you'd like to talk about, you know you can come to us," said Isabella.

"I know," replied the girl.

"So what are you planning to do today?" asked her father, changing the subject.

"My friends are coming round to help me find a spell to free you."

"Morag," said her mother, "you're working too hard on this. You've spent every day inside searching for a spell.

Please don't tire yourself out for us. We've wasted so long in here already. We don't want you wasting your life too. Please go out and have fun with your friends. Don't tie yourselves to spellbooks on our behalf."

"But Mum…!" she began. It still felt strange called Isabella 'Mum'.

"Sweetheart, we have tried every conceivable spell we could think of to free ourselves and nothing has worked. I think we all have to accept that your father and I will be imprisoned here forever."

"No," replied Morag. "I don't accept it. I'm going to prove you wrong. I'm going to find a spell to free you so we can be a proper family."

She stood up.

"Now, if you'll excuse me, I have to go and get ready. Bertie and Aldiss are coming round to help me go through the books in the library. One of them is bound to tell us how to free you!"

***

"So what are we supposed to call you now?" asked the dodo, Bertie Fluke, as he popped into his beak another juicy grape from the lunch platter. He reclined on the large floor cushion and mused: "Your Royal Highland? Your Majesterial? Madam Morag? Ma'ammy?"

"Just Morag," the girl replied, "like always."

"How about…" the bird went on, "your Royal Maj, or Queenie, or something like that?"

"*Just* Morag will do," she answered more firmly.

"Oh! Oh!" squeaked Aldiss Drinkwater — rat, best friend and fellow adventurer. "I've got it…how about Morag, Lady Empress of Marnoch Mor?"

Morag glared at her two friends. They had been at it, trying to think up newer and even more ridiculous titles ever since they had found out she was the heir to the Marnoch Mor throne.

"I know...how about you two just shut up about the titles and get on with it?" the girl growled. "I asked you round here to help me look for a spell that might free my parents, not to sit there being silly. Now come on, we've got all these to get through and one of them must contain it." She waved her hand towards a huge pile of old books lying on a table close by.

They were in the library of the Marnoch Mor Palace, searching for an enchantment to release Morag's parents from their oil painting prisons. Morag had been searching ever since they had last returned from the DarkIsle of Murst, but with many days now passed her heart was growing heavy with the knowledge — the fear — that she might never find one.

The library was a large pentagon-shaped room on the ground floor of the Palace. One wall was an enormous carved stone fireplace in which a large fire blazed. Leather settees and armchairs fanned out from the hearth and on the floor were cushions. The dodo and rat were sitting on one, busily scanning a dusty old spellbook.

A second wall of the library was floor to ceiling arched windows, each framed with their own heavy satin curtains. The three remaining library walls were lined from floor to ceiling with hundreds of shelves full of ancient and modern tomes, ranging from the most ancient of spellbooks to the latest human adventure novel. There had to be thousands of books there.

At each of those three walls of bookshelves there was a long wheeled ladder and it was on one of these that Morag perched looking for yet another book to research.

"Montgomery says it would be better if the spell caster performed the enchantment," Aldiss said, flicking through a copy of *101 Spells for Everyday Use.*

"Well that's never going to happen," replied the girl, "Mephista will never agree to it."

"She might," the rat — ever the optimist — replied.

Morag made a face that told her friends she didn't think so and continued flicking through the great tome on the floor before her, a 400-year-old edition of *Gull's Spells and Enchantments (fifth edition).* It smelled musty and old, just like the Marnoch Mor poetry book her parents had left her when they had disappeared. It was in the pocket of her dress as always and Morag smiled when she thought of it. Who would have thought that the book would have been one of a set now in the Marnoch Mor Museum of Weird Things and Magic? But then who had realised that her parents had not abandoned her (as her guardians Jermy and Moira had always insisted)? And she had not known that her father, Nathan, was Crown Prince of Marnoch Mor and heir to its throne, making her a princess.

The thought of being royal reminded her of recently deposed Queen Flora — her own grandmother and the woman responsible for having split Morag from her mother and father. All because Flora had felt Nathan had married beneath himself. Flora had decided that if Nathan's wife, Isabella, wasn't good enough then the couple's daughter, Morag, wasn't good enough either. Indeed Flora had even confessed to being *embarrassed* by her. It was why she had placed Morag with Jermy and Moira after Nathan had disappeared.

Morag shivered. At least the horrible woman was now in the town's high security prison where she couldn't hurt her any more.

"Are you all right, Morag?" Bertie asked as he placed a comforting wing on her forearm.

"I'm fine," she replied with a smile. "But I wish I didn't have to wear this stupid dress. It's so itchy and stiff."

She twisted her body in order to free it a little from

the iron grip of the dress, which had been specially hand stitched for her by Marnoch Mor's top fashion designer, a silly man called Oh! It was made of silk, spun by the silk worms of Cooradonga — or so Oh! had told her — and it was so tight Morag felt she was being squeezed from all angles.

"I hate this thing," she confessed. "I wish I could go back to wearing jeans and a t-shirt."

"Well, that wouldn't be very royal now, would it?" Bertie said.

"Yes, but I would be a lot happier," she grumped. "Besides, I never *asked* to be royal, now did I?"

"Well, there's not much you can do about that now," replied the bird as he took some sweet almonds from a little bowl on a nearby table and popped them into his beak.

"No, there's not," she admitted.

"Still, could be worse," said the dodo, munching. "You could still be living in that cramped little cottage with Shona. I mean," he continued, looking at the ornate and sumptuous surroundings of the Palace's library with wistful eyes, "who wouldn't love to live *here*? It's fantastic."

"Yes it is," she agreed. *But I'd be far happier with Shona than here,* she thought miserably.

Their conversation was interrupted by a polite knock on the door. A palace footman, in obligatory white wig, knee-length trousers and tights, entered and bowed low. All that made him a bit different from a bog standard footman were his horns and goats' legs. The faun bowed low again.

"Your Royal Highness," he began, "I apologise for interrupting you and your friends, but there is a group of people at the door who wish to speak to Mr Montgomery."

Morag frowned.

"But he's not here. Why don't they go to his house?" she

asked.

"They have tried that, but he's not at home," the footman said. "They thought perhaps he was visiting you today. They insisted they will *only* speak to him and no-one else."

"Well, he's not here," Morag repeated, wondering what she was supposed to do now.

"Perhaps," said the footman, whose name was Jed, "I should just tell them to go away."

"Okay, Jed," said Morag with a shrug, "I would appreciate it if you could do that."

"Yes, Your Royal Highness," he said and bowed low again.

Head still bowed towards Morag, Jed walked backwards towards the door — in the Royal Palace of Marnoch Mor it was thought rude to turn your back on royalty. Morag rolled her eyes and blushed. She hated all the deference. It didn't feel right, it was all too embarrassing.

Jed made it to the door without bumping into anything and was reaching behind him for the door handle when a thought occurred to Morag.

"Jed," she said, "did the people say where they were from?"

"Yes, Your Royal Highness."

"Well, what did they say?"

He opened the door and positioned himself to go out.

"They said they were from Murst, Your Royal Highness."

Morag flinched. What was a delegation from Murst — the DarkIsle — doing in Marnoch Mor?

"Did they give their names?"

"No, Your Royal..."

"What do they look like?"

"I don't know, Ma'am, they are all wearing dark cloaks with their hoods up. If you don't mind me saying, they look very mysterious."

Morag glanced at her friends, who were looking equally shocked by the news.

"Okay, put them in the drawing room..." she began.

"Ooh, drawing room, how posh," muttered Aldiss appreciatively.

Morag ignored the rat.

"...and send for Montgomery...wherever he is," she ordered. Jed bowed and made to leave. "And Jed," she continued, "make sure there are at least two guards in the drawing room with them."

"Yes, Your Royal Highness," he said before disappearing out the door.

Morag turned to her friends.

"What do you make of *that*?" she asked.

"Well I think *drawing room* is a really funny thing," Aldiss started. "I mean it's really a *living room* or *sitting room*, you don't actually do any *drawing* in it."

They all glared at him.

"What?" said the rat, beady eyes lacking any kind of understanding of what he had said wrong.

His friends chose to ignore him.

"I wonder what they want." Bertie said.

"Why do they want to speak to Montgomery?" Morag wondered.

"Only one way to find out," replied the bird.

***

They waited for Montgomery near the front door of the Palace. It was freezing in the square marble hallway despite there being fires merrily blazing away in three huge and ornate fireplaces. They sat on a large sofa next to the biggest fireplace and looked at the intricate needlepoint design of its upholstery and the many tapestry wall-hangings that were the main features of the room. Morag particularly liked the smaller one that showed an image of her father as a young boy, riding on his favourite pony. She smiled as she looked at it and it made her feel warm inside.

"Do you think he'll be long?" Aldiss asked Bertie as he examined the massive Christmas tree in the corner. The rat gave a nearby glass bauble a flick with his paw, it tinkled merrily.

The bird took a big pocket watch out of his magical satchel and looked at it.

"Well, it's been half an hour since we sent Jed to look for him. I think he should be here any time..."

"Now?" said the rat, watching as the great doors of the Palace opened and the wizard walked in. Montgomery was relaxed and unconcerned as he strode through the doorway, knocking off the morning's snowfall from his shoulders and hair. He removed his heavy woollen coat and handed it to a waiting maid, who curtsied as she took it. Something gold and heavy glinted around his neck: Henry the medallion was with him. Morag slid off the sofa and hurried to the wizard's side.

"Do you *know* who is here to see you?" she asked without even greeting him.

"Hello, Morag, how are you? Hi, Bertie and Aldiss," Montgomery said, ignoring her question.

"Montgomery, this is important, did Jed tell you about your visitors?"

"Yes," he replied. "I came as quickly as I could."

"Do you know why they are here?"

"I think so," he said and then would say no more.

"Henry, can *you* tell us?" she implored.

"Certainly not!" snapped the medallion, his face contorting into a scowl.

Morag frowned and looked into Montgomery's face, expecting an explanation. None came. The great man merely ruffled her hair and gave her a half-smile.

"How are you today, princess?" he asked again.

"*Morag*," she corrected.

"Morag then," he said. "How's life at the Palace? Are they treating you well?"

"It's boring and I have nothing to do," she complained. "And they won't let me do anything interesting like slide down the banisters or go sledging in the park."

"You're a princess now and you should act like one," he said, barely able to keep the amusement out of his blue eyes.

"That's what *they* say," she grumbled.

"So where are these visitors of mine?" he asked, looking around.

"In the drawing room." Morag motioned to a doorway at the back of the hall, forgetting that Montgomery knew the Palace better than her.

There was a snigger from Aldiss at the sound of 'drawing room', but Morag ignored him again.

"Good," was all Montgomery said. "Come on Henry, let's go and see what they want."

Tight-lipped, he gave Morag's head another ruffle and reluctantly (or so it seemed to the girl) crossed the hallway. His footsteps echoed across the cold, hard marble and his shoulders were hunched as if there was some great weight on them. He didn't look back.

Morag looked to Bertie and Aldiss.

"Ask him!" the bird hissed.

"Em...Montgomery," she called.

The wizard stopped mid step and turned around.

"Yes?"

"Do you think we could come with you?" Then, seeing the stern look in his eyes, she added: "I mean, as princess of the realm and the only member of the royal family able to attend the meeting, I should be there."

He smiled.

"This is one meeting you definitely don't want to be in on," he said.

"But..."

"No, Morag. Not this time."

"Montgomery...!"

"I said 'no'!"

Morag could see from the expression on his face that it would be pointless to argue so she let it go. Montgomery opened the door then carefully closed it behind him. The lock clicked loudly as he turned the key on the inside.

"What are we going to do now?" Aldiss asked.

"We're going to that meeting with or without his permission," Morag replied.

Chapter 2

It was one of the first places she had explored when she had moved into the Palace a week before. She had happened across the little doorway when examining the magnificent Christmas tree that the servants had erected in the hallway. Glittering baubles swung from its ample boughs and a pretty angel was perched on the very top, but it had been when she'd bent down to look at a particularly pretty tree ornament that she'd spied a tiny ring on a wooden panel on the wall behind it. Burning with curiosity, Morag had reached out and pulled it. With a small swooshing noise the panel had opened to reveal a secret passageway.

Morag had crawled through and found herself in a tunnel running right along the side of the hallway. Lit by tiny Half Moonstones, it was just tall enough for a fully grown adult to stand up in and just wide enough to allow one person to walk along. Morag had discovered that not only did it go around the hallway, but other tunnels led off of it and around other rooms. She knew this because every now and again she'd come across ventilation grates that gave a view into other rooms: the ballroom, the library, the Chief Footman's room; one grate on the floor had shown her to be above the kitchen, another above a storeroom.

"It also runs alongside the drawing room," she now told Bertie and Aldiss as she located the doorway behind the Christmas tree. She yanked on the ring and the little door swooshed open again. She pulled her skirt through her legs from the back and tucked it inside her waistband at the front to make a pair of trousers of sorts. Then she hunkered down and crawled into the secret passageway. "Are you coming?" she called as she disappeared inside the dimly lit space.

Her friends didn't need another invitation. The dodo, ever one for health and safety, pulled a bright-yellow hard hat out of his satchel, plonked it on his head and cautiously followed Morag inside the wall. The rat, wide-eyed with the excitement of another possible adventure, couldn't help but whistle merrily as he scampered in after them. He was met by a stern Morag.

"Shush," she whispered. "They'll hear you. These walls may be thick, but the sound carries along the tunnels."

"Sorry," the rodent replied. Then he said: "*Who'*ll hear me?"

But Morag did not respond. With a nod of her head she indicated for the friends to follow her...quietly.

After a few careful paces down the passageway, she stopped and knelt. There wasn't much light to see by, but Morag knew her way around. She felt about close to the ground and with a little snort of triumph found a ventilation grill on the wall. She lay on her stomach and Bertie and Aldiss followed her lead. Together they endured the dusty floor and peered into the room beyond.

The panel opened up a section of the wall of the drawing room; a wall against which sat a valuable antique display cabinet. It was this piece of furniture that hid them beautifully behind its low and heavy Queen Anne legs. They peeked through its bowed legs, ears twitching to catch what was being said by the room's occupants.

"Can you see anyone?" Bertie whispered. "Can you hear anything?"

"No," she replied. Then: "Wait, look."

From their place on the floor they had a rat's eye view of the room: all they could see were the rugs, the bottom of furniture and eight pairs of feet. One pair in heavy outdoor boots were obviously Montgomery's. Two other pairs, which were too large and cumbersome for normal humans (*Murst giant guards?* Morag wondered), stood at the door next to those of three Palace guards. The final two pairs were in leather boots, but were mostly obscured by ankle-length heavy woollen cloaks. These had to belong to the mysterious visitors, Morag deduced.

"Welcome," they heard the wizard say. "Please have a seat."

There was a shuffling as the two closest visitors sat down on the large sofas opposite where Montgomery stood. The wizard himself then sat down on a nearby armchair.

There was a pause and then he said: "To what do I owe this honour?"

At first the visitors said nothing.

"Can I ask that you remove your hoods so that I may at least see your faces?" Montgomery said. "I think if you've come to see me I should at least know to whom I am speaking."

There was a rustle of weighty woollen material being removed and then a gasp from the wizard.

"You!" he said with a growl.

***

Morag glanced at her two friends. "What does he mean? Who is it?" she mouthed silently. Bertie and Aldiss, their view equally restricted, could only shrug.

"Yes, it is I." Morag had to stifle her own gasp as the familiar voice of the witch Mephista rang out. What was *she* doing there?

"I'm sorry to arrive here unannounced and in disguise, Montgomery," the witch went on, "but I had to come. I had no choice. Trust me if I had had an alternative, I would have chosen it, but you'll have to do."

Montgomery's silence was overwhelming.

"I have come to ask for help," Mephista went on, hesitantly. "A great danger walks on Murst and will soon come to Marnoch Mor. I need you to get rid of it for me. I, unfortunately, can't do it myself."

The wizard sighed.

"I know about this danger of which you speak. I tried to warn you about it before, remember?"

"I know, perhaps I should have listened to you."

"So, you've finally found out that Amergin is real and occupying your father's body?"

"Is that his name? I had forgotten. Yes, that's why I'm here," Mephista said haughtily. "We are *all* in danger, not just those on the DarkIsle. So you'd better do something about it."

"Well, you were the one who resurrected him and set him loose in this world."

"Yes, you're correct, I did perform the ceremony, but I had no idea what I had done. I only wanted to bring back my father, not...not..."

"You've set loose a monster," accused the wizard.

"Yes, yes," she replied, her voice rising. "But surely you understand why I wanted to resurrect my father..."

"She saw him...in the mirror," said a new gruff voice, one Morag instantly recognised as belonging to a warrior long used to serving the Devlish family.

"MacAndrew!" Morag whispered to the others.

"She was going to speak to him in his chambers and she happened upon him as he was looking at himself in the mirror," MacAndrew explained.

"It was horrible," Mephista cried, "some sort of ancient demon with a red skin and terrifying eyes. It had horns, scaly skin and teeth so sharp they could cut away dragon flesh. It was horrible, terrible looking. I can't take that thing on by myself, not with the Girallons on its side. I found MacAndrew and we left Murst to seek your help."

"So what do you want me to do? You caused the problem, you should fix it," Montgomery growled.

"You're the only wizard powerful enough to assist us," Mephista stated. "You must help us rid Murst of this thing. He's already quelled the slave rebellion..."

Oh no! Chelsea! Morag thought as she remembered the maidservant who had helped them the last time they had been on Murst. Morag had promised her she would help her escape, but had been unable to. The last she had heard was that Chelsea and her friends were carrying out a revolt in Murst Castle against Mephista and the person they thought was Devlish. Her heart flipped as she thought about Chelsea and what might have happened to the revolutionaries.

"...and he's going to attack Marnoch Mor," she continued. "He's been talking about it for days. He's planning to attack on Christmas Day — when you'd least expect it."

"Tell him the rest," MacAndrew urged.

"He won't stop there. He's planning to take over the human world too," she added.

There was a weighty silence and the three friends hardly dared breathe as they lay in their hiding place waiting to find out what would happen next.

"When you kidnapped me and took me back to Murst," the wizard began, "when Morag and the others came to rescue me... we found out about Amergin and I knew this day would come. Ever since, I've been searching for some kind of clue that might enable us to vanquish him. He's extremely powerful — so powerful that his spirit can inhabit dead people...and bring them back to life. Something must have gone wrong with your spell; you must have called for *him* — Amergin — instead of your father.

"But, I *didn't* call for him," Mephista insisted. "I wanted only to bring back my father, not a demon!" She snorted loudly and with ill-concealed temper spat: "*Kang*! He must have meddled with the spell. It was he who brought that creature back, not me! When I get back to Murst he'll wish he'd never come to the castle of Devlish. I'll make him pay for this."

"*If* you get back to Murst," Montgomery corrected. "This demon Amergin is no fool. He will know his disguise has been discovered. Your absence from the castle will make that clear. So he will be awaiting your return."

"Well, what do you want me to do?" the witch snapped. "I can't stay here, because you'll put me in jail..."

"Where you belong, Mephista," he pointed out." You have a number of crimes to answer for."

"...and I can't go home because the demon will get me. So what am I supposed to do?" she growled.

Montgomery rose to his feet.

"I would suggest your best bet is to remain in Marnoch Mor until we know more about this threat and can work out a way to rid the island of it," the wizard said.

"Oh thank you, I knew you'd understand," she said, the relief audible. "We'll just stay at the Royal Hotel and..."

"Guards!" Montgomery said. The two men moved forward but were blocked by the Murst giants. MacAndrew unsheathed his sword. "Show the Lady Mephista and her people into the Palace's cells please. Make sure Special Chief Constable Shona is made aware of their detention and ask her to ensure no-one goes in or out of their cells without my say so. Murst guards stand down."

"Do as he asks," MacAndrew instructed his guards.

"But...!" the witch protested as the Palace guards lowered their pikes and motioned her and MacAndrew towards the door.

"Just do as he asks," the warrior said to his Lady.

"I'm sure you'd rather be safe here than be the next meal — or worse — of a demon, Mephista," Montgomery smirked.

"This is outrageous!" the witch roared. "If my father...!"

"You're father's dead, Mephista," the wizard pointed

out.

"He's right, Your Ladyship," MacAndrew said. "We'll be safer here, even if we are in jail."

"Leave me alone, don't touch me!" the witch complained as the guards moved to escort her and MacAndrew to jail. Her Murst giant guards followed meekly behind. "Stop poking me with that thing, I am quite capable of walking there myself."

In their hiding place, Morag, Bertie and Aldiss could only look at each other, numb with shock at what they had just witnessed and heard. Mephista had come to Montgomery for help, something they had never thought they would see. She had come to Marnoch Mor because she was frightened of Amergin. Morag let out a little sigh. She had been in Marnoch Mor less than four months and already her life had been in danger more times than she could count. Would this new threat mean she would be running for her life yet again? She was so tired of it.

"How much did you hear?"

A voice very close by made them jump out of their skins. They looked up to see Montgomery's boots standing at the cabinet. He bent down and peered underneath it. His blue eyes were serious but not angry.

"Um...all of it," Morag said.

He nodded. "Well, I would have expected nothing less from you three. Why don't you join me in the library so we can discuss it?"

"Okay," replied Morag. "We'll be there in a minute." She carefully led her friends back to the secret doorway in the hall. Not one of them said a word until they were all safely back in the library.

"Why is it we always get caught spying?" Aldiss muttered as they entered the room and took their seats on the floor cushions again.

"Because we are always doing it," the dodo replied

matter-of-factly. "You heard him — he would 'expect nothing less' of us."

"And it's always getting us into trouble," added Morag.

***

Montgomery positioned himself in a large old-fashioned wing chair next to the fire and solemnly surveyed the friends. Henry gleamed from a chain around his neck. The medallion was also looking stern.

"Morag," the wizard said, suddenly making them all jump, "why don't you organise some tea for us, while we chat about what just happened?"

As Morag summoned a servant by yanking on the giant tassel of an elaborately embroidered bell-pull that hung from the ceiling, the others drew closer to the wizard, eager to hear his plan to vanquish Amergin. They positioned the floor cushions at his feet and looked up at him expectantly. Montgomery, however, was not for speaking until Morag re-joined them.

As she took her place next to Bertie, the wizard looked them each in the eye and said: "Well, what did you think of Mephista's story?"

"I'm scared," Aldiss shivered. "I don't like the sound of this Amergin one little bit. I mean, what kind of person inhabits the dead body of another? It's horrible."

"He's one of the worst of the ancient demons," Montgomery told them as he handed Morag a copy of Azra MacNab's *Vanquishing Demons and Other Nasty Magical Creatures*. It was open at a page entitled Mitlock Demons. "That's why I've been at the Palace library a lot lately. I've been researching him; looking at every book I could find that mentions his name to see how I could vanquish him. I knew this day would come. This book has the most on him. Read it for us Morag."

The girl gazed down at the yellowing pages of the old book and began: "*Mitlock Demons were once plentiful on Earth and could be most commonly found in Africa, along the Gold Coast. These creatures are carnivorous and highly dangerous. They are violent and must not be approached under any circumstances. They have been known to kill and eat the residents of entire towns. During the War of the Demons in 3012 BC, the humans and the magical people joined forces to fight the main tribes of Mitlock Demons. They managed to kill them all — at great loss to their own troops — except for the demon King, Amergin the Destroyer. He managed to escape and was caught on the slopes of Mount Kilimanjaro by the Supreme Coven of Witches. This coven banished Amergin's spirit to the Dark Lands for good.*"

"So how *did* Mephista manage to release him?" Bertie wanted to know.

"*She* didn't…it was Kang. He must have tampered with the spell to ensure it was Amergin and not Devlish who returned to this world," replied Montgomery.

"Hold on," said Morag, "there's another bit. *Amergin must not be released under any circumstances for he will inhabit the body of a victim of murder until such time as he can grow stronger…*"

"That'll be Devlish," muttered Aldiss.

"*In order to grow stronger, he must take the life force of the murderer of the body he has taken over…*"

"Morag," said the rat.

"*…and forever more he will grow in strength until there is no-one who can stop him. Do not release this dangerous demon for he will kill and destroy everything and everyone in his path.*"

There was a silence whilst everyone took in this information.

"Those poor people on Murst are at his mercy with no-one to protect them," Morag said. "Mephista said Amergin quashed the slave rebellion. Does that mean he killed them all or has he enslaved them again? We need to help them!"

"I don't know what happened to them," said the wizard, "but I agree we need to do something, not just for the people of Murst, but for Marnoch Mor and the rest of the world. From what I've read of Amergin, and from what Mephista said, this thing will stop at nothing to take over whatever and wherever he can.

"And," the wizard added looking pointedly at Morag, "we need to protect you too."

"I don't understand."

"Didn't you hear the bit about him taking the life force of the murderer of the body he inhabits to become stronger?" Bertie said.

"But *I* didn't kill Devlish," the girl replied. "The Eye did."

They all looked at each other as the realisation dawned: once again Marnoch Mor was in grave danger. If the Eye was taken, the town would be annihilated.

"No matter who killed Devlish, we still need a plan," said Montgomery after some moments had passed. "There must be a way of getting rid of the Mitlock Demon once and for all."

"What can I do?" asked Morag. "Being a royal has some advantages. I am able to give orders in Marnoch Mor, so I can make sure you have soldiers and supplies, anything you want."

"Thank you, Morag, but I don't think force is what's needed. We need to work out what the demon is going to do first and how we can send it back to the dark prison where it belongs."

Morag looked at her friend's worried face. She leant over and put a hand on his arm.

"It'll be okay," she said, "we'll think of something."

Montgomery managed a tight smile, but Morag sensed

he was floundering.

"Perhaps the solution will come to me after a good night's sleep." He stood up. "I'll leave you now. I must get back home and think about the best solution for this new danger. I will return tomorrow and we can discuss it then."

Morag stood up too.

"Okay," she said. "We'll see you tomorrow."

He nodded, turned and walked slowly to the library door.

"Montgomery!" Morag called.

He turned.

"Why not pop in to see Shona on your way home?" she suggested. "As she's descended from an ancient Murst race perhaps she might have some ideas about how to stop the demon."

"Perhaps. And I will," he said. "Goodbye."

Aldiss yawned loudly.

"What time is it?" he asked the dodo. Bertie glanced at his pocket watch.

"It's nearly noon. Time to go, my little rodent friend," he said getting to his feet and waddling to the door.

"Where are you going?" Morag asked as she watched the rat join the bird at the door.

"My favourite programme is on the television," explained the dodo, "I have some books to look through and Aldiss here needs his afternoon nap. Perhaps you should think about having a nap yourself, Morag. You are looking awfully tired."

"Yes," said Morag, suddenly feeling exhausted. "I am tired. Perhaps I will go for a sleep."

She saw them to the door.

"See you tomorrow," she said giving them a hug in turn.

"We'll be all right, you know," the bird assured her thinking her worried look was all about the threat from Amergin. "Montgomery will think of something."

"I know," she said.

As she watched them stride across the town square, Morag thought about all the things that were worrying her at that precise moment: there was the release of her mum and dad; the threat from Murst; and her horrible haunted dreams. *Well*, she said to herself, *I can't do much about the other two right now, but I know someone who may be able to help with the dreams.* She closed the door and ran up the stairs to collect her duffel coat from her room. Quietly as a mouse, the girl slipped on the coat, swapped her shoes for wellington boots and slipped out of the palace, heading for Marnoch Mor's famous Museum of Weird Things and Magic.

Chapter 3

Elma MacPhail had a reputation in Marnoch Mor for being a bit of a clairvoyant ...with the emphasis on '*bit*'. While it was widely believed that she could indeed talk to the dead and see into the future, it was also known that what Elma did or saw was generally fragmented; her clients were given snippets of information. The witch did her best to hone her skills, but never got past the very basics in clairvoyancy and telling the future.

The witch was flustered when Morag appeared at the rickety door of the Museum of Weird Things and Magic where Elma was the assistant curator. Her candyfloss hair was sticking out at angles, her grey tunic top and matching trousers were stained with a strange yellow liquid and her glasses sat askew the bridge of her nose. On her feet, she wore threadbare woollen slippers that were made to look even untidier by the sleek black cat that was threading its body between her ankles. Looking at her, Morag finally understood why someone might say Elma looked like a burst cushion. The woman looked as batty as Morag knew her to be.

"Oh it's you!" muttered Elma.

"Can I come in?" Morag asked.

"The museum doesn't open till ten. Come back then," snapped the witch.

"I don't want to see the museum," Morag said. "It's *you* I've come to see."

"Me? Why do you want to see me?"

"Can I come in and I'll tell you?"

Elma shrugged. "I suppose so."

She opened the door wider to allow Morag in. As she did so the cat bolted.

"Grizzy! Come back here! I haven't finished bathing

you!" shrieked Elma to a disappearing black streak. "Dratted cat doesn't know what's good for her."

Morag stepped into the large hallway and was once more astounded by its grandeur. The Museum of Weird Things and Magic was built into the former home of Colm Breck, the founder of Marnoch Mor. The house was an ancient old shack. From the outside it looked as if it might give up trying to keep its timbers aloft and collapse at any time, but inside, now that was a different story. It was as if Morag had stepped into a grand stately home and, although she had been there before, she couldn't help but marvel once more as to how so much entrance hallway could fit into so small a building. Of course, the museum wasn't just on the one floor; it covered thirteen separate storeys. How they did it, Morag would probably never know, but she loved it anyway.

She followed Elma across the marble-tiled floor, under the giant crystal chandelier and through a small doorway at the back of the massive stone staircase. All the time the witch was muttering about the flight of her cat and, in barely audible words, blaming Morag for allowing the feline to escape. Morag, who heard it all, merely smiled to herself and was not offended. She knew Elma was always a bit strange.

"Come on, come on," Elma said to the girl as they stepped into a little corridor. "Just down here. I've got the kettle on. Would you like some tea or something a bit stronger?"

"Like what?" asked Morag, stepping into a large kitchen. The room had a huge stove at one end in front of which sat two of the squishiest chairs Morag had ever seen. On the adjoining wall was a row of cupboards and a sink, and over the other side was a long rectangular wooden table surrounded by eight wooden chairs.

Elma turned to her.

"Well, don't tell Montgomery, but I've been brewing a few wee things in the back," she said, pointing to a pantry door. "My famous Bee Thistle beer with added fizz. Would you like to try some?"

"No thank you," replied the girl.

"Why not?"

"Well...I'm only a girl," she said. "I'm not supposed to drink alcohol."

"What? Oh yes, so it is and so you are. Never mind. Cup of tea instead?"

"Yes please." Morag sat down on an armchair.

"Now why have you come to see me?" the witch asked, pouring the contents of a kettle into an enormous Brown Betty teapot. "Got pimples you want rid of? You need a love potion? No, that's not it. I know: you want your fortune told. I'm great at that." She gave the teapot a swirl and emptied its steaming contents into two mugs. She passed one to the girl.

"No," Morag said firmly to each suggestion. "I've come to ask if you can help me with some dreams I've been having."

As the girl explained the hideous images of her dream, Elma sat on the arm of the other chair and rocked back and forth, nodding her head and making little noises that sounded like: "Hmmm! Yes, I see. Is that so?"

"Well," said the witch when Morag's tale had finished, "let me think. May I?"

She reached over and gently placed two fingers on Morag's right temple. The witch closed her eyes and breathed deeply. Morag sat still and patiently waited and waited and waited. Elma sighed. Elma moaned softly. Elma began to rock gently from side to side. From the corner of her eye, Morag could see that she was also silently talking to herself. Then the witch removed her fingers and opened her eyes.

"Well, that was interesting," she said, getting up and plonking herself in the seat of the chair.

"What was?" the girl asked eagerly.

"You never told me you were royal," the witch accused. "If I had known I would have tidied myself up a bit."

"Everyone knows I'm royal," the girl snapped. "Anyone could have told you that."

"*I* didn't. No-one tells me anything down here."

"What about my dreams?" the girl asked exasperated.

"Well, that's also interesting," the witch said. "Your dreams aren't dreams at all but a channel to the undead. The person trying to talk to you is on the..." (and here she turned her loud voice down to a stage whisper) "...*other side!*"

"And what was he saying?" the girl wanted to know.

"Well, that was the tricky part," Elma confessed.

"You mean you don't know?"

"Um...yes. More tea?"

"No thanks," Morag said, her heart heavy with the knowledge that she had not escaped from Devlish even in death. "Is there any way I can get him to stop?"

"Who dear?"

"The warlock, Devlish."

"Who?"

"The man in my dreams!" Morag nearly shouted.

"What? Well, no, not really. Until you can work out what he's trying to tell you he will continue to visit you every night. He will never rest until he's told you his message." The witch stood up. "Now, is there anything else dear? I've got some lovely love potions bubbling up in the pantry?"

"No thanks," Morag said, getting to her feet. "I need to go home now, back to the...er...Palace. Thanks for your help."

***

Morag dragged her heels returning to the place that she called her new home. She was in no mood to be feted and pampered and called 'ma'am' by the servants. She wanted peace and silence and to be left to her own thoughts. So she took her time wandering through the busy streets of Marnoch Mor's centre, dodging busy Christmas shoppers as they scurried from shop to shop picking up last minute presents for their loved ones. Morag stopped to gaze into her favourite shop window: Erbium Smyte's Department Store, which sold '*everything you never knew you needed or wanted*'. A tiny snow fairy was putting the last touches to a polar-themed window display in the shop's two huge windows and she waved to the sad girl before returning to her job of spraying an icicle display with tiny glittering snowflakes. Morag waved back. The fairy flew up to her and through the window the fairy mimed 'Why so sad?' Morag shrugged. The fairy smiled, waved her tiny wand and the window's inside was immediately framed in a beautiful blue ice. 'You like?' the fairy mimed. Morag nodded. 'Thank you,' she mouthed back.

"That was amazing!" said a high-pitched voice somewhere near Morag's feet.

The girl looked down to see Aldiss looking up at her. He smiled and waved at her.

"Hi Aldiss," she said gloomily. "What are you doing here?"

"What's the matter?" he asked.

"How long have you got?"

"Not much time. Shona's on the warpath."

***

Shona was pacing the library when Morag returned to the Palace with the rat. The dragon scowled as the girl threw herself on the sofa and folded her arms. Aldiss discreetly sat at the other end of the room and pretended to read a book.

"Where have you been Morag MacTavish?" Shona growled. "I've been worried sick. You left here without a guard or one of us to accompany you. You didn't even tell anyone where you were going. *Anything* could have happened."

Morag remained moodily silent, wondering whether or not to confess to the dragon that she had been to see Elma. She knew that Shona and the assistant curator did not get on, especially as Elma's boss, Muriel Burntwood had been so scathing of the dragon when she had gone to the museum to investigate the theft of the tooth of the witch Mina MacPhail.

"Well? I'm waiting for an answer," the dragon demanded.

Morag let out a melancholy sigh.

"What do you want from me?" the girl snapped.

"I want you to be straight with me," Shona replied. "I don't think that's too much to ask, is it? Well? Morag... what's wrong?"

"I'm fed up with you being so bossy all the time." Morag surprised herself by bursting into tears. Through snottery sobs she told the dragon the whole story about the horrible dreams, how they were becoming more frequent and how they were disturbing her sleep.

"How can I help Montgomery find a way to deal with Amergin if I'm too tired to do anything?" she cried. She was exhausted trying to keep up the pretence that everything was all right and it felt good to tell her former guardian. When she had finished, Shona's scaly face softened and she knelt to give the girl a hug.

"It'll be all right, you know," she said gently.

"How will it? Elma says I can't get rid of these dreams until Devlish has delivered his message, but I can't make out what he's saying," replied the girl, gently blowing her nose into an electric blue handkerchief proffered by the rat, who had leapt up from his chair to comfort his friend. "Thanks, Aldiss."

The dragon chewed her lip thoughtfully. Then an idea suddenly formed.

"Stay here," she said, getting to her feet. "I won't be long."

Without giving a word of explanation, Shona hurried out of the library. Moments later, the library door opened again and this time a distracted Bertie scuttled in to return a book he had borrowed the week before. He was surprised to see a teary Morag and concerned Aldiss looking over at him.

"Is this a bad time?" he asked, placing the book carefully on a table. "Do you want me to leave?"

"No, it's fine... I'm fine," the girl replied.

"I've just seen Shona running out of the Palace as if her tail were on fire. She's got a face on her that would frighten Devlish himself if he were still around!" He guffawed, flapping his tiny wings with mirth until he realised Morag was not seeing the funny side of his comment. "What? What have I said?"

"Nothing," replied the girl, "it's just that Devlish is kind of the reason why Shona has gone out."

She was just about to tell the dodo the whole story when the library door opened once more and in stepped a triumphant dragon carrying a strappy item in one claw. She held it up excitedly.

"That was quick!" said the rat, eyeing the contraption suspiciously.

"I knew I had one somewhere," the dragon huffed, still trying to catch her breath from her sprint. "I took this one off an illegal trader in Central Station two weeks ago."

She held it up. It was some sort of head-gear made up

of several straps of leather, including a chin strap with a little silver buckle.

Bertie stared at it.

"Is that what I think it is?" he asked, almost breathless with wonder.

"Yes," said the dragon, eyes bright with excitement.

"What? What is it?" Morag asked, not understanding why the others were so excited about such an unfashionable hat. She certainly did not intend wearing it around Marnoch Mor. People would surely laugh at her.

Shona handed it to her with a huge grin.

"Yes, what is it?" the rat squeaked from the sofa.

"This," said the dragon, "is something that will help Morag get rid of her dreams. This is a dream enhancer. You wear it when you go to bed so that when you dream you hear and see things more clearly."

"You expect me to wear *that* tonight?" Morag asked incredulously. It looked like some sort of torture device.

"Yes."

"But..."

"Do you want to continue to be haunted by that horrible warlock?"

"No."

"Do you want to get your normal dreams back and to sleep a whole night without being disturbed?"

"Yes."

"Well then, I would advise you to give it a try."

Morag examined the dream enhancer carefully. *Well,* she thought to herself, *it can't hurt.*

"Thanks, Shona," she said. "I'll try it tonight."

Just then Jed appeared at the door and instructed Morag that Mephista wished to see her in the dungeon right away. The girl gave the footman a look that would have felled lesser men.

"What does she want to see *me* for?" she demanded.

Then realising how rude she was being, she added: "I mean: did she say what she wanted?"

"Yes, ma'am, she wanted to see Mr Montgomery," he said apologetically.

"Well, could you please go and get him for her?" she asked.

"I can't, ma'am," the footman replied.

"Why not?"

"Mr Montgomery is not here," he said. "That is why the Lady Mephista is asking to see you."

Morag looked at the man, dumfounded by what he was asking. She wanted nothing to do with Mephista, the witch who had imprisoned her, enslaved her and tried to murder her. Why should she give her the time of day?

"He's telling the truth, Morag," Shona said, interrupting the girl's disturbed thoughts. "Montgomery left Marnoch Mor on urgent business about an hour ago. He's not due back till tonight."

"Where is he?" squeaked Aldiss before Morag could ask.

"He's gone to seek the advice of an old friend of his who lives somewhere further north," the dragon replied.

"The Lady Mephista is causing quite a disturbance in the jail, ma'am," Jed said. "She claims she will break out and start causing trouble, starting with — and these are her words, not mine ma'am -, 'that girl upstart and her little friends too'...I think those were the words she used...," he said, "...if you don't go and see her."

"Can she really do that?" Bertie wanted to know.

"She seems serious in her threats, sir," the footman admitted.

"And is it all right for Montgomery to leave? Remember what happened last time? The town crumbled around us when Mephista had him kidnapped from his study," the bird reminded them all.

Shona shook her head. "Montgomery was taken without

his permission," she said. "He is able to leave for short periods without the Eye of Lornish destroying Marnoch Mor...provided he leaves of his own free will." On seeing the doubt in her friends' faces, she added: "He'll return tonight, don't worry."

There was another polite cough. They turned to look at the footman again.

"What shall I tell the Lady Mephista, ma'am?" he asked.

Morag thought for a moment.

"Tell her nothing. I'll go and see her."

"You can't!" Bertie said, aghast at the thought. "She's evil. She might do something to you to escape."

Morag smiled at her friend.

"I can and I have to. Who knows what she'll do if I don't!"

Chapter 4

The Palace's cells were situated in the basement and until the previous day had not been used for twenty years. So dirty was the basement, and so full of unwanted furniture, that it had taken five servants a full two hours to clean it before it was habitable enough for Mephista, MacAndrew and their two giant guards. The witch was in one cell, the warrior in another, the guards in a third and, sitting between them at a small wooden table, were two of the Palace's guards. They snapped to attention when they realised Morag, Shona, Bertie and Aldiss had joined them.

"Oh, I might have known," drawled the witch from behind bars, "you've come with all your little friends. Am I so frightening, Morag? Do I still terrify you?"

The girl looked steadily at Mephista.

"No," she replied. "You don't scare me one little bit. Now, why did you ask to see me?"

Mephista, who had until that moment been lounging on a hard cell bed, sauntered over to the bars that separated her and the group of friends. Although she was smirking, Morag could see her hands trembling as she grasped the cold hard metal of her cage.

"Well, with Montgomery away, you, as his lackey, were the only person I could talk to," the witch said. "Have you rid my island of that creature yet?" Her voice wavered.

"We're working on it," Morag said. "I'm sure we'll come up with something soon."

"Well, hurry up, I'm getting tired of being trapped in here," snarled the witch.

"You're in here because of what you did to Morag and Montgomery!" shouted Bertie.

"Yeah!" said Aldiss.

Mephista turned her gaze to the bird and rat.

"Shut it!" she hissed. "I don't talk with vermin."

She turned back to Morag.

"Well, *when* do you think it'll happen?" she asked.

"Things will happen when they happen," the girl replied, taken aback that even now, locked in a cell, having come to Marnoch Mor to beg for Montgomery's help, Mephista was still trying to act as if she were the one in control.

"What kind of answer is that?" sneered Mephista. In fact, why am I bothering to even speak with you? You're a nobody, a nothing. After all I've been through, I shouldn't have to deal with a mere girl, especially a girl who did what you did." She peered at Morag.

"The Eye killed Devlish," Morag said firmly.

"*You* killed my father," snapped the witch. "You have no idea what it feels like to lose a dear father, do you?"

At this, Morag's face paled.

"I know only too well what it's like to not have a father. Or a mother!" she shouted. "You and *your* father made sure of that!"

Mephista pursed her lips and casually flipped her long red hair. "Oh *that*, I'd forgotten all about that. They got what they deserved. Nathan was supposed to marry *me*, *not* that upstart pretender to the throne. Did you know your mother claims to be descended from the great Colm Breck! How funny is that? Everyone knows he didn't have any children. What a stupid woman."

Morag looked at her, her face a stony mask. Her friends held their breath, waiting for her to snap, but she kept calm and said nothing, merely stared as Mephista laughed long and loud.

Then: "Free my parents!" Morag demanded.

"Why should I?" the witch sneered.

"Because we're your only hope of defeating that demon," said Morag.

That wiped the smile off the witch's face. She looked

D A Nelson

uncomfortable as she returned Morag's gaze.

"I tell you what," she said, "you rid my island..."

"*My* island," Shona corrected.

"Back off, lizard," Mephista hissed. She turned her attention back to Morag. "You rid *my* island of that demon and I'll free your parents."

"Deal," said Morag immediately.

But no sooner were the words out of her mouth than she was regretting them. Could she fulfil the promise?

***

Morag went to bed that night with fresh hope that she could free Isabella and Nathan from their oil-painting prisons. Before she turned in for the night, she spent half an hour with them in their room chatting about her day as she normally did. Not wanting to give them false hope she kept Mephista's promise to herself. The witch couldn't be trusted.

Nathan and Isabella's portraits were propped up against a mound of pillows on top of a large four-poster bed in the room next to Morag's. Their daughter smiled when she saw them and ran over to the bed to join them.

"How was your day today, my dear?" her mother asked. The frozen painted face in the picture did not move, but Morag heard the words anyway.

"Uneventful," Morag lied. "I spent most of the day in the library with Bertie and Aldiss again. I feel we are close to finding a spell to free you."

"Morag," her father said, "while we appreciate what you are doing, we feel you are spending far too much time with your nose in dusty books. You should be out having fun with your friends."

"I'm fine, Dad, honestly," she assured him.

"But..."

"I'm fine."

"Well, all right, if you are sure," he said, sounding unconvinced.

Morag quickly changed the subject and told them a funny joke Aldiss had told her about some cheese and a cockroach. As she told the punch line, the little clock on the mantel above their fireplace chimed 10pm and reminded her how tired she was. She yawned.

"Time for bed, my dearest angel," said Nathan.

Morag leant over them and planted a quick kiss on each painting.

"Good night, Dad," she replied, still feeling awkward about calling anyone, let alone a painting, 'Dad'. "Night, Mum."

"Goodnight, Morag," her mother replied.

Leaving them with a smile, she exited their bedroom and sleepily trudged to her own room next door. Without really thinking about it, she pulled on her pyjamas, jumped into her enormous bed and pulled up the covers.

"Oh!" she said, sitting up suddenly. She looked around her and found what she was looking for on a bedside cabinet. She plonked the dream enhancer on her head and lay down. It was surprisingly comfortable to wear and she barely felt it as it enclosed her head like a soft pillow, lulling her into a deep sleep.

***

Morag didn't know how long she had been sleeping for — hours could have passed — but when the dreams came, she soon found herself wishing she was awake again. Devlish appeared as soon as she entered the dream state, his twisted white face writhing and squirming as if someone were distorting the image. He flashed a nasty smile before calling her name.

"Morag!" he said. "Morag MacTavish...murderer!"

"Morag, beware! The demon Amergin has taken over my body. You must stop him," the warlock's spirit warned.

"I know, I know," Morag said.

Devlish seemed surprised. His eyes widened and then he smiled.

"At last you can hear me!" he said. "I knew I'd get through eventually."

"What do you want, Devlish?" Morag asked.

"I want you to get rid of that demon!" the warlock spat.

"Why me?"

"Because...as much as I hate you for doing what you did to me..." Here he paused and grimaced. "...there *is* no-one else. Yours is the only conscience I've been able to reach. It's probably something to do with the fact you killed me... some sort of connection, I don't know."

There was a silence. Then the warlock started again.

"He's using my body and he plans to take over the world. You must do something about it."

"Isn't that what *you* planned to do?" the girl asked accusingly.

"Yes, but that was different. I wasn't trying to do it in someone else's body," he snapped, "and I had Mephista at my side. I'm worried for her safety. Amergin is a powerful and deeply evil monster. He's unpredictable. He'll use Mephista and cast her aside."

"Well *do* something about it!" said the girl.

"How...? When...? How can I do something about it the way I am now? I am just a spirit floating about in the darkness. I can't even leave this place, this purgatory. I'm stuck," he replied. "It's up to *you* to do it, Morag."

"Do what? What are you talking about?" the girl said, suddenly afraid.

"*You* can stop him. You have the heart of a lion. You showed that when you stood up against me. You are my only hope. Vanquish Amergin and put my daughter back on the throne of the DarkIsle."

The girl didn't know what to say. She didn't want this job, hadn't asked for it, but knew that she had to do something to clear Murst of the demon if she was to have any hope of saving Marnoch Mor and the human world. There was also the bargain she had made with Mephista to free her parents. The thought of putting the witch back in power sickened her, but she couldn't see any other way.

"What do I have to do?" she asked quietly.

"You...have..." the demon tried to say, but something was happening...it was as if the signal was waning.

"What? What are you saying?" the girl cried.

"Take the..."

"What?"

"...The Destine...you must...use it...him," Devlish said, the signal interrupted by static. "It's the only way... defeating him..."

And then he was gone.

Morag awoke with a start, cold sweat pouring down her face, her heart beating harder than it had ever beaten before. She scrambled out of bed, switched on a lamp and raked through a bedside cabinet for a pen and paper. Finding both, she quickly scribbled down what she hoped were the correct words: *The Destine.* Then she wrote: *Only way of defeating him.* She placed the pen and paper on the cabinet and got back into bed. As she slipped her feet beneath the warm covers, her mind was trying to work out what had just happened. One thing was for sure, the dream enhancer had worked and she had been able to hear him, to talk to him. His voice had been as clear as a bell, as if he had been standing right next to her.

Why was he so keen for her to vanquish Amergin? Was this is a way for Devlish to somehow wreak revenge on her for having killed him? Or was he simply a father worried for his daughter, crying out for help from the only person he could? Suddenly the warlock didn't seem so frightening any more, he seemed...human. Morag almost felt sorry for him as she remembered his pinched, sad face. The clock on her mantel chimed 3am and, with a yawn, she removed the dream enhancer, laid down and closed her eyes. For the remainder of the night, Morag slept more peacefully that she had done in weeks.

***

The next morning, Morag shared her news with Shona, Bertie and Aldiss over breakfast. Her friends had arrived early, eager to find out if the dream enhancer had lived up to its name. They joined their royal friend in the morning room for hot buttered pancakes and tea. Sitting at the table, Morag could hardly contain her excitement.

"I know how to defeat Amergin," she said before they had even sat down, "and once we do that Mephista will finally free my parents from the paintings."

"So...it worked!" Shona gasped, barely able to believe it. "I wasn't sure if it would or not."

"Yes, yes, this time I could hear him, though it was a little crackly in places. I couldn't make out some of the words, but I think I got most of it...the important stuff at least," said the girl between bites of pancake. She wiped a drip of butter from her lips with an embroidered napkin.

"What did he say?" Aldiss squeaked.

"Tell us *everything*," Bertie pressed.

"He said I had to use The Destine to defeat the demon."

"What's that?" Aldiss, who was sitting next to Morag, asked. "I've never heard of it before."

"Dunno," Bertie replied before Morag could. "Shona, any ideas? Shona?"

They turned as one to face the dragon who was sitting

on the floor at the head of the table. Her face had turned a nasty shade of puce.

"Shona? Are you okay?" Morag asked.

"What? I'm...fine," she replied, getting to her feet. "I need to go," she said.

"Shona! Wait! What's wrong?" Morag asked, running after her. "You can't just leave." Then realisation dawned: "You know what The Destine is, don't you?"

With doleful eyes, the dragon turned to look at Morag.

"Yes," she said, then recommenced her journey.

Morag, unwilling to let it go at that, raced ahead of her friend and blocked her exit. Shona could easily have shoved the slight girl out of the way, but instead sat back on her haunches and glanced up at her, a defeated look in her eyes. Morag was puzzled, she had never seen Shona react in such a fashion to any kind of challenge. The dragon was normally so brave.

"Shona, what's wrong?" Morag asked, wrapping her small arms around the dragon's muscular neck and giving her a gentle hug.

"There's only one place you can find The Destine," the dragon said, and Morag felt her quiver.

Morag released her and looked into her great yellow eyes.

"And where's that?" she asked quietly.

"It's in a temple in the kingdom of Graar, deep within an extinct volcano," Shona replied.

"Well, that doesn't sound so bad," Morag said. "Is it far away from here? How do we get there?"

"You don't understand!" The dragon was gruff. "We can't go there, it's too dangerous. It's forbidden."

"But why? What's so wrong with this place Graar? I don't understand."

"Graar," said a familiar voice, "is the ancient kingdom of the Klapp demons." Bertie stepped out from behind the dragon and waddled towards Morag.

"Uh-huh?" Morag waited for more.

"The Klapp demons no longer live there," he continued with an audible gulp, "because it's guarded by Felix Saevus."

"Felix *what*?" Morag said with a half smile. "Felix isn't a very scary name!"

"No," agreed the dragon, "but the creature whose name it is, is *very* scary." She shivered.

"I'm sure he can't be *that* bad," said the girl. "Why don't we just go down there and ask him nicely for The Destine. He might give it to us. Or maybe we could pay him."

"You don't *pay* Felix for anything," the dodo said.

"Why not? Who *is* this Felix anyway?"

Bertie looked at Shona and neither seemed prepared to speak any further on the matter.

"Only the biggest, scariest he-dragon this world has ever seen!" squeaked Aldiss from between Shona's great claws. The dragon recoiled from the rat instinctively. She had never liked rodents and was still a little uneasy in the rat's presence, especially when he was speaking about Felix Saevus.

Morag looked to Shona for clarity.

"I thought most of the dragons were dead. I thought that apart from the ones who live in the caves around Marnoch Mor, you were the only one," she said, confused.

"I'm the only *pigmy* dragon still alive," Shona replied. "Felix is *not* a pigmy dragon."

"Well, what is he then?"

"Dragon Gigantasaurus," Bertie said with authority and before Shona could say it. "It means: giant dragon."

"I kind of got that," the girl said.

"A giant flying dragon with a famous bad temper and a taste for humans, birds and other dragons," the rat said with relish.

"I'm sure he's partial to rats too," grumbled the bird.

"Probably puts you all on sticks and eats you as a cocktail snack!"

Aldiss stuck out his little pink tongue and blew the dodo a raspberry.

"Bertie! Aldiss! Stop it!" Morag scolded. "This isn't helping."

"Sorry," they said in unison.

"So you can see why I'm very worried," Shona said. "I need to discuss this with Montgomery. Maybe he can think of a way of getting around Felix to get The Destine."

***

"No," said the wizard, stroking his chin thoughtfully, "I can't see how you can get it without coming up against Felix. According to the Klapp demons, he sits on top of their temple guarding the gold and jewels inside. No-one can get close to it, for if he even thinks someone is nearby he breathes fire and eats them for a snack. That's why the Klapp demons — what's left of them — have never returned to Graar to collect their treasure, but instead live on Murst.... We'll have to find another way."

He placed his teacup on its saucer on the table and scooped up a cupcake from the three-tiered cake stand. He stuffed it into his mouth, crumbs bouncing off Henry and falling on to his lap.

They were all sitting in the living room of the wizard's mansion on the edge of Marnoch Mor. Montgomery was comfortably ensconced on a large armchair next to the fire; Morag, Bertie and Aldiss were on the sofa; and Shona was sitting on the floor, her long body snaking behind them. There were three other large sofas in the huge room, a massive marble fireplace and lots of little tables strewn with magic books and old copies of *The Wizard* magazine. The flock-wallpapered walls were covered in large oil paintings of long dead magical folk, with the exception of one picture that hung over the fireplace: it depicted Montgomery in 18th century tailcoat and breeches.

Morag, who up until that point had contributed nothing to the conversation, suddenly broke the gloomy silence that had descended upon the small party.

"If this Graar was the kingdom of the Klapp demons," she began, "surely it will have more than one way in? You know what the Klapp demons are like. They are sneaky, as well as repulsive. They must have created other ways in and out of their city. All we need to do is find one. Then we could sneak into the kingdom, get The Destine and leave without Felix Saevus ever knowing we were there."

This caused Montgomery and Shona to start, Bertie to puff his feathers and Aldiss, who had been sitting preening his whiskers, to suddenly jump up and down on the sofa shouting: "Of course!"

"By 'we' I assume you mean you and your friends, in which case the answer is 'no'," said the wizard. "It's too dangerous. You're not going, Morag, and that's my final answer."

He rubbed his face with his hands, a gesture Morag had seen him make when he was stressed.

"But...!" she replied.

"No!"

"What if we sent an elite group of guards instead?" Shona suggested.

Montgomery thought about it.

"It could work," he conceded. "I could ask for volunteers..."

"No, that *wouldn't* work," said Morag, "we need as many guards as we can to watch over Marnoch Mor. If what Mephista says is right, then we'll need every man we have here to defend the town if Amergin attacks."

At that point, Montgomery's face turned a little shifty.

"What is it? Have you something to tell us Montgomery?" Morag asked.

"Mephista was telling us the truth. Amergin is getting ready to invade," he confessed. "When I was away, it was to meet with one of my spies. She's a trader who regularly visits the DarkIsle, so she knows a lot of what's going on there. She told me Amergin is definitely raising an army and he's planning to attack Marnoch Mor before the New Year."

"Why didn't you say something before?" Shona wanted to know.

"Didn't have the chance," he replied.

"Well that settles it," Morag said. "I'm going to go to Graar to get The Destine. It's our only hope."

"Well we'll come with you!" squeaked Aldiss excitedly.

"Will we?" hissed the dodo, fear tingeing his eyes. "And face the giant dragon?"

"Yes," hissed the rat behind a furry paw. "Morag needs us."

"I'm going too," said Shona.

Morag looked at Montgomery triumphantly.

"It looks like we're *all* going to Graar!" she said. Montgomery did not reply, but Morag could see he knew there was no other way.

"Only one problem," said Shona. "No-one knows where Graar is."

The group fell despondent again.

"There is one person who might know," Morag said.

They held their collective breaths.

"Well?" squeaked Aldiss, unable to contain his excitement.

"Tanktop," the girl said. "He's a Klapp demon, so he must know where Graar is and how to get into it."

"Tanktop?" Bertie said with disgust, remembering the stinking, sneaky creature — the same creature who had kidnapped Montgomery, taken Morag and generally been a nasty little sneak. "Him? You think *he'll* help us?"

"Why not?" asked the girl.

"Well, for one thing," the bird said, "nobody knows where he is. He didn't come with Mephista and MacAndrew. He's probably still on Murst with that demon and the Girallons. He's probably become their pet or something."

"He's a tricky one alright," Aldiss agreed.

Morag thought for a moment.

Then she said: "Bet he's not on the DarkIsle. Bet he's here in Marnoch Mor somewhere. He worships Mephista, he would do anything for her. There's no way he's going to leave her side, not even if she's in jail. He's bound to be somewhere close by, acting as her spy."

"Stinking, horrible little creature," snarled Shona, "it would be so like him to spy."

Just then there was a rustle and all eyes turned to a large fern sitting in an antique pot in the corner of the room. In an instant, Shona was over at it. She dug her claws into the large fronds and felt about a bit. There was a girly scream as she pulled out a struggling Klapp demon.

Chapter 5

"Tanktop!" the friends gasped when they saw who had been spying on them.

The Klapp demon, dangling by the neck from Shona's great claw, sheepishly waved at them.

"How did we not smell you?" Aldiss wanted to know, nose quivering as he sought the creature's normally pungent scent. There was none, just the faint smell of roses.

"Bleurgh, ack, hmmpffh," replied Tanktop.

"Shona, put him down, you're choking him!" Morag said.

Reluctantly, the dragon opened her claw and the mangy Klapp demon fell to the ground with a bump and a whimper. He got to his feet and smoothed down his matted fur.

"That's better," he said with a grin that showed off his two rows of sharp, yellowing teeth.

Everyone stared at him. He coughed and looked down at his feet, embarrassed at being caught. Still no-one spoke.

"Hello," Tanktop said.

Morag stepped forward, her forehead creased into a worried frown.

"How did you get in here?" she asked.

"Through the door," he replied.

"How did you get by the guards and the security spells?" she wanted to know.

"Ah, well, that's kind of a trade secret," he replied with a sly grin. The smile was soon wiped off his face when the dragon, already annoyed at him being there, swept the gangly creature up by the throat again and held him over the roaring fire in the fireplace. Morag wrinkled her nose as the smell of singeing fur filled the room.

"Eeeek!" screamed the Klapp demon. "Okay! Okay!"

"Put him down, Shona," said Morag.

"Do I have to?" the dragon replied. "I'm quite enjoying toasting this stinking thing."

"Yes."

Once again, Tanktop found himself unceremoniously dumped on the floor, a furious dragon breathing down his neck.

"I'll ask again: *how* did you get in here?" Morag asked.

"I... um... climbed up through the sewers," he replied.

The girl stepped forward and took a sniff of him.

"You don't smell like you've been in the sewers. In fact, you don't smell like a Klapp demon at all," she said.

"That's because I used a special spray to get rid of my normal manly scent," Tanktop replied. "You see, I knew that you lot — especially that vermin over there..." he said, pointing a long bony finger at the rat — Aldiss bristled — "...would be able to detect my presence, so I used a bit of a disguise." He pulled an aerosol out from nowhere. On the can, in big red letters, were the words "*Stinko: Get rid of that body odour fast!*" Morag rolled her eyes.

"And it worked!" the Klapp demon added with another huge grin. "You lot did not know I was there."

This was a worrying confession for Morag, who had increased the security spells around the Palace, the Museum of Weird Things and Magic and Montgomery's house after Tanktop had been able to get in before. Then he had stolen a magic tooth and kidnapped Montgomery. Now he was telling her he had been able to get round all the additional security she had organised. She glanced at Shona, whose face was set in a deep worried frown, and knew she was having the same thought.

"How long have you been here, spying?" the dragon asked through gritted teeth.

The Klapp demon looked down at his monkey-like feet and muttered something.

"What? I can't hear you," Shona hissed. "Lift your head

up and say it loud enough for us to hear or I'll hold you over the fire again."

"Two days," he said and then looked down again.

Shona let out a puff of smoke and sat back down on her haunches. She looked at Morag who was equally shocked by the confession.

"*Where* have you been hiding all this time?" Morag wanted to know.

"Um...around..."

"Be more specific," Montgomery demanded.

"Er...in here," Tanktop said, "and in the palace library. I've been following you around," he added, nodding towards Morag.

There was a loud gasp from everyone in the room. That meant that over the past 48 hours the Klapp demon must have heard everything they had said and seen everything Morag had done.

"Well we won't have to bring you up-to-date with all that's happened," growled the dragon, looking away from him in disgust, "because you already know everything."

Tanktop didn't dare respond. No-one said anything for a moment.

Then Shona, in her role as Special Chief Constable of the Marnoch Mor Volunteer Police Force, made a decision: "I think we had better take you to the cells where you can wait until we can bring you to trial for spying, kidnap and generally being a nasty piece of work. I think you'll find that the judge, whoever that might be, will have no doubts of your guilt and will send you to prison for the rest of your miserable little life," she spat.

The Klapp demon quivered and whimpered and looked like the coward he truly was.

"Please don't put me on trial!" he wailed. "I don't want to go to jail. There are nasty horrible things there."

"Then you'll fit in perfectly," growled the dragon.

"Well you should have thought about that before you committed those crimes," Morag said. She turned to Shona: "Please take him away, Shona. We'll let the judge deal with him." To Tanktop she said: "And I hope you get everything you deserve."

"No! No! Wait! I don't want to go on trial! I can help you," Tanktop said desperately. "Please don't send me to prison. I can help, I can help!" Then he added desperately: "I know where Graar is."

Morag looked at him, searching his monkey-like face for any sign of duplicity. There was an earnest look in his eyes and he seemed genuine enough.

"How do we know we can trust you?" she asked.

"Because I want something from you," he said, his deep brown eyes looking straight into hers. "I want what my mistress wants. I want to return Murst to my Lady Mephista..."

Shona snarled.

"...and rid the land of that creature Amergin," he finished. "He's worse than Devlish and does not treat the Klapp demons with respect. He needs to be sent back to wherever he came from."

Morag looked round at her friends, who seemed as sceptical as she felt, but she knew they didn't have a lot of choice in the matter. They would have to let the Klapp demon show them the way to Graar.

"And do you know of another entrance into Graar — one that will take us past Felix?" Morag wanted to know.

"Yes."

There was a pause.

"Okay," said the girl. "Are you okay with that, Montgomery?"

The wizard nodded. "Do we have any other choice?" he replied.

"So," the girl said, turning to face Tanktop once more,

"where is this entranceway to Graar?"

"I need a map of Scotland," the creature said.

Montgomery went to a large leather trunk sitting in a dark corner in one side of his study and flipped the lid open. He rummaged through a large pile of scrolls until he found what he was looking for. He pulled one out, shut the trunk lid and walked over to the desk. Untying the red satin ribbon that held the scroll closed, he smoothed the paper open on the desktop to reveal a beautifully hand-painted map of mainland Scotland. He motioned for the Klapp demon to join him at the desk. With a fearful glance at the dragon, the demon slunk over and climbed up onto Montgomery's large leather chair so that he might have a better view of the map. Morag, Shona, Bertie and Aldiss gathered at the other side of the desk.

"Show us," the wizard demanded.

The demon looked down and stared at the map. He scratched his head and made a lot of 'um' and 'er' noises.

"Do you know where it is or don't you?" Shona snarled.

"Give me a minute!" snapped the Klapp demon.

The dragon roared at him and made to grab him again... this time with her teeth.

"Shona!" Morag warned.

The dragon stopped herself inches from Tanktop's face and pulled back.

"Find this place, demon, before I snap you in two!" she warned the whimpering Tanktop.

He glanced down at the paper and then back at her.

"Could you...could you...maybe go and wait over there?" he asked. "Your proximity is making me nervous."

"Shona, please can you do as he asks?" Montgomery said.

Shona's green lips pursed and she was about to say something, but must have thought better of it. Without another word, but with an evil look cast at the quivering

Klapp demon, she turned around and stomped to the other side of the room, where she sat on the floor with her arms crossed and her back to everyone. All eyes turned back to Tanktop.

"Where is this entrance?" Morag wanted to know.

"Do you really know where it is or are you just having us on?" said Bertie.

"I think he's lying," added Aldiss.

"I do know, I do know!" squealed Tanktop. "Just give me a minute! It's here somewhere if only I could remember."

"What do you mean: 'if only I could remember'?" asked Morag. "I thought you knew where Graar is."

"I do...it's just...well, it's been a long time," he confessed.

"So do you *actually* know where it is?"

"Yes," he replied. "The entrance to Graar is a cave on the far north coast of Scotland. It's near a place called Durness in Sutherland, but I can't see it on this map."

Morag peered closely at the north western coastline. The names of the places written there were quite faded, but she could just about make out what they said.

"Hmmm, does the cave have a name?" she asked.

"Um...Soo or Boo or...or...Poo...I don't know. Something like that," he stuttered.

"Is it Smoo? Smoo Cave?" the girl asked excitedly.

"Yes, yes, that's it!" he squeaked in delight. "Where is it?"

He studied the map as Morag pointed to the place.

"There!" she said, stabbing the paper with her forefinger.

Sure enough, above her finger, written in curling Copperplate lettering, were the words: *Smoo Cave.*

"And there's Durness," she said, pointing to a dot on the map where the tiny hamlet was marked.

Montgomery, Aldiss and Bertie looked at it too.

"Well," said the girl, "now we know where to go, let's get ready."

"Um," said Bertie, "how are we going to get there?"

"Underground?" Morag suggested.

"No good, trains don't run that far north-west," said the bird. "We can go as far as Tongue by train, but no further."

"Could Kyle meet us and sail us round the coastline?" Aldiss suggested.

"No, he's away on family business this week," said a voice from the other side of the room.

Everyone turned to look at the grumpy dragon and all their faces said: *How do you know?*

"I went fishing with him two days ago. He said he wouldn't be around for ten days, something about a big family do in the south. We'll have to find some other way of getting there."

Morag turned to Montgomery.

"Do we have anyone already up there who could help?" she asked.

The wizard rubbed his chin.

"Well, there is someone, but whether she'll help us or not is another question," he said.

"Why not?" the girl wanted to know.

"She's kind of not speaking to me at the moment," he said. "In fact, she hates me."

"Hates you?" Aldiss squeaked. "Who *is* this woman?"

"Her name is Claudine. And she's my wife."

Before they could fully take in what he was saying, he quickly added: "We had a difference of opinion a few years ago, she left and I haven't seen her since...if that's what you want to know!"

Morag was the first to find her voice. Still shocked that Montgomery was married and none of them knew, she said: "Do you think she will help us...if she knows how serious the situation is?"

"Only one way to find out," Montgomery said. "We'll need to ask her."

***

Montgomery's face was ashen as he took his place on the red velvet bar stool underneath the stairs in the hallway. Unlike the beautifully wood-panelled majesty that was Montgomery's entrance hall, the under-stairs cupboard that housed the telephone was plain and a little bit dingy. A single Blue Moonstone lit up the tiny space and there was flowery linoleum on the floor. The telephone, a large black Bakelite creation from the 1950s, was screwed to the back wall. The wizard lifted its receiver and stuck a finger in its rotary dial. He hesitated.

"Morag, I can't!" he gasped.

"You can," she assured him. "We need her help, you said so yourself."

"I've not spoken to her for years, she might slam the phone down on me," he said.

"And she might not," replied the girl. "Phone her."

With a trembling hand and a loud sigh, Montgomery began to dial. The telephone's rotary dial whirred as it went through its rotation then, when Montgomery had finished dialling the number, there was a pause before Morag could distinctly hear the faint brrring... brrring... brrring of the call at the other end of the line, the call that would take them through to Claudine Montgomery.

Brrring... brrring...

Brrring... brrring...

...the phone went.

Seconds that felt like minutes came and went.

Brrring... brrring...

Brrring... brrring...

"She not in." The relief in Montgomery's voice was palpable. He was about to put down the receiver, but Morag stopped him.

"Give it another wee minute," said the girl.

Brrring…

"*Hello*?" a woman's voice rang out of the receiver causing the wizard to start. "*Hello?*"

Montgomery lifted the handset to his ear and spoke.

"Hello Claudine," he said…his voice almost a whisper. "It's James. I need a favour." Morag, who could no longer make out what the woman was saying, stood patiently at his side listening to his end of the conversation.

"Claudine I need your help. Please listen. Wait! Don't put the phone down. Marnoch Mor needs you!" pleaded the wizard. Then he whispered something into the receiver that Morag could not make out, but it seemed to do the trick. This mysterious woman, Montgomery's wife, listened and stayed listening as the wizard told her all about what had happened — about Amergin and what he hoped she could do to assist.

"I need you to meet them at the station and take them to Smoo Cave," he said. "That's all, you don't have to do anything else."

Morag could hear Claudine responding, but could not make out the words clearly. Then…

"Yes, I know I could just as easily take them… no, I mean I can't. I need to be here to try and work out a way of defeating him. Besides, you know I can only leave Marnoch Mor for a couple of days at a time," he snapped. "Yes, I'm still tied to the Eye. No, no, Claud, don't hang up. We need your help."

She must have said something to Montgomery about Morag, for he glanced down at her.

"Yes, it's true. She's the lost princess…Mmmmm…She's going on the mission with some others…Of course I don't want her to go, but she's adamant…If you help us you'll get to meet her so you can ask her that yourself. Come on, what do you say? Are you up for it? If you can't do it for me, do it for yourself, for your friends. If we don't stop Amergin, no-one will be safe."

There was a pause whilst, Morag assumed, Claudine was thinking about it.

"Thank you, Claud… Claudine, you'll not regret it. I'm putting them on the afternoon train. That should give them enough time to gather together all the things they might need," he told her.

There was another pause.

"Thanks for this Claudine, I really appreciate it."

He put the receiver down and turned to Morag. She was smiling.

***

It took the band of friends less than an hour to gather all the items they thought they might need for the trip. They ran back to the Palace and raided its extensive kitchens, large workshops and stables of various items on a list that ran like this:

- ✓ Torches
- ✓ Ropes for climbing
- ✓ Hard hats
- ✓ Warm clothing (waterproof)
- ✓ Food and drink (Bertie's magic satchel)
- ✓ Sturdy boots (Morag, Bertie to wear his winter boots)
- ✓ Map of the north of Scotland (just in case)
- ✓ Magical mobile phone for emergencies
- ✓ Claudine's telephone number
- ✓ One bag of lemon bon-bons for the journey (Aldiss's request)

Morag also had the perfect excuse to change out of her

restrictive 'princess' dress and slip into a pair of jeans and a t-shirt. For the first time in ages, she felt herself again. She was smiling as she went downstairs to join the others.

"Well, that's everything," Shona said as she surveyed the pile of stuff piled on the marble floor of the Palace's reception hallway.

"Not everything," Morag replied.

The friends turned as one to look at her.

"What do you mean? We've got hard hats, boots, torches, a map..." Aldiss said.

"Yes, but I haven't told my parents yet," the girl sighed. *And I'm not looking forward to it*, she thought.

Chapter 6

Morag did not know how best to break the news of her departure to her parents. On the one hand, she was going to do something that would, she hoped, eventually lead to them being freed. On the other, she was putting herself in grave danger — again — and she knew they weren't going to allow her to do that. She rehearsed what she was going to say as she leapt up the stairwell to the first floor, where the bedrooms were. Her parents, still trapped in their now re-framed oil paintings, were watching television in their room when she came to say goodbye. Their bedroom, like Morag's, was sumptuously decorated in rich brocades and velvets. The paintings were propped up in their usual space on the multiple pillows and cushions that were piled on their four-poster bed. At the end of the bed was a large flat-screen television. An American sitcom was showing and Morag could hear her father chuckling as she opened the bedroom door.

"I love this show," he said as she peeked around the door. "Oh! Morag! Come over here and see this, it's hysterical."

Meekly, the girl did as she was asked. She ran across the floor, around the chaise longue and launched herself, as she always did, at the bed. The shock of her weight hitting the mattress caused the two paintings to rock violently, so much so that Isabella's toppled over. There were muffled sounds of laughter as a horrified Morag quickly moved to set her right again.

"Sorry," she said as she placed her mother's portrait back against the pillows.

"Don't worry about it, Morag," Isabella replied, her voice warm and soft. "It's so nice to be able to sort of move that I really don't mind being toppled on to the bed. I missed seeing you do silly things like that when you were growing up, so you jumping on the bed is just heavenly."

Morag smiled. Heavenly was the right word for it. It had been like a miracle when she had found out that Nathan and Isabella were her own long lost parents. Her heart soared with love and relief and happiness that the three of them were together at last, even though they could not hold each other. And, despite their imprisonment and Montgomery's inability to free them, Nathan and Isabella remained cheerful throughout.

"How are you today, daughter of mine?" Nathan crowed from the other side of the bed. "Been up to anything interesting?"

"Well..." Morag began.

"I'm just asking, you understand, because I'm interested, not because I want to get you into trouble or anything like that," he added hastily.

"I didn't think you were..." the girl continued.

"Of course, if you *have* been up to no good, as your father I should be disciplining you," he said more seriously. Then: "Feels good to say 'as your father'. We didn't think we'd ever see you again after we were trapped..."

There was a heavy silence, which Morag knew meant her parents were thinking of the ten years they had all been apart: Morag with her guardians living in a draughty old guesthouse on Irvine Beach; and Isabella and Nathan stuck inside the paintings not knowing what had become of their baby daughter. There they had stayed until Morag had escaped from the Stoker's guesthouse, gone to Murst and stumbled across the paintings in Mephista's bedroom. For some reason, only she could hear them talking and they had struck up a friendship without knowing who the other really was. Morag had rescued them and it was only later, when they had escaped from the DarkIsle, that their true relationship was discovered.

"Let's not talk of such sad things," said Isabella suddenly. "Morag, you look as if you've come to tell us something. What is it child?"

Morag grabbed the TV remote and turned down the volume. They weren't going to like this. With a deep breath to give her courage, Morag told them of her conversation with Mephista and how the witch would only free them if she, Morag, rid Murst of Amergin. She told them what Montgomery had gleaned about the demon and how there was only one thing that could rid the Earth of the creature once and for all and that was The Destine in Graar.

"Tanktop has reluctantly agreed to come with us," she explained, "to show us a way into Graar that will not take us near Felix Saevus. Montgomery's wife, Claudine, is helping too."

"What!" roared Nathan. "What is Montgomery thinking about letting our daughter, our only child, put herself in such danger?"

"We have no choice," said Morag, "there's no-one else."

"What about the Volunteer Police Force? Can't they do it?" her father demanded.

"Shona's coming with us," replied the girl.

"Fat lot of good a pigmy dragon will do coming up against something like Felix. He's enormous."

"And he can fly," interjected Isabella.

"And he's got a stinking temper. That's why he was banished to Graar when the Klapp demons moved out," Nathan continued.

"I thought he'd forced them out," Morag said.

"Well, okay, he did force them out. Many of them had already gone to Murst anyway, into the employ of Devlish, and Felix was attracted by their vast treasure so he chased the remaining guards out," he admitted. "But, that's beside the point! I don't want any daughter of mine putting herself in such danger! I forbid you to go!"

"But dad...!"

"No Morag, you've not to go!" he demanded.

"But dad if I hadn't put myself in danger the last time, you and mum wouldn't be here now and Montgomery would be dead. Marnoch Mor would be just a pile of dust. I can take care of myself. I've done it before and I will do it again," she shouted. "Besides I've got loads of help..."

"A rat, a dodo and a dragon? What kind of help is that?" he rasped.

"And Henry and Claudine and Tanktop. There are lots of us and we'll keep each other safe."

"No! I forbid it!"

"Nathan." Isabella's voice was soothing. "I don't like it any more than you, but I don't think we're in a position to dictate to Morag. She's right, she has done this before. We need to let her go."

"But, it's dangerous and we've only just got her back," he replied emotionally.

"I know, but I trust her and I trust Montgomery. He would never let her go if he didn't think she was capable of doing this."

While Morag bit her lip, Nathan mused over Isabella's words and the only sound in the room was the soft burble of the television. The tension was finally broken by her mother.

"Besides, Nathan," she said, "in our current position, trapped as we are, with only Morag able to hear us, how on earth could we stop her from going anyway?"

There was a harrumph as Nathan acknowledged she was right.

"Okay," he finally said, "you can go, but don't come running to me if Felix gobbles you up for breakfast!"

Morag laughed at how absurd her father sounded.

"Okay dad," she said, relieved the first hurdle was over. Now she just had to get by Felix, get The Destine and come home. "I'll be careful, I promise."

"You'd better be!" her father warned. "Now come and give us a hug."

Grateful there would be no more fighting. Morag pulled the two paintings to her and hugged them tightly. She knew her parents couldn't feel her doing this, but it was the principle of the act that mattered: her hug showed them she loved them and that was good enough for her.

"Morag, before you go," Isabella began, "there is something I must warn you about. The Klapp Demon is not to be trusted..."

"I *know* that, mum," the girl interrupted, "but it was *he* who offered to lead us to Graar."

"He's tricky and sneaky and a downright little...!" Nathan growled.

"Yes, he's all those things," Isabella continued, "but he also has his own reasons for going back there."

"What do you mean?" Morag asked.

"I believe the Klapp demons have some sort of magic of their own," her mother continued, "and it's all centred within some object that was lost to them when Felix decided to move into Graar. The Klapp demons weren't always the servants of the Devlish clan, you know. They were a strong race. They had their own kingdom, their own ways and they worked for themselves, not for some warlock and his horrible daughter." The last words were almost spat out and Morag didn't blame her mother for feeling so passionately about Mephista. After all, it was the witch who had imprisoned Isabella and Nathan, forcing them apart for eternity whilst being so close. "Their ways were dangerous and they lived wild and violent lives."

"What I'm saying," Isabella continued, "is don't be surprised if he tries to get away from you when you are down there. Watch him carefully, make sure he never leaves your side. The Klapp demons must not become magical again. That would cause chaos."

"Okay," Morag replied. An icy chill ran down her spine. There was more at stake than she imagined. "Maybe we shouldn't take him."

"No," her mother snapped. "He must go if he's the only hope of getting The Destine..."

"And of getting out again," Nathan finished.

"Mum, this magical thing you think Tanktop will be after," Morag said, "you don't think it *is* The Destine?"

There was a pause.

"It's possible," Isabella admitted.

"Now you must get going," she continued. "You don't want to miss your train."

"Okay, mum."

Morag got up to leave.

"Be safe, child," Isabella said, "and come back to us in one piece."

"I will," Morag promised.

"Remember that we love you," her father added.

Leaving her parents' bedroom was one of the hardest things Morag had ever had to do, but she knew she had to go because she was their only hope of freedom. With this in her mind, she gave them one last smile before closing the door behind her and hurrying back downstairs to where her friends were waiting for her.

Shona gave her a huge toothy dragon grin as she approached.

"Everything okay?" she asked as the girl put on her red duffel coat and scooped up her rucksack.

"Yes," Morag replied. She glanced behind the green scaly body of her friend and saw Tanktop sitting there looking all innocent. He looked up, saw her and grimaced. "Yes, everything is all right," she said. She would tell Shona all about what her mother had told her at a later date. She did not want Tanktop to know she suspected him of anything.

"Good," her friend replied. "Now, come on, let's go. We've got a train to catch!"

***

"Good luck," said Montgomery, worried eyes on the girl. Morag seemed oblivious to his fears. She grinned back at him. "And be careful," said the wizard.

"We will," she replied, giving him a hug. "We'll be fine. We'll grab The Destine and be back in Marnoch Mor before you know it, I promise."

They were standing on an underground platform of Marnoch Mor's Central Station, surrounded by rucksacks, discarded gloves and a small lump of cheese tied in a red spotty handkerchief. Aldiss, the owner of the handkerchief, was sitting on Shona's backpack pulling on a tiny pair of thermal boots. The dragon was checking the efficacy of her compass and Bertie was standing guard over Tanktop, who was looking like he might bolt for freedom at any minute. The Klapp demon, like the rest of them, was swathed in warm, waterproof clothing and on his monkey-like feet he wore glove-like rubber boots. He glowered at Morag and the wizard.

Montgomery took his magical medallion Henry from around his neck and offered him to Morag.

"Here, take Henry, you may just need his talents."

"Hey, wait a minute!" the medallion complained, his tiny gold face screwing up in annoyance. "I'm fed up with you just giving me up for these missions," he continued. "It would be nice to be *asked* for once, not just handed over like a...like a...piece of jewellery."

Montgomery sighed

"Would you *mind* going with Morag?" he asked. Then he added: "Please?"

"Hmph," replied Henry grumpily. If he could have (and

if he had had them), he would have folded his arms and turned his back on them, but being a medallion this was an impossibility.

"We don't want him anyway," said Shona, who was still engrossed in the compass. "He doesn't bring anything to our adventures."

"What?!?" Henry snarled. "I'll have you know that I am a very magical medallion and I can perform lots of different magic that *has* come in very handy on previous adventures and *will* come in very handy on this trip."

"Name one!" the dragon goaded. She was looking at him now with narrowed eyes and there was a small smile playing about her green lips.

"I can...I..." replied the medallion, who was so furious he was unable to answer.

"See!" said the dragon triumphantly. "I told you so!"

"I can freeze and stun people and bring others back from the dead — like I did with Aldiss — and... and..." Henry stuttered. Then he went quiet. "I *will* come on this mission," he decided, "whether Shona wants me there or not."

"Oh I don't mind you being there," replied the dragon. "I just don't want you doing your usual thing of trying to get us all to cajole you into coming so that you can somehow feel all superior. We don't have the time for that."

"Well!" replied the medallion in a rage. "Of all the...! You sneaky...!"

"Henry! Shona! Enough!" snapped Morag who was getting more than tired of their bickering. She reached out and took the medallion from Montgomery. "Thanks," she said to the wizard.

"No problem," he replied, bemused by the arguing of the tiny medallion and the *much* bigger dragon. "I just hope they can behave themselves enough to complete this mission."

"They will, I'll make sure of it," Morag told him. She turned to her friends. "Okay," she said, "do we all have our rucksacks?"

There was a round of 'yes's and a jiggling of bag straps.

"Good." She glanced down at a pink watch on her wrist. The face was smiling adoringly at her, its little eyes crinkling up into a smile when it realised she was looking at it. It had been an early Christmas gift from Shona. It was supposed to digitally display the time when the owner looked at it, but the little watch was so busy loving Morag that it continually forgot its purpose. Morag cleared her throat to remind it.

"Oops!" the watch said in a tiny tinkling voice. "Sorry!" Then with a burst of pride it displayed 14:00.

"Where's the train? It's supposed to be here by now," grumbled the girl, looking up the tracks. Just as she said this there was a low rumbling. It grew louder and as the sound increased, the platform began to vibrate like a washing machine on full spin speed. Rumble, rumble, RUMBLE! It got so bad that the band of friends were forced to cover their ears from the sound whilst trying to keep on their feet as the vibration grew to epic proportions. Then suddenly a train flew into the station and came to a screeching halt right next to where they were all standing.

"Oh my!" shouted Bertie in excitement, eyes twinkling. He flapped his wings and hopped from foot to foot. "She's back!"

Everyone looked at the engine that had caused all the fuss and a collective groan went up. For there, standing before them, whinnying gently, was the love of Bertie's trainspotting life: the ancient steam engine, The Flying Horse. She was in great condition: gleaming from wheels to whistle and pulling an old First Class carriage behind her.

"Hello, my beauty," the dodo crooned as he gently stroked the engine's boiler with a tiny wing. The train gave a little shudder of pleasure.

"Oh boy," muttered Aldiss, "we're never going to hear the end of this! The last time we rode *this* train, Bertie did nothing but speak of it for two whole weeks. I wouldn't mind, but he talked about it through breakfast, lunch and ten episodes of my favourite TV programme."

"Well, she's here now, so I suppose we'd better just make the best of it," said Morag, watching in amusement as Bertie cuddled the steam train. "Let's go. We don't have a lot of time."

She turned back to Montgomery.

"See you soon," she said. Then: "Do you have a message for Claudine?"

He shook his head.

"Okay, I'll see you later, then," she replied.

"Take care, Your Highness," he replied.

Morag sighed.

"Please don't call me that," she complained as she scooped up her bag and slung it round her shoulder. "My name is Morag, plain old Morag."

The wizard smiled and watched as she led her friends on board the luxurious carriage linked to the train. It was made of wood and painted a deep red with gold scrolling highlights. Inside were little wooden tables, carved with woodland creatures of all sorts, and great big leather chairs that had been made with comfort in mind. Bertie did not join his friends inside, but instead leapt up the footplate of the engine and stood beside an Instant Driver created to drive the train. His little black eyes shone with delight as he made himself comfortable for the journey ahead.

"Where to sir?" the Instant Driver asked, his grey powdery face serious to the task ahead.

"Tongue. And don't spare the horses!" the bird squawked.

In the carriage, Morag carefully placed her bag on the

luggage rack and plonked herself down on a seat near a window overlooking the platform. As the train drew away from the station, she gave Montgomery a wave and then settled down for the hour-long journey ahead. Henry felt reassuringly heavy around her neck and she stroked him absentmindedly as she thought about their latest adventure. It would be dangerous, of that she had no doubt, but she had her friends around her to keep her safe. She closed her eyes and relaxed, lulled into a dreamy, calm state by the low purring of the medallion. Soon she and Henry were fast asleep, oblivious to their friends and the Klapp demon sitting nearby and of the various underground stations they passed through en route. The train chugged gently on.

Chapter 7

"Morag, time to wake up!" a voice broke into her slumbers. She felt hot breath on her cheek and she stretched and slowly opened her eyes. Someone was staring intently at her. She started and pulled back before realising the large yellow eyes peering at her and the burning hot breath belonged to Shona. The dragon grinned.

"Sorry, I didn't mean to make you jump," her friend said, her voice soft and reassuring, "but I thought you'd want to know we have arrived."

Morag sat up and in doing so woke the slumbering Henry. His tiny almost-not-there eyes sprang open and he shouted out: "Don't shout at me! I was only saying!"

"What?" said Shona.

"What?" said Morag.

"What?" replied Henry. "Er...oops, I must have been dreaming. Are we there yet?"

"Yes," replied the dragon. "Come on, let's get going, Claudine will be waiting for us."

Tongue station was tucked away underground and lit by softly glowing blue Moonstones. The friends exited the carriage, collected a disgruntled Bertie from the cab (he did not want to leave his beloved engine) and made their way up a set of slate stairs. Shona led the way, a Moonstone lodged on a band around her head which made Morag think of a miner's helmet. Its dim glow gave the dragon enough light to see where she was going, but the stairs were small and narrow, causing her claws to slip and miss a step as she tried to get a proper footing. Morag and Henry followed close behind with Bertie and Aldiss bringing up the rear. Tanktop, their reluctant companion, was dangling by the neck from one of Shona's claws. He winced and whined every time the great lizard "accidentally" banged him off a wall. The stairwell was badly lit and it took them all their time to stumble up the steps and feel their way along the cold earthen passageway, moving carefully to make sure they did not bang into each other.

Ten minutes into the climb, the dragon suddenly came to a stop, causing each friend behind her to bump into the one in front. She reached out and her claw hit a bank of earth.

"Shona? What's the matter?" Morag asked, squeezing alongside her friend's scaly body to get a better look.

"We seem to have come up against some sort of barrier," the dragon replied, her nails scraping off great clods of earth as she ran them down the wall. "This appears to be a dead-end," she added.

"Let me see," Morag said. "Shine the Moonstone slowly over the wall so that I can get a good look at it."

The dragon did as she was bid and in the dim light of the stone they could make out a great wall of earth that blocked the passageway. Morag searched for some sort of doorknob, thinking there might be one like there had been on the wall of the cave on Irvine Beach some months before, but she could find none. All she could see was a rich, dark earth, plant roots and stones. She reached her hands up and felt along the wall. It was cold and damp and pitted with sharp things, but no door handle.

"Hmmm...that's odd," the girl said aloud.

"What's the matter?" Bertie called from behind. "What's going on? Why have we stopped?"

"We can't go any further," the girl replied. "The way is blocked."

"What do you mean 'the way is blocked'?" the bird wanted to know. He tried to peer round Shona, but could only see the dragon's great scaly behind. "Can you see what's going on Aldiss?"

The rat also peered around Shona, but could only see

feet and said so.

"Well this is a bit of a nuisance," the dodo went on. "I wonder if I've got anything in my satchel that might help."

"Cheese?" Aldiss asked.

"No, I was thinking more along the lines of a shovel," the bird snapped. "Now let me have a look…" His voice became muffled as he stuck his beak into his magical satchel. Bertie's bag was by now legendary amongst the friends, having furnished them with food, spell components and other vital things during their previous two adventures. All he had to do was to ask it for something and it generally gave him what he wanted. There were limits to what it could provide, but Bertie was very pleased with it nonetheless.

There was a very loud sigh from Morag's neck. The girl glanced down at Henry. She couldn't see his facial expression, but knew by the sigh that the medallion was feeling impatient and annoyed with them.

"Are you all right Henry?" she asked.

"No I'm not!" he snapped. "I want to get out of this place. It's quite horrible and I'm sure the dampness down here is wasting my gold."

"But, didn't you hear? We can't go any further," the girl said.

There was another audible gasp from the medallion.

"Yes I did hear and I don't understand why we're still here," he said. There was silence. "Give it a shove," he said.

"What?" said Morag. Give *what* a shove? She didn't know what he meant.

"Morag, I know you're a princess now and everything, but I hope wearing a crown has not affected your intellect!" he replied officiously. "I said give it a shove. Give the earthen barrier a shove."

"Okay," replied the girl uncertainly. She didn't know what the medallion was playing at. There was no way she could move this mound of earth on her own, but she decided to go along with what he was asking. She put her hands out and pushed.

"Harder!" urged the medallion.

"I'm trying!"

"Harder than that!" he said.

"I am!"

Then the earth began to dissolve around Morag's hands and if it hadn't been for the quick thinking of Shona grabbing her coat, she would have overbalanced and fallen through the hole that suddenly appeared before them. As they watched, the wall melted away, revealing the outline of a tall, thin person. They squinted to see who it was as the figure stepped forward into the blue light of the Moonstone. It was a woman. She was tall and beautiful with long dark hair and dark eyes. She was swathed from head to foot in a padded red ski suit, wore heavy walking boots and a stylish woolly hat.

"Hello!" she said, removing a glove from her right hand and extending it to Morag. "I'm Claudine and you must be..."

"Morag," said Morag, shaking the woman's hand. It was soft and warm.

"Great to meet you at last Your Royal Highness," she said, dropping into a neat curtsey.

"Please call me Morag," said the girl, "and please don't feel you have to curtsey."

After introductions were made to the rest of the party, Claudine led them out into the sharpness of the open air. After the too-comfortable warmth of the train and the stuffiness of the station, the cold air was just the tonic they needed to wake them all up. Morag was the first to have a good look around. It was by now late afternoon and the sun had almost completely set over the northern Scottish sky, which was thick with a blanket of heavy grey clouds. It was getting dark and she could not see much of the cold wintry landscape she knew she was standing in. Morag shivered as she felt the sting of an icy December wind on her cheeks. There was a sharp tang in the air that told of an impending snow shower and she pulled her duffel coat closer around her small body.

"Come on," Claudine instructed, "over here. I've got transport waiting. Watch your feet, it's been pretty icy around here lately."

In the unfolding darkness, the friends cautiously followed the willowy figure of Montgomery's wife. The ground was hard with frost and full of grass clumps and ruts that caused them to stumble and trip. Once Bertie nearly took a header over a particularly large tuffet of grass and was prevented from a certain fall by Shona. The dragon caught a hold of his little white tail feathers and yanked him back.

"Ow!" Bertie complained as the dragon released him, sending a couple of his tail feathers fluttering to the ground. "My tail!"

"Well that's gratitude for you!" she muttered.

"Sorry!" the dodo began, but the little speech he had conceived about how grateful he was to her for saving him despite the loss of the feathers was stopped before it could begin by Claudine removing something from her jacket pocket, holding it up and…

"Beep beep beep!"

Headlights flashed across their path, lighting up bleak moorland and the first flurries of snow.

"Whaaaa…?" exclaimed the bird in surprise, for he could see nothing there.

"Transport," replied Claudine. "Come on, let's get in before this snow gets any worse."

She beeped the keys again and this time the dark outline of an old-fashioned bus revealed itself to them. First the bumper with the headlights, then the driver's seat, the door and row after row of old leather and metal seats and lozenge-shaped windows. The interior lights flicked on, bright and glowing and then, finally, the rear of the bus appeared. Vrooooom! growled the engine and the headlights blinked on once more.

The snow was getting heavier and was starting to lie on the ground. Claudine quickly opened the bus's door and ushered everyone inside. It took several minutes to get Shona into the bus, but a little pushing from Claudine and pulling from Morag and Aldiss soon did the trick. She squeezed in, Klapp demon still dangling from one claw, and sat down in the aisle between the seats. Bertie and Aldiss raced up the bus to bag the back seats. Dispatching their luggage on to the row in front, the rat squeaked in delight as he took his seat; for, as Bertie loved old trains, Aldiss was a bit of a vintage bus buff. Morag sat near the front next to Shona and loosened her coat. The bus was warm and comfortable, and smelled of ancient leather and furniture polish.

"Everyone in?" Claudine asked. "Good. Let's go."

She climbed into the driver's seat and grabbed the wheel. The bus's door swooshed shut and the interior lights extinguished themselves as the bus began to roll forward into the snowy night. Morag leaned on the back of the seat in front of her, head resting on her arms, and looked out of the windscreen. The wipers were swishing furiously across the glass, wiping away the snowstorm, as the little bus bumped and banged its way over the rough ground.

"Claudine?" Morag called loudly in order to be heard over the roaring sound of the engine and the creak of the wipers. "Are we going straight to the cave?"

"Whaaat?" the woman shouted over the melee.

"I said ARE WE GOING STRAIGHT TO THE CAVE?"

"I can't hear you!" Claudine yelled back, using a hand to

pat one ear to make her point.

Morag rose from her seat, carefully stepped over Shona's green tail that snaked down the aisle, and walked unsteadily to the driver. The bus jostled and jolted as it went, sending the girl this way and that way, but by clinging on to various metal handholds along the way, Morag was able to reach Claudine.

"I SAID ARE WE GOING STRAIGHT TO THE CAVE?" she shouted at the woman.

Claudine nodded.

"OF COURSE. THIS IS JUST A GENTLE FLURRY. YOU SHOULD SEE IT IN THE MIDDLE OF WINTER!"

"Oh!" replied Morag, not sure whether she was relieved or upset at this. She peered out into the bleak landscape. There was not much to see for there were no streetlights, but even if there had been the constant sprays of snow on the windows would have blocked out most of it.

***

Tongue's magical underground station was not in the village itself, but in a field about half a mile away. Claudine carefully drove the little bus across the open ground until it joined a single track road, the main thoroughfare in that part of the country. And by then the snow had eased and turned to sleet.

Claudine steered left, heading west, and then, without so much as a 'by your leave' to her passengers, she put her foot down. The bus's engine roared in protest as the woman pushed it on faster and faster along the sleet-laden coast road. As the bus swung from side to side, Morag grew fearful that the vehicle, ancient and rickety as it was, would suddenly leave the road and plummet down the cliffs she knew were to their right. She closed her eyes and tried to relax. Montgomery would not have delivered them into the care of a madwoman, no matter how crazy her driving...she hoped.

The journey only took about five minutes according to Henry — who seemed excited by the rush — but felt much longer to the girl. She was delighted when, at the medallion's prompt, she opened her eyes to see the white of a little cottage looming into view. The house was typical of a Highland croft, a small home with no garden to speak of, but set in acres of wild countryside.

"That's Claudine's home," Henry said with glee.

"How do you know?" she asked.

"I've been here before," he replied in a tone of voice that made Morag feel a little stupid. "She *is* married to Montgomery you know."

"Oh, yes, I'd forgotten," the girl replied, straining to see more of the little house.

"As you can just about see through this sleet," the medallion said, "the outside it is small and neat. But, once through the little black wooden door, it is no ordinary house. Inside it is a little bit like stepping into the Museum of Weird Things and Magic back in Marnoch Mor. It's not as grand or as richly decorated; but, like the museum, it is much, much bigger on the inside than the outside."

Almost as if able to read their lips, Claudine shouted from the front of the bus, "I WOULD NORMALLY INVITE YOU IN. BUT WE HAVEN'T TIME TO STOP.

***

The bus trundled on with its journey for more than half an hour and Morag was just drifting into a half sleep when, without any warning, the bus groaned loudly. The brakes screamed and the vintage vehicle came to a sudden stop, sending all its passengers forward with a violent jolt. Ignoring the protests of her passengers, Claudine opened up the driver's door and slipped out. She turned to look back at Morag and her friends, who were in the process of picking themselves up from the bus floor. In the light of the headlamps, Morag could see her frown.

"What are you all waiting for?" Claudine shouted. "Come on!"

"A better driver," Bertie muttered as he hauled himself to his feet from under the chair where he had fallen and gave his little white tail a quick flick. To the bewildered Aldiss, he added: "Remind me never to get into any sort of moving vehicle she's driving."

"Me too!" the rat replied, brushing himself down.

Carefully, the friends followed the tall figure of Montgomery's estranged wife off the bus.

"Why do you think Montgomery and Claudine live apart?" Morag whispered, suddenly wanting to know.

"Dunno," replied Bertie, "I didn't even know he was married."

"Me neither," agreed Aldiss.

"Do you know, Shona?" the girl asked the dragon, but Shona merely shrugged.

All eyes fell on the smallest of their number.

"Henry?" Morag asked. The medallion looked a little uncomfortable.

"How would I know?" he muttered.

"Because you are always with Montgomery," replied Morag.

"And you've been his magical medallion for a long time," added Bertie.

"It's none of our business," the medallion snapped.

"Yes, but it would be good to know," Aldiss squeaked.

"I'm not at liberty to say," Henry replied, "so I'll thank you to stop asking."

"Stop asking what?" Claudine wanted to know. Morag hadn't noticed that she had stopped, allowing her to hear their whispers.

"Why you and…" the rat began.

"Aldiss, shush," scolded Morag, "Henry's right, it's nothing to do with us."

Claudine smiled.

"You're wondering why Montgomery and I don't live together," she said.

Morag looked down at her feet, ashamed at her own curiosity.

"Yes," the girl murmured.

"We had a difference of opinion…" the woman began.

"That's what *he* said!" shrilled Bertie.

"…and I left," she continued, "That's all you need to know."

Chapter 8

Claudine's sudden breaking had caused Tanktop to bang his head on the seat in front. However, even that had failed to revive the Klapp demon from the deep sleep he had settled into the minute he had boarded, so Shona had to go back and fetch him from the bus. She returned with a dishevelled and sleepy creature who could barely open his eyes. Tanktop resented having been woken. He glared at them all.

Morag shoved a dark green waterproof jacket at Tanktop.

"Here, put this on. We're going now and I don't want you to get cold."

"I haven't eaten yet," he complained.

"Tough," replied the dragon.

"But I'm hungry!" he wailed. "I need at least three cups of swamp mud to drink before I can even get going."

Morag audibly sighed.

"Bertie's satchel will give you what you want," she said. "Now come on, you've got work to do." She offered him the jacket again, which he reluctantly put on.

"Everyone ready?" asked Claudine. "Then let's go."

***

A blast of icy cold wind hit them as they set off, but at least the sky was now clear and the full moon was shining. Morag found herself wishing that her parents were there with her. But she had a job to do and she could not forget it. She pushed thoughts of Isabella and Nathan from her mind and pressed on.

Claudine gathered them at the clifftop.

"Do any of you have a light?" she asked, brandishing

a now lit storm lantern. The light from the gas flame illuminated the cold faces of the friends. They each nodded and held up a Moonstone. "Good," said the woman. "We'll be able to see a lot with the moonlight, but it's always good to have extra. Now follow me and watch your step."

They followed Claudine down a winding track on the hillside that led to a wooden staircase set into the cliff. One-by-one they carefully descended the steps to the shoreline below, occasionally slipping on the snow as they went.

The beach was deserted and the only sound was the sea lapping gently against the cold beach. Morag breathed in the salty air and enjoyed the whoosh of sensation its freezing temperature produced in her nostrils. *Best enjoy it while I can,* she thought, *because who knows when or if I'll ever smell it again.*

"The cave is over here," she heard Claudine say.

Morag looked to where her guide was pointing and just made out a large dark slit in the dark rock. There was something foreboding about it, something unworldly, and she shivered as she thought of their underground journey ahead. There was a cough behind her and she turned to see Shona frowning at her.

"We have to, Shona," Morag said, looking at her friend who still had her Moonstone strapped to her head. "It's the only way. *You* know that."

"No, I don't. There has to be some other way. I'm not happy about going down to Graar. We need to find some other solution."

"You know there's no other. Montgomery wouldn't have let us go on this mission if there was," said the girl. She moved towards the cave, the shifting sand underfoot turning to rock the closer she got to it. "Come on, let's go. The sooner we go in here, the sooner we can leave again."

The dragon snorted, let out a frustrated sigh, but argued

no more. She knew Morag was right.

A little wooden walkway, constructed by the local tourist organisation to allow visitors into the cavern, snaked across a stream and into the main chamber. There the rush of the cave's waterfall could be heard. One after another, the friends carefully walked along the slippery planks until they were all gathered at the inside end of the jetty. There was a pause whilst they turned to say their farewells to Claudine, but Montgomery's wife had other ideas.

"I'm coming with you," she said. "I can't have you all going into Graar alone. What if something happened to you? Besides, I might be useful. I have a lot of survival skills," she assured them.

"You are very welcome to come with us," replied Morag, "but only if you're sure."

Claudine smiled. "I'm sure," she said. "Besides, if you fail then it won't just be Marnoch Mor that Amergin will attack. He'll try and take over the *entire* magical world, not just that found within the town." There was a silence whilst they each contemplated failure. Then Claudine frowned and said: "Where's that Klapp demon? We need him to show us the way from here."

Torches were held high as they looked for the creature. Tanktop was nowhere to be found. There was no sign of his matted, stinking, furry body anywhere. Aldiss, whiskers twitching, sought him out by scent and followed a very faint trail back out of the cave to the beach. He found the demon cowering behind a rock, whimpering to himself.

"You're needed inside," the rat said.

"No! No! Don't make me go in there," squealed the creature, his eyes glittering in the moonlight. "I don't want to... It smells all wrong. It smells of dragon."

"That's just Shona!" Aldiss said.

"No, it's not. It's Felix. I can't believe how strongly

that creature smells. It's like he's *all* evil. The deal's off, I'm going back to Marnoch Mor to be with my mistress," whined the creature.

Aldiss, normally a kindly soul, looked at Tanktop with disdain and did something that he would normally not have done: he threatened Tanktop with Shona, reminding him what the dragon would do to deserters. "She has been known to bite their heads off and munch on their bones," the rat lied.

The Klapp demon's eyes widened at this information and he quivered all the more. Go and face Felix or leave and face the wrath of Shona? "I don't know what to do," Tanktop whimpered and the torment was clear on his already ugly face

"I'll tell you what to do," said the rat, feeling very brave. "Get up and get into that cave or I will be forced to call her."

Tanktop squealed in horror. "No no! I'm going, I'm going," he said as he scrambled to his feet and ran howling into the cave, leaving a stunned rat behind.

"I must be scarier than I thought," Aldiss said to himself. "Wow! I have real power!" Then from under his hat he produced a tiny wand — a wand he knew he shouldn't possess. He had been banned from practising magic following an unfortunate incident with a policeman near Oban. He gave it a little flick, sending a teeny shower of pink sparkles through the air. *I am Aldiss the Powerful right enough!* he thought.

"Aldiss!" came a stern voice from the cave. "Stop mucking around and get in here. We're going into Graar!"

"Okay Bertie! I'm coming!" he called, stashing the wand back under his hat and scampering back into the cave to join the others

Shona shoved the squealing Tanktop forward with a "You go first!" His cries echoed around the cave giving even the loud woosh of the cave's twenty-metre high waterfall a run for its money and causing everyone to wince. Claudine grabbed one of his scraggy arms and pulled him towards her.

"Stop yelling and get a grip of yourself," she said. "You're only here to help us find Graar. Where's the antechamber?" she asked.

"I don't know what you mean," he replied huffily.

"The smaller cave where the Graar entrance is," she said. "We all know about it, it's in every Graar legend. So, where is it?"

Tanktop shrugged and shook his head.

"I thought the only reason you were here was to help us into the Klapp demon city," hissed the woman.

He nodded.

"So take us there."

"Can't," he said.

"Why not?" It was the question they all wanted the answer to.

Tanktop sighed and looked worried. "I don't actually know the way. I've never been to Graar. I was born on Murst," he confessed. He looked at his feet, ensconced in their waterproof boots, and scuffed the ground a couple of times with them.

Unwilling to suffer the Klapp demon any longer than she had to, Shona stomped forward, steam rushing from her nostrils and mouth, eyes wild.

"You little liar!" she snarled, looked as if she were about to chomp Tanktop up. Morag quickly stepped in between them.

"Why didn't you tell us this before?" the girl asked.

"Because I didn't want to go to prison. It's cold and horrible and not comfy at all," he said. "I thought if I came along I could maybe escape, but she..." he looked at Shona, "...kept her horrible big yellow eyes on me at all times, so

I couldn't."

"Well, you must have been told stories about Graar when you were a little...little..." Morag searched for an appropriate word to describe an infant Tanktop.

"Cub," offered Tanktop.

"Yes, cub. Surely your parents told you about Graar."

"Yes and no. Most Klapp demons don't want to talk about it. They are embarrassed about being chased from the ancestral home by nothing more than a dragon." His eyes flickered to Shona, who growled menacingly.

"Well, what *do* you know?" Bertie asked.

The Klapp demon sighed again.

"Well, there *was* a rhyme that my mother used to recite to get us to sleep and it was about Graar," he said. "It goes like this...

Stomp, stomp, stompity stomp, into the hole we go;
Slip, slip, slippery slip, where we land we know;
Chap twice on the door, knock once on the floor, dance and you're almost there;
Welcome, my dear, to the place others fear, you've come to our home of Graar."

"Well that's not much of a rhyme," grumbled Henry from Morag's neck. She shushed him.

"What does it all mean?" she asked.

Tanktop shrugged. "No idea," he said.

Bertie let out a long sigh.

"Well," he said, "it looks like we're never getting to Graar."

"I wouldn't be so sure," Aldiss's voice sounded from *somewhere.*

They all turned, but could not see him.

"Where are you?" Bertie snapped. He wasn't fond of games in such soul-destroying conditions.

"Behind the rock," the rat said. "I think I've found the entrance."

They all ran over and sure enough behind the biggest boulder Morag had ever seen was a large doorway leading into a tunnel dimly lit by Half Moonstones.

"How did we not see this before?" she wondered aloud.

"Optical illusion," Claudine said. She stepped past the girl and went into the corridor. "The rock looked like it was part of the wall. It's a clever way of hiding things..." Her voice trailed off as she went deeper in.

"Optical illusion or not, this is our chance to find Graar," said the girl, following Claudine, "and I'm taking it."

Bertie followed with Shona and Tanktop behind. The dragon snarled at the Klapp demon when he suggested he was of no use any more and therefore should leave.

"I don't think so," the dragon replied. "You're coming with us."

"But...!"

"No buts, get going!"

Whining with fright, Tanktop slipped into the entrance, the green dragon snapping menacingly at his back.

"I'm going! I'm going!" he yelped. "Stop trying to eat me. I don't taste nice!"

"You don't smell nice either! I think your cologne is wearing off, your odour is foul."

"You don't have to be so personal!"

"Just get going," snarled Shona. "And behave yourself, Stinky, or you'll have me to deal with...you're already in my bad books!"

Chapter 9

The entrance led into a wide corridor dimly lit by Moonstones and it was down this passageway that the friends headed. They walked for five minutes, turning this way and that as the corridor snaked through the rock, and Morag was aware that the floor was gently sloping downwards. After another five minutes they turned a bend and found themselves in a rocky antechamber. It was about the size of Shona's small living room in the cottage she had shared with Morag before her move to the palace. It was brightly lit by one large Full Moonstone right in the centre of the rocky ceiling. There were no other doors or visible ways of moving into Graar. The friends looked at each other in dismay.

"*Now* what?" said Morag, fearing this was going to be the end of their journey.

"Now the Klapp demon earns his money," snarled Shona, shoving Tanktop forward.

"You're not paying me for this!" he snapped.

"And it's still a terrible bargain!" hissed the dragon.

"Tanktop," said Morag in a nicer tone, "can you tell us what to do next?"

The Klapp demon shrugged, his large dark eyes popping.

"Dunno," he said in a quiet voice.

Morag looked to the others.

"There must be a way in," she said, "we've just got to find it. Bertie, Aldiss and Shona, you search that side of the room. Claudine and Tanktop, you're with me over here. If we all work together, one of us will surely find the door or the trigger. Remember how we found the entranceway into the underground at Irvine? We searched the walls for a door handle. Let's try that here."

Within twenty minutes of feeling the wall and searching

the floor for clues, it became apparent that there was no secret doorway into Graar.

"This is hopeless," said Aldiss, whiskers drooping.

"Failed before we've even begun," said Bertie with a sigh.

"Oh listen to you two!" said Henry from around Morag's neck. "Harbingers of doom! There must be a way in we just haven't found it yet. Now all of you think! What would the Klapp demons do to protect their homeland?"

"Hide the entranceway," said Morag, "which is what they've done."

"Correct," said the medallion. "So, they've hidden it, but how would they let other Klapp demons know about it?"

Morag thought for a moment.

"They would tell them?"

"Too risky," said the medallion, "then others would know."

"They would have a secret word?" Aldiss squeaked excitedly. He loved secret words and messages.

"Possibly," agreed Henry.

There was silence as everyone thought about what Henry might be getting at.

"Or a rhyme?" Morag suddenly said.

All eyes turned to Tanktop. He squealed in fright.

"What? I've not done anything!" he said.

"What was the rhyme you told us earlier?" Morag wanted to know.

"It was nothing. Just something my mother used to...," the trembling Klapp demon began.

"Tell us it again."

And so he repeated it...

Stomp, stomp, stompity stomp, into the hole we go;
Slip, slip, slippery slip, where we land we know;
Chap twice on the door, knock once on the floor, dance

and you're almost there;

Welcome, my dear, to the place others fear, you've come to our home of Graar.

"That's it!" said the girl. "That's how we get in."

"I don't understand," the rat confessed. "What does it all mean?"

"Must be a secret spell or something," the dodo replied.

"No," said the girl. "It's instructions! Follow me. First we have to '*stomp, stomp, stompity stomp*'."

She demonstrated with her feet and a loud crunching rose from somewhere in the antechamber, as if rock were scraping against rock.

"It's working," she breathed. "Come on, everyone do it."

She gathered them into the middle of the room: a dragon, a dodo, a rat, a Klapp demon and a tall willowy woman, and she talked them through the rhythm.

"On three..." she said. "One, two, three."

Together they each did it: stomp, stomp, stompity stomp. And then they stopped and waited and looked at each other with wide-eyes wondering what was going to happen next. Within half a minute, they found out. As Bertie opened his mouth to speak, a hatched door that covered the entire floor opened and they found themselves hurtling into the blackness below. A long loud scream rang out as they hit a wide rocky chute and slithered down, down, down. The scream continued until moments later they saw a bright light and, with a whack, landed on a pile of old sacking, breathless and exhilarated.

"That was fun!" said the rat. "Let's do it again."

"Let's not," said the dragon, who was panting on the floor. She looked around. "Who was screaming? Was it you, demon?"

Tanktop, who was standing up brushing down his matted fur, shook his head. The dodo stepped forward, sheepish and embarrassed.

"I'm afraid that was me. That rushing downwards gave me a bit of a turn," he said. He was unable to look at anyone.

"Where are we?" asked Henry, who had become lost inside Morag's duffel coat. She pulled him out. "Oh!"

They were in another room, but this one was enormous. Morag looked up to see the source of the light, but could make out neither the ceiling nor what was giving off the strange yellow glow illuminating them. Before them was an enormous doorway. Its double doors were made of a green metal that had been carefully and intricately carved with the snaking branches of a huge tree laden with fruit. Within the branches sat strange creatures not unlike Klapp demons...except they were smooth and unmatted and as sophisticated as bronze carvings of such creatures could look. Over the tree, in large bronze letters were the words: *Welcome to Graar! Tourists welcome any time for dinner. Hawkers use the trade entrance round the back.*

"Well, it looks like we've found Graar," said Claudine, gazing in awe at the door. "Now how do we get this open?"

"What's the rest of the rhyme?" said Morag. "Oh yes... '*Slip, slip, slippery slip, where we land we know.*' Well we've done that part. Then it's '*Chap twice on the door, knock once on the floor, dance and you're almost there; welcome, my dear, to the place others fear, you've come to our home of Graar.*'"

She approached the door. Down at the bottom, at Klapp demon height, was a door knocker in the shape of a human head. She lifted it and chapped twice. Then she bent down, knocked once on the floor and did a little wiggly dance. She took a step back and waited. There came a screeching and then a smaller door cut into the large entranceway popped open. Morag opened it wider and stepped inside.

"Come on," she called, "follow me!"

"Trust the Klapp demons to be all show and no

substance," muttered Shona as she followed the girl through the tight doorway.

"What do you mean?" Aldiss asked.

"I mean, they've created that fantastic big door, but does it open? No. We have to use this tiny little entrance instead."

"It's more convenient," muttered Tanktop as he too stepped inside.

"I'll say," said the rat.

Claudine went in last. She checked they were not being followed before closing the door behind her.

The first thing that struck Morag was the sheer size of the cavern they now entered and how much was inside it. It was as if someone had carefully built a city then dug it up and transplanted it into a massive cave with no roof. The doorway led them onto a large ledge high enough to allow them to gaze right across the Klapp demon city for miles. Encased and protected in the walls of an extinct volcano, Graar could not be seen by the outside world yet was still able to bask in natural light thanks to a huge opening in the ceiling. Morag strained to see out of it, but snow clouds were gathered like a marshmallow plug in the volcano mouth. The whole thing was illuminated by a dull golden light.

"I can't believe how beautiful it is," said Shona. "Are you sure we are in the right place?"

Morag looked at her friend and smiled, for she had had the exact same thought. Whereas the Klapp demons themselves were stinking, matted, stringy creatures with poor personal hygiene, their city was the epitome of charm: classic archways, Roman-style pillars, expertly constructed multi-storied housing and pretty parks and open spaces could be seen throughout the homeland. Here and there was the gleam of gold: picking out features on sloping ornamental rooftops, covering statues of prominent Klapp demons and shining from every doorway in the form of doorknobs and letterboxes. Dotted around were little houses that reminded Morag of bungalows. There were also tall towers, palaces and mansions with sweeping driveways. Trees and ferns grew freely and the whole thing was covered in a thin blanket of crisp, white snow. Everything looked so nice that she couldn't believe Klapp demons had once lived there.

Tanktop was evidently as surprised as the others, for he gaped at his spiritual home.

"I suppose the demons must *once* have been cultured creatures," Henry speculated, "for no smelly creature created this wonderland!"

"I had no idea," Tanktop gasped as he surveyed the empty streets. "It looks like new, as if everyone's in hiding ready to jump out and say 'Boo!'" The tales of Graar never once said it was so...so...pretty. Why did we ever leave?"

"Pretty except for that over there," said Shona, pointing a green talon into the distance.

Morag peered at it. It was as if a great dark shape that had been poured over a large building like hot tarmac. She screwed up her eyes to try and make out what it was. As she did so, the shape shifted and a loud snore resonated throughout the city.

"Is that...?" she began. For if this was what she thought it was then they were in even more trouble than she had imagined.

"Felix Saevus?" replied Aldiss, sniffing the air. "Yes, that is the very distinctive odour of dragon...pungent, gamey and with more than a hint of ash."

Shona snorted, causing the rat to jump.

"Except you...you don't smell like that, Shona," he added hastily.

"He's huge," gasped the girl. "I thought all dragons were the size of you, Shona. I had no idea they could grow so big."

"I'm a pigmy dragon, remember," Shona explained, "and he's something altogether quite different." Felix growled softly in his sleep, causing them all to jump as the sound rumbled over them. Shona added: "I think it would be best if we got what we came for and left as soon as we can *without* waking him."

"Agreed," they all said at once.

"So let's quickly and *quietly* find The Destine and get back out of here,' the pygmy dragon declared. 'Klapp demon: where is The Destine kept?"

All eyes were on Tanktop, who looked like he was desperately trying to disappear.

"Er...um..." he stuttered.

"We're waiting," said Bertie impatiently.

"Yeah, hurry up," added Aldiss.

"Think!" Shona demanded.

The Klapp demon's eyes widened and he seemed paralysed with fear. Morag stepped between him and the others and said more kindly: "Please think hard Tanktop, this is important. And not just to us, but to you and your family too. We need to stop Amergin before he takes over everywhere and puts us all in danger. None of us want that, do we?"

He shook his head.

"I think it's in the Great Temple," he whimpered. "My mother told me about it when I was a cub. Our people put all their treasures there. That's where I would have put it if...if...I was in charge of it."

"And where in the city is that?" Morag wanted to know.

He leaned to the side and stared past her, eyes widening with every passing moment until the girl was sure they would pop right out of his head.

"I think Felix is lying on it," he said at last.

They turned as one and looked once more to the distant hill with the ruined building and the large black slumbering shape of Felix.

"Drat," said Morag, "I was afraid you were going to say that. Bertie, could your satchel conjure up some binoculars? I want to have a better look at what we are up against."

The dodo, always happy to oblige, slipped a wing inside his little satchel and pulled out a pair of black binoculars. He handed them to Morag. The girl put them to her eyes, adjusted them a little and then trained them at Felix.

"His tail is blocking the main doorway," she said, "and his body is covering all the downstairs windows. I can't see any other way in, but if there's a back door, I think it might be around about where his head is."

She lowered the binoculars and sought out Tanktop, who was trying to hide behind a rock.

"*Is* there another way in?" she asked him.

He shrugged again: he didn't know.

"This looks like a pretty sophisticated kind of place," said Claudine, surveying the city. "It looks like there might even be a proper sewerage system and waterways."

"I hope you're not suggesting what I think you're suggesting," said Bertie haughtily. "There's no way you're going to get me down a sewer. It would ruin my feathers!"

"And it's taken my family centuries to get *out* of the sewer," piped in Aldiss. "There's no way..."

"No-one's suggesting that!" snapped Claudine. "I was just thinking that there might be a cellar or something at the temple...another way in."

"Well there's only one way to find out," said Morag. "We need to go there. Come on, we've got a long way to go to the other side of Graar."

She looked at their journey and sighed. The walk ahead was miles long and would probably take them all evening... if they were lucky. She turned to Tanktop, who was also looking at the city in dismay.

"Did your people have any form of transport?"

"We cling on to the underside of cars, that's how we get about," he said.

"But what about here?"

"Dunno."

"Okay, walking it is then." She adjusted her backpack and straightened her coat before taking her first step.

"Morag, wait!" said Claudine. "Let me go first, there may be traps."

Morag nodded her consent and moved aside to let the tall woman pass. She then fell into line behind Claudine and the two set off, followed by Bertie, Aldiss, Tanktop and Shona. They descended a wide stone staircase into the city below, their quiet footsteps and nervous breathing the only sounds in the silent, ghostly town. Claudine paused at the bottom and waited until the dragon joined them.

"Be careful everyone," the woman warned, "stay behind me at all times and don't touch anything. Klapp demons are a tricky bunch at the best of times..."

"Hey!" Tanktop protested.

"...so keep an eye out for traps or weapons," she continued, ignoring him. "Keep quiet and keep close and we may just get to the Great Temple undetected by Felix. Ready?"

Everyone nodded.

"Follow me."

Cautiously, Claudine led them into the eerily still streets of Graar. From up on the vantage point the city had looked perfect, but here they could see that decades of neglect and decay had taken their inevitable toll on the place. Nettles and purple thistles grew through cracks in the paved road and a street light leant to one side, its roots undermined by those of a nearby oak tree. The glittering houses and apartment blocks, so stunning from a distance, were yellow with damp, and here and there windows had been smashed by some unknown force. A headless bronze statue of a once prominent Graarian stood in the centre of a little market square, its plinth deeply scarred. *Dragon claws did that*, thought Morag as they carefully walked past. Abandoned carts and egg-shaped vehicles littered the roads and, lying in a gutter, deep in melting snow, she found a furry Klapp demon toy that must have once belonged to a cub. Further down the street, several faded, shredded flags hung from the wall of a restaurant. Unable to curb her curiosity, she ran over and pressed her face up against the dirty glass. Inside there were tables laden with discarded plates, bowl-shaped glasses covered in scum and chairs upturned on the floor. *They must have left in a hurry when Felix showed up*, Morag thought as she rejoined the others.

They followed a narrow side street north for about half an hour until it dissected one of the main arteries of the city. The new road, two broken carriageways wide and lined with overgrown trees, appeared to travel towards the temple, so they took it instead and trudged on.

They stopped for dinner three hours later, eating from Bertie's enchanted satchel and warily gazing up at the slumbering black form of Felix in the distance. He had his head tucked beneath one of his huge leathery wings and his long tail wrapped tightly around his great body. As he slept, the beast's back, with its armoured spikes, rose and fell gently with each quiet breath and Morag wondered how something so big could make so little sound.

"Do you think he's nocturnal?" Aldiss, who was more of a night person himself, speculated as he sat next to her. He popped a raisin in his mouth and chewed it hungrily.

Morag was about to reply, but the dodo got in first.

"I hope so — if he doesn't wake 'til later that should give us more time to get to The Destine," answered Bertie, getting to his feet and beckoning to the rat. "Come on, Aldiss, old friend. Time to go. We've still got a long way to go yet."

By eight o'clock, they were about a quarter of a mile from the Temple. Half an hour later, footsore and tired, they had almost reached their destination. They stopped a little bit downwind from the huge dragon and hid behind the wall of an overgrown garden. Wet ferns and grasses tickled them as they crouched down to take stock. It was Morag who stood up first to take a good look at Felix, who was still snoozing quietly, his great dark body wrapped possessively around the temple like it was a pile of gold. He was even more imposing this close up and Morag estimated his body alone was the size of eight double decker buses sat two up and four along. His tail was as long as his body and his head was at least the size of Shona's house in Marnoch Mor. And then there was the smell. They had been aware of the dragon's ripe stench for some time now, but this close it was an overpowering mix of rotting flesh and fish. She wrinkled her nose as she sat down again.

"I don't know how we're going to get into that temple," she said. "Felix is covering the whole building."

"Now what are we going to do?" Aldiss whispered.

"I don't know," Bertie whispered back. "But I could do with a rest, my feet are sore."

"I know, mine too," the little rodent admitted as he removed a boot and rubbed a claw. "I have blisters on my blisters."

"Shhh, keep it down," Claudine warned as Felix shifted in his sleep and let out a little grunt. "You'll wake him."

"It's getting really dark in here," Morag said, "perhaps we should find somewhere to stay while we try to work out what to do next."

Sure enough the Klapp demon city had been steadily fading into almost pitch darkness for the past hour. The yellow glow that had lit their way was now down to just a peep and they had to use their own equipment to see. It wasn't even nine o'clock and Morag wondered how they were going to get The Destine in this blackness. She peeked over the wall at the temple, a fortress of crumbling sandstone and dragon flesh, and her heart sank. The front door was just visible behind a thick chunk of Felix's scaly black tail and there was no other obvious way in. *Now what indeed?* thought Morag.

Just then, as the black gloom of despair descended on her, there was a loud bang. The friends spun round as a yellow flame shot out of a parkland area to the north and whooshed to the open roofs like a rocket to the moon. It reached its maximum height in seconds and burst forth in a shower of glittering stars, each of which streamed over the streets. They hit them as one and as their glorious bodies fell to the earth every streetlight in the city blinked on with a strange and magical tinkling. The friends looked at the Klapp demon in surprise. But Tanktop's mouth was open and his eyes were goggling. He was as stunned as they were at the beauty of what they had just witnessed.

"Wow!" was all he could say.

At that moment, a low rumbling rose from the direction of the temple.

Felix was waking.

Snorting and snuffling out of sleep, the great dragon slowly opened an eye. He blinked. He stretched his neck and the stretch travelled all the way down his long back and out to his tail, which flailed up and round, swiping over the friends in their hiding place, causing them to throw themselves down and cover their heads with their arms and wings. The tail thumped against the wall of a neighbouring store, sending tiles flying off the roof and rubble crashing to the ground. Felix yawned loudly, filling the air with the smell of rancid meat and the heat of his breath. He lifted himself into a sitting position, shook his head and looked around sleepily. A loud belch escaped his black lips and he stood, causing the ground beneath him — to say nothing of the band of friends — to quiver and quake.

Morag looked round to check her friends were all okay and was met with five pairs of frightened eyes. There was a heavy downdraft and she looked up again. Felix had unfolded his wings and was preparing to take off. As she watched, the dragon pulled himself up and launched himself out of the large hole in the volcano roof. Within a few seconds his huge dark shape was lost to the dark cloudy sky.

"Where do you think he's going?" Morag gasped as the pointed end of his tail disappeared into the blackness.

"To eat," replied Shona flatly.

"Eat what?" asked Aldiss, his little black eyes glittering with fright.

Shona shrugged. "Perhaps it's best not to know," she replied.

Bertie shuddered and Aldiss shook.

"Shona's right, let's not think about it," Morag said. "Come on, this is our chance to get The Destine. Look!"

She pointed towards the temple's main entrance, which was illuminated by a row of streetlights that had somehow missed being destroyed by the dragon. At first no one could see what Morag was meaning. The main door was blocked by a huge pile of rubble. The only sign of it ever having been an entrance peeped out at the top in the form of ornately carved wooden double doors.

"It's blocked," said Tanktop, stating the obvious.

"Not that one, *that* one!" replied the girl. She was pointing at a much smaller door some five metres away from the same entrance; a door that was ajar, a door that promised entrance to the temple.

"Come on!" Morag cried as she got to her feet and

jogged towards the large blocks of stone that formed the temple steps.

"Morag! Wait!" hissed Shona, but it was too late. The girl was already on the bottom step. With a shrug, the pygmy dragon raced after her, followed by the others.

Morag was the first to reach the top of the steps. She paused and eyed the hole in the top of the volcano, fearful that Felix would return at any time. Keeping a wary eye out for him, she crept towards the door. Step by careful step, she moved forward, hardly daring to breathe. Then, out of the corner of her eye, something moved. She glanced to the side just in time to see a flash of matted fur as something hairy raced towards the door. And, before she could protest, it blew her a raspberry, then slammed the door shut behind it. The bang reverberated across the still city. Morag froze and raised her eyes to the sky, but there was no sign of the giant dragon. On tiptoe, she hurried to the door and tried to open it. It would not budge.

"What was *that*? Who slammed the door?" Claudine whispered as she caught up with the girl.

"I think..." the girl began, keeping her voice low. She looked around her friends to confirm her suspicions were correct. "I think it was Tanktop. He's shut this door and I can't open it." She gave it another push.

"Let me have a go," said Shona. She put her shoulder to the door and shoved. Nothing. She put her back to it and shoved. Nothing. She used her fists and pounded. Yellow sparks flew off it, causing the others to return their gaze to the dark sky in alarm. No Felix.

"Magic. He must have used magic to lock the door," gasped Bertie. "The little...! He's forbidden from practising magic."

"Hey, let us in!" Morag hissed, but nobody answered and the door remained steadfastly shut.

"Now what?" Shona asked, staring at the door as if it

ought to have been afraid of her.

"We'll have to find another way in," replied the girl.

Chapter 10

Window smashing was not something either Morag or Shona liked to do, but having walked right around the temple only to find no entrance other than the two unopenable doors (not even a space big enough to allow Aldiss through), they felt they had no other option. Besides, the temple was already damaged by Felix, so one more smashed window wouldn't really matter.

They found a window that seemed big enough to allow Shona to climb through and which was also at the same level as the main door. Morag picked up a piece of rubble the size of a child's fist and weighed it in her hand. It would do. Shona gave her a boost up and held her while Morag smashed a large pane. The glass tinkled and dissolved into nothing, allowing Morag to slip her hand through and undo the latch. The window swung open and the girl climbed through, relieved to be inside at last but wary of what might lie within. Shona attempted to squeeze through after her.

Morag looked around as she waited for her friend to join her. It appeared they were inside the main worshipping hall of the temple. The large domed room was held up by marble pillars carved in the ornate Corinthian style. The floor was tiled with marble and arranged in geometric patterns. The four walls were mainly made up of large windows like the one through which they had entered, but in between them, and burning brightly against the stonework, gold sconces held aloft white church candles. Here and there Morag could see paintings of neat Klapp demons in grand clothing. Polished wooden benches set out in rows faced the middle of the hall. And in the centre was a large, octagonal glass display case bejewelled with the finest of precious stones. The glass was opaque, revealing only the vaguest outline of the contents, but there certainly was something inside.

Morag stole towards it. "Do you think that could be The Destine?" she gasped.

"Yes. No. Maybe. I don't know," replied the dragon. "Wait!" warned Shona, holding out a claw to stop her from going any closer. "This could be a trap. Remember that stinking Klapp demon is about."

They were both conscious that Tanktop was nowhere to be seen.

The pygmy dragon's eyes darted around the room, looking for hidden danger. At her side Morag also glanced around and it was only then that she noticed a smallish figure hiding behind a pillar at the opposite end of the room. Tanktop waved at her before bolting towards the glass case. His feet skittered across the marble floor and he grinned manically as he ran.

However, the smile was soon wiped off his face and replaced with a look of terror as he was scooped into the air without warning.

"Aieeeeeee!" he screamed as he flew up, his voice echoing around the hall.

Morag and Shona could only watch as he came to a stop about six feet above them. And it was only then that Morag noticed the faint glisten of a magical net.

"Get me down! Get me down!" shouted the Klapp demon from the trap. "Let me down, mistress Morag," he pleaded.

"Well, lookee here!" Shona smirked. "That sneaky little liar Tanktop...trussed up like a Christmas turkey. Well, this serves you right doesn't it? Trying to get in and take The Destine for yourself."

"No no! It wasn't like that," the unfortunate Klapp demon cried. "I only meant to get it *for* you and I ended up caught in this trap. Please let me down, I'm beginning to lose all feeling in my left leg. I'm really, really sorry," whined the creature. "Please free me."

Morag glanced at Shona, who was still staring up at the demon, delight playing about her lizard features.

"We could just take The Destine and leave him here for Felix to deal with," the dragon suggested, eyes shining with the thought of it.

"We can't do that!" gasped Morag. "That would be cruel!"

"I'm joking!" laughed the dragon. Then she said: "Honestly...I am."

"I think it's a splendid idea," said Henry with glee.

"No, we're not leaving him," Morag decided, her warm heart horrified at the thought of leaving Tanktop to either starve to death or be eaten by Felix. "He'd die if we left him here!"

"Hmph!" said Shona.

"Well I can't see how you can get him down. We don't have a knife to cut the rope," the medallion said.

"What's happened?" asked Aldiss, who had just arrived.

"Is that...is that...Tanktop?" Bertie wanted to know. He was standing behind the rat, staring up in awe, beak open. "What happened to him?"

"It was a trap," said the girl. "We need to help him." She looked around and her eyes rested on a nearby pillar. "Look! That's how we'll do it." She pointed to a large hook sticking out of the column. Wound around the hook was very thin glistening thread that was, in turn, attached to Tanktop's prison. She ran across to it and, with a little difficulty, unwound it. Taking the slack and holding on tightly, she struggled as she slowly lowered the pathetic figure to the ground.

"Are you all right?" she asked, helping him to take the net off. It was heavy and sticky and it took them some time to unravel him.

"Yes, thank you, mistress," the demon simpered as he peeled off the last of it. He glanced fearfully at Shona who was staring at him menacingly. "I did not know this temple was booby-trapped."

"Serves you right!" snarled the dragon, taking a step forward. She looked as if she wanted to snap his head off.

"Oooooh, don't hurt me, madam dragon, I was only following orders!"

Morag caught Shona's eye and could see the same thought in her head: *'following orders'? Whose orders?*

"Leave him, Shona," said the girl, "we can think of a suitable punishment later. Right now we've got more important matters to deal with."

"Hmph," said the dragon, unconvinced.

"Couldn't have put it better myself," the medallion muttered.

"Now," said Morag, "we still have to get The Destine."

She took a step towards the plinth.

"Morag! No!" The dragon acted instinctively, shoving a large wooden bench forward so that it skittered across the marble floor. It came to a halt right in front of the girl. As the shocked Morag leapt back to get away from it, a wooden spear with a sharp metal head flew out of a hole in the wall and embedded itself with a 'doiiiinnng!' into the side of the bench. Ashen faced, Morag could only stare at it in horror.

Shona hurried to her friend's side.

"Are you okay, Morag?" she asked, placing a muscular arm around the shivering girl's shoulders.

"We could have been killed!" said Henry.

"*Morag* could have been killed!" the dragon corrected. "You could have been turned into gold leaf!"

"I'm fine, Shona," said the girl in a small voice. "I just got a bit of a fright, that's all."

"You're safe now."

Shona looked around at the assembled people and made a decision.

"I think it would be best if we got that stinking Klapp demon to get The Destine for us," she said, looking for Tanktop. "Hoi! Where do you think you're going?" she snarled.

The Klapp demon was on tip toe and sneaking towards the door like a guilty thief. He stopped in his tracks and turned to face the dragon sheepishly. With a face painted with a slimy, pandering grin, he said: "I was just going to get some tools to help us."

"Uh-uh! I don't think so," said the dragon. "You stay here where I can see you."

Under her stern gaze, the Klapp demon trembled.

"Now, Stinky," began Shona, "here's a little task for you. I want you to go over there and get The Destine for us. It should be a simple task for a creature of your abilities."

Tanktop looked round fearfully at the bundle of rope that had only moments ago bound him high in the air, then looked back to the dragon.

"I don't want to," he said. "I will fall into another trap and die a horrible death full of pain and suffering."

"Your people are from here. You know what to do," Shona added menacingly.

"I *don't* know how," he whimpered. "Please can I go now? This place reeks of dragon...er no offence intended...I mean it reeks of the big dragon."

"Haven't you got another rhyme that will give us clues?" asked Bertie, settling down on a nearby bench.

"No. Please let me go. The dragon's coming back, I can smell it."

"What about a poem? I like a good poem," said Aldiss, scurrying up to be beside his friend.

"No. I have nothing."

They lapsed into a silence so thick it could almost be cut.

"I have an idea," said Morag suddenly. "Let's put some

more benches out between here and the plinth to act as a lure for the traps. Then we can use them as a bridge to The Destine."

Shona blew out a few thoughtful smoke rings. Then she shrugged.

"Well, I can't think of anything else to try," she said.

If dragons had had sleeves to roll up, then that's what Shona would have done right then, for she took to the new task with gusto. Grabbing one wooden bench after another, she shoved them in the direction of the plinth, creating a wooden walkway. As each bench slid into place a new trap sprung: a swarm of poisoned darts embedded themselves into the wood of one; a small circular saw came out of nowhere and sliced the nose off another; a barbed net fell; and finally there was a small explosion. Everyone let out a sigh of relief when the smoke and splinters cleared and they saw that most of the benches remained intact.

"Now wha...?" Bertie began, but his words were left hanging in the air and his eyes popped as he witnessed Morag leap on to the first bench and sprint towards the plinth. Before anyone could say 'Morag, no!' the girl had reached the glass case and was gingerly removing it. Collective breaths were held.

There were no more traps.

"Phew," said Aldiss, his whiskers twitching with anxiety. Morag placed the case on the bench behind her and stretched her right hand towards the item inside: a little wooden goblet carved with mystical markings.

"Be careful, Morag," Aldiss warned.

She gave him a small smile and felt the tips of her fingers touch the cold wood of the chalice. Whooosh. Morag had the feeling she was being compressed and stretched and moulded. Before she had time to decide whether or not she felt sick, the feeling passed and she found herself standing on the soft spring green grass of a beautiful flower meadow. Above, the sun split the sky and a light breeze teased her hair. Around her were flowers of all shapes, sizes and colours; their scent was light and pleasant. Now, feeling uncomfortably hot, she undid the toggles of her coat and removed it, all the time gazing around at this beautiful place.

"Where am I?" she wondered aloud.

Just then, there was a loud buzz and the flickering image of a Klapp demon appeared before her. This was unlike any demon Morag had seen before, for he was dressed in beautiful blue velvet robes decorated with gold embroidery; and his hair, instead of being matted and dirty, was smooth and silky. He was...clean.

The creature bowed.

"Good day," it said. "My name is Toga and I'll be your hologram for today."

"H-hello," said Morag hesitantly as an 8mm projector and a white screen appeared before her. The daylight dimmed, the projector whirred and images of herself appeared on the screen.

"You are Morag MacTavish," Toga continued as the film played.

"Yes, but how do you know who I am? Where did you get those pictures?"

"Please don't interrupt," he said. "You are a princess of Marnoch Mor, daughter of Isabella and Nathan. You were raised in a house in Irvine by Jermy and Moira Stoker and rescued by Albert Fluke and Aldiss Drinkwater..."

Images of each person and creature appeared before her.

"Yes, but..."

"Don't interrupt!" Toga scolded again. "You are a friend of Montgomery and murderer of Devlish..."

"The Eye killed him!"

"Your greatest enemy is Mephista Devlish, but she is

also one of your greatest allies."

"What? Mephista? No!"

"You're biggest regret is that you left a friend to become a slave to a demon on Murst."

Here the film showed Chelsea and her mother Esmerelda being rounded up by four Girallons and forced into a wooden cage. 'No!' mouthed Morag as she saw one of the Girallons hit Chelsea as she tried to resist.

"You are here for The Destine," Toga concluded.

"Yes, can you tell me where it is?"

"You are in it."

Morag frowned.

"How can I be in it? I just reached out to touch..." she began and then it dawned on her: "The chalice *is* The Destine! I knew it!"

"Yes."

"How do I get back out so I can take it?"

"That's easy," he said, "you must give me a memory in which you have been kind."

"Is that all?" She wondered at the simplicity of it.

"Yes."

"Deal. Please, take my memory," she said, keen to get it over and done with so she could get back to Marnoch Mor.

The hologram floated towards her, monkey-like hand outstretched. She felt a cold draught on her forehead as his fingers touched her and it was as if someone was rummaging about in her head.

"Uh-huh..." said the hologram, "...no, not that one. Hmmm. Yes, this one will do."

There was a slight tug and Toga removed his hand from her head. He turned and flicked his fingers at the screen. The memory suddenly appeared there and Morag saw herself in the library at the Palace talking to Bertie. The bird asked to borrow her book of Marnoch Morian poetry for a project he was doing for magic school. Her parents had given her the book when she had been a baby and it was so precious to her that she had hesitated before handing it over to him. The bird, however, could not have finished his work without it, so she let him have it. The last thing Morag saw was the delight on her friend's face as he faded from the screen.

Unconsciously, she felt for the book in her coat pocket and smiled as she found it there. Bertie had borrowed it and returned it the next day.

"Thank you, Morag MacTavish, you are now free to go," said the hologram. "Oh, before I forget...you have given me only one memory, so you can use The Destine only once. Please return it to Graar when you are finished."

"Can't I give you more memories for more tries?" she asked desperately.

He merely smiled and shook his head. The hologram faded before her eyes.

"Wait! How does The Destine work?" But before she could say another word Toga, the screen and the projector vanished. Then she felt the sickening sensation of being tugged and pulled and stretched. She closed her eyes tightly and fought the urge to vomit.

"You're back!' cried Shona. 'We were so worried!"

Morag opened her eyes to see she was still in the temple, lying on the floor with her friends gathered around her. They were staring at her with real concern. She sat up.

"I'm fine," she said as she picked up the chalice that was lying at her side.

"What happened?" the dragon asked, helping her to her feet. "Where did you go?"

"No time to explain now," she said, gazing at the chalice. "We need to get this back to Marnoch Mor."

She was about to say something else when there was a swoop of leathery wings and something huge and scary rested on top of the temple. The ceiling creaked and bowed under his weight.

"Oh no!" squeaked Aldiss, staring up at the ceiling, nose quivering with the stench of dragon.

"Felix is back!" squawked Bertie.

"Run!" shouted Shona.

Chapter 11

Shona reached the open window first and without really thinking about what she was doing, picked up Bertie and Aldiss and threw them outside. Next it was Morag's turn. She placed her on the sill. The girl jumped and landed on her feet on the walkway. Claudine, with a push from the dragon, came next. A high-pitched screaming followed, alerting the friends — who were now gathered outside the temple — to the fact that Tanktop was swiftly following. It was all they could do to get out of the way as the scraggy Klapp demon flew past them and landed on his backside nearby. All this time Felix was shifting his weight on top of the temple, cracking walls, shifting roof tiles and sending debris flying from the building. It smashed all around them, forcing them down the steps. Shona, last one out, found herself dodging tiles and stones inside the temple. Above her, the ceiling groaned and buckled and gave way with a sickening crash as she pulled herself up on to the window sill. She threw herself out, whipping her tail to safety just in time.

Rolling to a stop close to Morag, the pigmy dragon scrabbled to her feet and turned around to see where the window had once been. It was now a big pile of rocks. She gulped.

"That was a close one!" she said, voice wavering. "Too close." Again she examined her tail and found it all present and correct. As she was doing this, the rat was hopping about from foot to foot. "Ur...Shona!" said Aldiss. His bright black eyes were fearful as he stared up at the space behind the dragon. His whiskers quivered and his paws trembled as he stabbed the air with one tiny claw. "L-l-loooook! Felix is...is..."

"What is it?" she asked, turning to see what the rat was

staring at.

Before she could take in what was there, a loud whoosh brought a downward draft that forced them to the ground, flattening them all against the cold cracked flagstones. Felix was flapping his wings. One final flick of the great leathery spans caused a rogue gust that sent Aldiss rolling over and over, squealing at the top of his voice as he tumbled to his doom.

Quick-thinking Morag grabbed his hairless tail just as he teetered on the edge of the walkway. Fighting against the wind, she hauled the little rodent to safety and pulled him to her. He was okay...for now. Above them, Felix got to his feet, threw his great scaly head back and let out a deafening roar as he called out to the night. Morag immediately plugged her ears to drown out the terrible sound. The call rose in pitch until it was almost a shriek, one so loud it made her head throb and her ears ring with pain. She fell to the ground and curled up in a foetal position, keeping her fingers in her ears and eyes shut. Here she stayed until at last, after several agonising minutes, the sound stopped. Then there was silence. She took a breath and gingerly opened her eyes. Her friends had also been forced to the ground and were in different stages of recovery...all except for Tanktop, whose mouth was moving but producing no sound.

"Tanktop, are you all right?" the kind-hearted girl asked as she got to her feet. "Tanktop?"

His trembling hand pointed.

"Fneurgghhhh," was all the stricken Klapp demon could say.

It was then that Morag was suddenly aware of a growing heat behind her. The girl turned her head to see that Felix had discovered them and was now staring down. He leaned over for a better look, intensifying the heat from his breath and making Morag feel like a roast chicken in an oven. Hardly daring to move, the girl peeped up at the giant looming before her and stifled a scream. This close up Felix seemed even more enormous, easily the biggest creature she had ever seen. His teeth alone were as big as the chairs in the palace's stateroom. Yellowing and razor sharp, they gleamed like stalactites in the dark cavern of his mouth. His cruel green eyes with their black slit-like pupils showed only a hunter's steely concentration. They were cat and mouse now.

A forked tongue, long and dark grey, flickered out from Felix's mouth and just missed the girl. She flinched, unsure whether to stand still or flee.

"Oh my goodness!" squawked Bertie, flapping his own tiny wings as he tried to get to his feet. "He's going to eat us all! Look at those teeth! Run everyone! Run!"

That was enough to get Morag out of her stupor. She came to and ran for her life, urging her friends on as she did so. They raced towards the stairs, but were prevented from escaping by a huge dragon claw. Felix had cut them off. As one they turned to discover their fate.

"Well, what have we here?" the giant dragon said as he looked down on them. His voice was deep and melodious. "More Klapp demons? I hate Klapp demons. Nasty, horrible creatures. Not even very tasty. I thought I told you lot to leave."

"No, we're not Klapp demons!" said Morag, finding her voice. "We're just some people and creatures who... er...have come to Graar to...um..." She ran out of things to say. Felix narrowed his huge emerald eyes and studied the group more closely. Morag bravely stood her ground as his scaly face drew nearer. His hot breath stank of soot and fish and was so rank that it made her eyes water. She closed them and pulled away. Felix studied her, sniffed her, wrinkled his nose and frowned. His tongue flickered out again and this time licked the girl on her face. She grimaced in disgust.

"Now would be a good time for you to use some of that magic of yours, Henry," Morag muttered to the medallion hanging round her neck.

"He's too big to render motionless," replied the medallion.

"What about magicking us out of here?" she suggested.

"Too many of us."

"Why are you here?" Felix demanded of those cowering before him. "Did you come to steal my treasure?" he growled.

"N-no," stuttered Morag.

"Then what is that in your hand?" he accused, staring down at the magical chalice Morag was carrying. She tried to hide it behind her back. "You liar, you *have* been stealing from me."

"I..." she began, trying frantically to explain. But Felix's attention was suddenly on someone else. He was sniffing in the general direction of Tanktop, who was whimpering next to Shona. The Klapp demon was frantically re-spraying himself with Stinko.

"What's that? A Klapp demon?" He took a long sniff. "Doesn't smell like a Klapp demon. Hmph."

Then his eyes rested on Shona and for a moment he looked like he was about to smile.

"Another dragon," he said. "By the look of you, you must be from Murst."

Shona gazed up at the huge creature before her and tried her hardest to keep the fear out of her voice.

"Yes," she said. "Nice to meet you. Now we really have to go."

But he ignored her and sniffed again. He frowned and his face wrinkled up in disgust.

"What *is* that odour I can smell? It's almost like...like...is there a rat with you?" He drew back from them and Morag was sure she saw horror on his face.

It was Shona's turn to narrow her eyes. She had an idea. Quick as a flash, she whipped Aldiss out from his hiding place behind her and held the trembling rodent up to Felix. Aldiss squealed and tried to jump off her claw, but the dragon held him tight. He covered his eyes and waited for the bite.

"Eugh! A rat! I hate them. Nasty biting creatures full of diseases and fleas. Get it away from me, get it away!" screamed Felix. He shuffled back from them, making sure his feet were nowhere near Aldiss, who had suddenly realised what Shona was doing. Felix was scared...*of him!* With a great deal of glee, he pulled faces at the giant dragon and blew raspberries.

"I'm coming to get you, dragon!" the tiny creature shouted. "Be warned!"

Morag saw their chance as the claw that was blocking their escape was hastily removed.

"Come on! Let's get out of here!" she hissed. Clutching The Destine in one hand, she and Claudine ran to the stairs. At the top, she picked up a startled Bertie and tucked him under her arm. As the bird squawked in surprise, Morag ran down the stairs towards the road. Shona, still holding Aldiss, ran after Morag, closely followed by Claudine who grasped Tanktop by the scruff of the neck and hauled him along. At the bottom of the stairs, she heaved the Klapp demon over her shoulder and followed the others.

The band of friends ran for their lives, darting down the streetlamp-lit side streets of Graar, heading for the entranceway several miles across the cavern. None dared look around, for they could hear Felix raging.

"Thieves!" he roared. "Come back here! You have my treasure! It's mine! Not yours! Come back and I promise death will be swift! I'll enjoy chomping on your bones!"

"Is he coming after us?" Shona puffed as she scampered

along, Aldiss now riding her back like a rodeo cowboy.

Morag glanced around. Felix was in a temper, stomping from foot to foot, crushing the temple beneath him.

"Hopefully he'll not come while we still have Aldiss here. He seemed really scared of him. Do *all* dragons dislike rats?" she asked breathlessly as she ran along.

"Yes," replied her dragon friend. "We learn from an early age not to trust the sneaky little sewer dwellers. No offence, Aldiss."

"None taken," replied the rat, who was too busy watching the giant dragon behind them to think about what she had said.

But Morag had spoken too hastily, for no sooner had she asked the question of Shona than they heard the beat of Felix's wings, felt another powerful downdraft rush towards them and heard a great bang as the dragon pushed off his nest.

"Come back!" roared Felix. "Come back!"

"Oh no!" Morag puffed, hardly daring to look back. But look back she did, only to see Felix unsteadily lift off the ground and lurch towards them. "He's coming! Keep running!"

What Felix hadn't accounted for, and what now saved them from his terrible jaws, was the arc of the inside of the volcano. It was causing the huge creature real problems in getting airborne. Whilst he could rise out the huge opening at the peak, flying *across* the city was much more difficult. Every time he got some height, he banged off the sloping walls, causing rocks to fall on the buildings below.

"Keep going!" Morag urged as Felix landed on the road and stalked them that way instead, his feet stomp stomp stomping, causing the ground to tremor and crack beneath them.

"There's no way we're going to get to the exit before he catches us. It's too far!" Bertie shouted from under

Morag's arm as she ran on. "We'll never make it. We'll need a miracle to get out of here alive!"

He's right, she thought looking at the entrance in the far, far distance, *but we must try.*

They rushed on, the great black dragon in hot pursuit, his huge body crushing buildings and toppling street lamps. Smash, his tail brought down an apartment block. Crash, a wall fell. Boom, the road cracked and buckled. On and on they ran, down narrow streets in an effort to lose their pursuer. Morag pulled up behind a garden wall and stood there, catching her breath. She waited until they had all joined her.

"We're never going to outrun him," she said, glancing around the wall to see where Felix was. The giant dragon was standing sniffing the air, searching for their scent. "Anyone got any ideas?"

"I could try magic," Bertie offered, "but I've only reached my Grade 3 magic exams. I don't know if I can conjure up a powerful enough spell to stop him."

"It's worth a try," the girl replied.

The dodo removed his silver wand from his satchel and peered around the wall. Felix was sniffing the road they had just travelled and with a growl of delight was following their trail.

"Now, Bertie! Before he gets any closer!" hissed Claudine.

Bertie said some magical words, whirled the wand around and flicked it towards their foe. A shower of red hot sparks shot out of the wand and blasted the dragon in the face. Startled and howling with pain, Felix withdrew quickly and grasped his face in his claws.

"My eyes! My eyes!" he screamed.

"You got him!" squeaked Aldiss excitedly. He high-fived the dodo: claw to feathered wing. "That'll teach him to take us on!" he added with glee.

"That'll show him to mess with us!" agreed the bird.

They were so proud of themselves they did not realise that Felix seemed to be recovering quickly from the blast. Eyes streaming with cleansing tears, the huge dragon blinked rapidly and suddenly he could see properly again. With a snarl, he turned towards his prey, now doubly intent on catching it.

"Yes, but instead of scaring him off, you've succeeded in making him angrier!" Henry sniped as Felix bellowed in fury.

"What?" Bertie squawked.

There was a loud rumble and the crash of falling masonry. Felix shoved buildings out of the way, searching for the small creatures who had caused him so much pain.

"If I were you lot, I'd run!" the medallion added.

No-one needed a second invitation. They rushed down the narrow street and turned a corner into a wide main road. Now out in the open, they sprinted along the boulevard, frantically searching for somewhere dragon-proof to hide. As Felix pounded towards them, an escape route offered itself to them...Morag spied a ramp leading down into a subterranean tunnel.

"Down here!" she shouted as she ran with Bertie towards it. Claudine, Tanktop still on her shoulder, swerved across the road to follow her, with Shona and Aldiss close behind. Boom, boom, boom, Felix's footsteps echoed across the city.

"Thieves!" he yelled as the friends rushed down into a brightly lit underground foyer. Dodging ticket booths and leaping over turnstiles, they pushed on, putting as much distance between them and Felix as possible. All the while they could hear the dragon drawing closer and closer above them, shouting and screaming at them to give up their booty. Then he fell silent.

The tunnel darkened and they heard a sucking noise. It was as if Felix was taking a deep breath.

"Round here," shouted Morag as she led her friends into a side passageway. She paused to ensure everyone had followed and was safe: Claudine and Tanktop, Bertie... where were Shona and Aldiss? Still running down the tunnel! She could hear Shona's claws on the tiles. Morag stuck her head around the corner.

"Come on!" the girl screamed as she heard Felix exhale.

Shona tore down the tunnel and leapt into the side passageway, Aldiss hanging on to her scales, terrified. A wall of flames shot down the tunnel and licked at the air around them. But Shona and Aldiss had reached safety. Just.

"Everyone down!" shouted Shona, throwing herself to the ground.

The flames shot harmlessly over them, then died out, leaving the walls and friends covered in a rotten mess of black soot.

"That was close!" said Bertie, getting to his feet.

"*Too* close!" replied Morag.

"Ooohh!" whimpered Tanktop nearby. "Why did I come here? I could have stayed safe in jail in Marnoch Mor!"

Everyone ignored the Klapp demon, including Claudine who was standing next to him. She seemed lost in thought. They heard Felix exhale again.

"Everyone down!" Morag ordered. They all flattened themselves on the floor again, all except for Claudine, who disappeared around the corner. "Claudine! Don't!"

As Morag watched, she saw the woman stand with her feet apart, raise her hands before her and chant strange and mystical words. The flames once more shot down the tunnel and, although terrified for Claudine, Morag could do nothing but leap to the floor, cover her head with her hands and wait for the flames to hit.

But nothing happened.

Morag removed her hands from her head and risked

looking up. No flames. She sat up. Still no flames. She scrambled to her feet and peeked around the corner to witness an astonishing sight: Claudine was single-handedly holding back the searing hot flames. Then, with a flick of her wrists, she turned the fire around and sent it racing back up the tunnel. The stunned Felix reacted too slowly and got the full force of his own fire in his face. Morag thought his screams of pain might burst her eardrums.

Claudine, unscathed and decidedly pleased with herself, rubbed her hands on her trousers.

Morag gawped at her. "How did you do that?" she asked.

"Och, it's an old trick," Claudine answered. "Come on, let's join the others."

Morag's friends were lying on the floor around the corner, waiting for the danger to pass. Shona, unaware of Claudine's intervention, was first to get to her feet and looked impressed when Morag told her how Claudine had saved them.

"What's that old dragon doing now?" Bertie wanted to know. But he was too scared to look, so Shona tiptoed to the corner and peered around. She could just make out Felix's great black body at the other end of the tunnel.

"He seems to be lying down…Oh! Get back!" As Shona said this, Felix's forearm shot down the tunnel and his large claws scrabbled at them. Shona pushed Morag away and ushered the others further down the corridor. Loud scraping and screeching filled the tunnel as Felix's hard nails scratched the floor. He was after them again.

"What are we going to do?" Bertie wanted to know.

"Sit it out?" Claudine suggested.

"We have no time for that," Henry said. "We need to get back to Marnoch Mor."

"Can't you use The Destine?" asked Tanktop, who was greedily eyeing the wooden chalice in Morag's hands.

"I can only use it once," replied the girl regretfully. "Is

there another way out?"

They looked around. There were only two options open to them: go back up the tunnel they had just come down or see where the passageway led them. They unanimously agreed on the latter. The passageway was brightly lit and curved round to the right. As they followed it the corridor came to an abrupt end at three doorways: one yellow, one red and one blue.

Aldiss, keen to show off how clever he was, ran up to each of the three doors and sniffed under them. None smelled dangerous and he told them so, but from under one came a smell that was familiar to him, though he couldn't work out why. It was a musty, slightly oily odour. Puzzled, he said nothing about it. Morag assessed each door, trying to decide which one to open. She noticed that over each was a sign written in ancient Klapp demon. Despite his protestations that he wasn't a good reader, Tanktop was brought forward to translate.

"This way to down, this way to up and I think the other one says something about a park," he read.

"Was the way out up or down?" Morag asked. Bertie and Aldiss shrugged and Tanktop could offer no guidance. It was Claudine who came up with the answer.

"Down, definitely down," she said.

"Well, down it is," Morag decided. She moved towards the door Tanktop had indicated and put a hand on the wooden handle. "Here goes!"

"I'm not sure about this," Aldiss confessed to Bertie, but his mind was soon changed, for as the girl opened the door, Felix began another assault on their hiding place. He shoved an arm down the tunnel again and felt for them with his claw. They could hear the awful scraping and scratching.

"Come out, come out. You can't stay in there forever!" he roared. His voice was muffled by the passageway, but terrifying nonetheless.

"Wait for me, Morag!" the rat shouted as he bolted for the door. Morag held it open as the friends made their escape into yet another tunnel, which seemed to take them deeper underground. This one was also brightly lit and painted white. It led out on to a little platform of an underground railway. Bertie flapped his wings in delight.

"Why can't it ever be an underground *bus* station," muttered Aldiss.

"You don't think this is linked to the Marnoch Mor Underground do you?" asked the dodo, eyes shining brightly with delight.

Morag looked to Shona, who shrugged.

"Why do you ask?" the girl wanted to know.

"Because if it is...watch," said the bird mysteriously. He put a wing into his satchel and pulled out a brass train guard's whistle. He put it to his beak, took a deep breath and blew with all his might. A piercing shriek ripped through the air, causing them all to clutch their ears. The bird lowered it and looked from one rail tunnel to the next expectantly.

"What is it? What are you looking for?" Morag wanted to know.

From around her neck, Henry sighed loudly. "Only the love of his life," he muttered.

As he said this, The Flying Horse chugged into view with a loud whinny, still towing the carriage from before.

"I think I've just come up with our escape route," said the bird proudly.

"How did *that* get here?" Henry wanted to know. He had no faith in the dodo as a magician or wizard or anything else magical. "There is no railway into Graar, not any more, not since the Klapp demons moved out."

"I took the liberty of fitting her with a device of my own invention, a device that allows her to go anywhere I go that has rail tracks," the dodo said. "It's a kind of transporter." He held up the whistle again and waggled it enthusiastically as he added: "She responds to this."

"Wow," said Morag.

"I suppose it's interesting," admitted Henry.

"That's really impressive," said Aldiss, wide-eyed. His whiskers twitched with pride that his friend had been so clever.

Claudine, who had been inspecting the steam train, rolled her eyes and said: "When you've all quite finished giving him a big ego, could we leave?"

Morag nodded.

"Where to, Morag?" called Bertie. He was already in the driver's compartment and standing next to the Instant Driver. "Marnoch Mor? I'm not sure where these tunnels lead or if they are still open, but we can only try."

"No," she said, "Head for the coast. We're going straight to Murst."

Chapter 12

"Murst?" the bird asked, puzzled.

So Morag quickly told them what she had seen in the film shown to her by the hologram. She spoke of watching the people of Murst being horribly treated by Amergin and his Girallons and reminded them that Chelsea — who had been so helpful to them in the past — was still there.

"I think it would be better for us to go straight there. They really need our help. People may be dying," she said firmly. "We'll also have the element of surprise. Amergin won't expect us to attack him in his own fortress." Then she added sadly: "Marnoch Mor will have to wait."

The friends quietly nodded their agreement, each lost in their own thoughts for the people on Murst. Then the silence was shattered by the rat.

"Bags I ride shotgun with Bertie," squeaked Aldiss, running up on to the metal footplate. "And he can tell me all about this new whistle invention."

As the others boarded the carriage, she smiled to hear the rat ask his friend whether or not the whistle could bring anything else.

"Anything like...cheese for instance?" was the last she heard as the steam engine began to chug out of Graar station.

***

Morag, Shona, Claudine and Tanktop made themselves comfortable in the little carriage. They were all exhausted from their recent run-in with Felix and glad of a soft chair to sit on. For a while no-one felt much like talking, so the carriage was silent but for the soothing chackity-chack of the train as it moved along. Morag placed The Destine carefully on a little table next to her, leant back on her seat and briefly closed her eyes. She was so tired that, had a small sound not alerted her, she would have fallen sleep there and then.

It was almost a nothing sound, a tiny scrape on the floor, but it was enough to force open her eyes. Tanktop was at her side, staring at the chalice, one long straggly arm reaching towards it.

"What do you think you're doing?" Morag snapped. He jumped out of his hairy skin.

"Nothing, young mistress."

"It didn't look like nothing to me. What were you doing? Were you trying to steal the chalice?"

"No...I...!"

"You were, weren't you?"

"I only wanted to look at it," he whined, as only a Klapp demon could. "It's so pretty."

"Well look at it from over there," the girl ordered. She pointed to the other end of the carriage.

"What's going on?" Shona wanted to know. She had the startled look of a dragon jolted awake.

"Tanktop was trying to steal The Destine," her friend replied.

"No I wasn't!" muttered the Klapp demon sulkily as he slunk over to the furthest corner of the carriage. He sat down on the floor and glowered at them.

"He was, I saw him," the girl said.

"Stay over there and don't move!" the dragon hissed at Tanktop. "Or I'll throw you off this train...while it's still moving!"

The Klapp demon did not reply, but threw the dragon and girl a disgusted look and turned his back on them. He pulled his knees up, wrapped his long arms around them and buried his head inside. It looked as if someone had decapitated him.

"If I were you, Morag," said Henry from inside her coat, "I would sleep with it tucked under your arm. You can't trust a Klapp demon and we can't afford for The Destine to go missing."

"Agreed," said Morag, snatching the chalice from the table and stuffing it in beside the medallion. "We'll keep an eye on it together," she added.

"Try and get some sleep, Morag," said the dragon. "We've a long journey ahead of us."

"I will," she replied, fighting the urge to close her eyes. Soon she nodded off and dreamt of happier times with Isabella and Nathan.

Morag was asleep for a few hours before awaking refreshed and still clutching The Destine. As she opened her eyes, she was aware that Shona and Claudine were head-to-head having a whispered discussion. Curious, she kept her eyes closed and strained to hear what was being said.

"I think I know who you really are, Claudine," Shona said.

"Really?" said the woman casually. "And who am I?"

"I've heard the stories, but I had no idea you and Montgomery had actually married," the dragon continued. "I didn't think your kind could marry humans."

"James isn't entirely human anymore," said the woman regretfully. "The Eye saw to that."

"But without it, he wouldn't have lived so long," the dragon reminded her.

"True, but his overarching sense of decency and his link to that stone caused our marriage breakdown," Claudine said.

"Is that why you argued?"

"Yes. He wouldn't leave Marnoch Mor and live with me in the north. I couldn't live in Marnoch Mor, I found the town stifling. So we parted."

"I'm sorry."

"It happens."

"How long has it been since you last saw him?"

"One hundred and thirty years," answered Claudine.

At this point, when Morag heard the answer, she could no longer pretend she was still sleeping. Her eyes flew open and she gasped out loud.

"What *are* you?" The question was out of Morag's mouth before she could stop it. Shona and Claudine looked at the girl in surprise and it was Henry who answered.

"Mrs Montgomery — Claudine — is...you don't mind if I tell her, do you Claud?" he asked. Claudine shook her head. "She's an elf. More accurately, she's an elemental elf."

"That will do, Henry," Claudine warned.

"I don't understand," said the girl. "What's that?"

Claudine smiled at her. "I am fire, water, earth and wind," she said. "My people and I control the elements. We make the rain come, we create the storms, we bring the sun, we control the rivers and seas and make things grow. Without us, this planet would fail."

"But you're Montgomery's wife," the girl replied, puzzled.

"I *was*," said the elf, "but he chose his people over me."

She paused, sorrow playing about her face, then seemed to brighten.

"Anyway," she said, "enough of my woes. There are more important matters to attend to. There won't *be* a Marnoch Mor or northern Scotland if we don't defeat Amergin."

"How long until we reach the coast?" Shona wanted to know.

Morag peered out of the carriage window. It was still dark outside, but they had by now left the safety of the Underground tunnels and *The Flying Horse* was chugging along on a magical overground track that followed the coastline. It was a crisp clear night and she could see the moon's reflection on the sea just ahead of them.

"I think we're almost there," she said and held The Destine all the tighter.

***

"Now what?" Morag despaired. They were standing on a deserted beach somewhere on the north-west coast of Scotland, with no boat. The sky was a murky morning-grey and just starting to lighten. There was the sharp tang of rotten seaweed and salt in the air, and some small black and white seabirds were beginning to stir on the cold shoreline. They cried out to each other as Morag tried hard to think of a solution. Kyle was away and they had no *Sea Kelpie* to rely on this time, so how were they going to get to Murst?

"I'll ask my friends for help," said Claudine mysteriously.

Morag saw that she was winking. Before she could ask what she meant, Claudine strode towards the gently lapping sea, cupped her hands around her mouth and shouted: "Ooooh! Eeeeeee! Oooooh! Eeeeeee!"

"What's she doing?" Aldiss whispered to Bertie.

"I don't know," replied the bird.

"Well I wish she would stop it!" complained the rat clamping his paws over his ears. "That sound is dreadful."

"I agree," replied the bird, "but it seems to be working."

With an outstretched wing, Bertie pointed out towards the dark sea and sure enough the water seemed to be churning. As they watched, the churning became more violent until Morag was sure a whirlpool would appear at any moment and suck everything down into it, she and her friends included. But no whirlpool appeared. Instead she was surprised and delighted to see a number of heads push up through the water. Seals? She wondered. They were certainly about the right size, but she couldn't see them properly in the half light.

"Here they come," said Claudine, smiling.

There were around thirty of them and they swam towards the shore in one pod. As they drew closer Morag gasped. They weren't seals at all but strange men and women with pale green skin and round fish-like eyes. The women had long dark green hair which they had adorned with shells and pebbles. The men wore their hair tied back in ponytails and carried tridents and other weapons.

"Mer people!" exclaimed Morag, unable to keep the wonder out of her voice. She had heard from her mother that mermen and mermaids actually existed, and since finding that out it had been her dearest wish to talk to one. Now here were *thirty* for her to talk to.

As the mer people drew closer, Claudine began to wade into the sea.

"Claudine! No! You'll freeze to death!" Shona warned, but the woman seemed oblivious to her. She did not seem to notice the ice-cold of the water either, but continued to wade in until the sea reached her chest. She greeted the nearest mermaid in a strange high-pitched language that no-one else could understand and the mermaid smiled and put her arms out for a hug. As they embraced, the rest of the mer people gathered around Claudine and an animated conversation began. The friends watched on, unable to make out what the group was saying. As Claudine talked, a few mer people turned to peer at Morag and her friends standing self-consciously on the beach. A few narrowed their eyes and grimaced, showing off horrible sharp teeth. Others smiled and waved, but even though they appeared to be friendly, Morag couldn't shake off the feeling that the mer people did not want them there.

"What do you think Claudine is saying to them?" Bertie asked Morag.

"I don't know," replied the girl, "but I hope she's asking

them for a boat because it's really cold standing here." As if to prove her point, she shivered.

"I'm sure it won't be long now," said the bird kindly, although what 'it' was he didn't know. To make his friends feel better, he reached into his satchel and brought them each out a mug of steaming hot chocolate. Even Tanktop, who was not a fan of sweet drinks, took his gratefully.

"Morag! Morag!" Henry called from inside her coat, where he was taking refuge from the winter weather. "Pull me out, I want to see what's going on."

She did as he bid and the magical medallion watched Claudine with interest.

"What's she doing?" Morag wanted to know.

"Oh! Don't you know? I forgot you wouldn't be able to understand them," he replied a little smugly. "She's asking them to help us, she's requesting some sort of transportation...something like a cup."

"A cup?" said Morag, alarmed. She hugged The Destine tightly to her.

"Oh, she's finished now. They've agreed to help. Here she comes," the medallion added.

Sure enough, Claudine, the elemental elf, was already saying her goodbyes. She turned and waded gracefully out of the water. On the beach, she stood and shook herself dry, reminding Morag of the dogs she had seen on Irvine Beach a lifetime ago. They had done the same thing after getting out of the sea.

"That's better," said Claudine. She smiled. "They've agreed to help us get to Murst." She turned and gazed out to sea. "In fact, here's our ride now."

They all turned to look and were astonished to see one half of a huge white scallop shell rise to the surface of the water. It was the size of a minibus and boasted three rows of seats. Attached to the shell was a set of long reigns and attached to the reigns were four playful dolphins. They cackled their welcome to Morag and her friends. Shona's eyes looked like they were about to pop out of her head.

"There's no way I'm getting into that," she said firmly. "We'll all drown."

"You'll be fine," Claudine assured her, "it's perfectly safe."

"Morag," said the dragon, "I really think we should think this through. I don't think the shell thing is safe and you don't even have a plan for when we get there! We'll be caught before we can even get to Amergin."

The girl knew her friend was probably right, but the memory of Chelsea and the others being treated terribly by Amergin and the Girallons would not go. She knew in her heart of hearts that this was the right thing to do. She would figure something out on the way.

"We *have* to go," she said firmly, "we have no choice and I don't think Claudine would put us in any danger. Come on. Oh! Tanktop! I didn't see you there." The Klapp demon was standing at her back and Morag nearly walked right into him as she turned towards the craft.

But Shona was adamant and Tanktop backed her up.

"Nasty freezing water," he said, "it's too dangerous for me!"

"Well you can both stay here then," Morag snapped. She didn't have time for dissent. "*I'm* going! Bertie, Aldiss, are you coming?"

The dodo looked at the rat and then they both looked at Shona and Tanktop. Neither really wanted to go to Murst aboard a giant shell and they didn't want to leave Shona either. However, they both wanted to help Morag. They stood silently trying to decide, but unable to for fear of insulting one or other of their friends. It was Aldiss who made the final decision. He climbed up Morag's leg and sat on her shoulder.

"I'm in," he said.

"Me too," said Bertie, going to stand beside Morag.

The girl looked pleadingly at the dragon.

"Shona, please change your mind," she said. "We need you. *Murst* needs you."

The dragon pursed her lips and seemed to think for a bit. Then she closed her eyes and snorted, sending little puffs of white smoke up into the air.

"No, I just can't," she said. "I can't. I'm sorry, it's the water." She turned to Tanktop. "But there's no reason why you can't go," she told him.

The Klapp demon, who liked being near water even less than Shona, whimpered and backed away, shaking his head violently.

"I think I'll stay here on dry land," he said quickly, "It's much warmer." He clutched his jacket closely around his skinny body. "Anyway, you don't need me anymore, so I'll just be off!"

And before anyone could stop him, he turned tail and bolted towards the sand dunes.

"Tanktop! Come back!" Morag called, but it was too late. He was gone.

"He would only have held you back," muttered Shona as she watched the shell boat being brought close to shore. "Don't worry, *I'll* go after him." She helped Morag to board the boat, being careful not to get her scaly dragon feet and tail wet. "I'll find him and take him back to Marnoch Mor," Shona promised as she gave her friend a hug. "That little sneak still has to be punished for what he's done! Spying in a royal palace should get him a least a year in jail."

"Please come," said Morag, tears pricking her eyes. She had never been on an adventure without her dragon companion. "We can catch Tanktop later."

"I can't, Morag. That craft just looks too dangerous. I'll die if I fall into the water, you know that. My inner core will go out, I won't be able to create fire and my life force will be lost. It's better I stay here and get the Klapp demon back." She hugged her friend again. "Take care. I'll send reinforcements, I promise."

Morag took a seat near the front of the shell boat, sitting next to Claudine. Bertie and Aldiss sat behind them. The girl turned to see her friend waving her off.

"Good luck!" Shona shouted as the four dolphins dragged the boat out to sea.

Morag waved to her friend until she was a small dot on a distant beach. Upset Shona wasn't coming with her, she felt that her mission was now doomed to failure.

"Are you all right, Morag?" Henry asked. His voice was soft and kind.

"Not really," she replied.

"We will all miss her," the medallion said, "but we can't let Shona's absence stop us from fulfilling our goal. We *must* vanquish Amergin and save Murst before he grows even stronger."

***

The seashell boat was surprisingly comfortable, despite its lack of shelter, for it skimmed above the waves like a hovercraft as the four dolphins pulled it along. Bertie handed them all lap rugs he had obtained from his magical satchel and they wrapped themselves in them as snug as bugs. Morag was delighted to see some of the mer people swimming alongside and was impressed by how well they kept up with the little ship. She smiled as one — a female with a sparkling glass bauble in her hair — came close; but instead of returning the greeting the mermaid hissed at her and pulled away.

"They are not the friendliest of the sea people," Claudine said. "Come, sit closer to me and I'll tell you stories of the elemental elves."

The hours passed by in a blur. Lulled by the monotony

of the journey and Claudine's soft voice, Morag drifted in and out of sleep. They ate breakfast and lunch on board, meals requested from Bertie's satchel, and kept their spirits up by singing songs. As the early afternoon sped away from them and the sky began to darken, Morag sank into silent brooding about returning to the DarkIsle once more. Twice she had gone before, twice her life had been endangered and twice she and her friends had escaped. Would she be so lucky third time round? She hoped so.

"I see it!" Aldiss squealed excitedly. "The DarkIsle, Murst, it's over there."

Sure enough, black against the dark grey sky, were the now familiar point of Ben Murst and the tall thin outline of Murst Castle. Her heart sank. She could not believe she was here again. She felt for The Destine, safely tucked away inside her coat. And she felt for her book of Marnoch Mor poetry. Despite their reassuring honest hardness, neither gave her the comfort she craved.

"Morag where do you want us to disembark?" Bertie's voice broke through her thoughts.

The girl stared at the dark island. For once she was out of options. They couldn't dock at the castle for they would be caught immediately. She thought about doing what they had done the last time, climbing the cliffs on the west of island. That would take them up to the village of Dragon's End, but day had turned to night and it would be too dangerous. She looked at her friends in dismay.

"I don't know," she said. She suddenly felt hopeless, exhausted and unable to think clearly.

Claudine put her arm around her and gave her a hug.

"It'll be okay," she reassured her.

"But we can't even get onto the island," the girl wailed, "and if we can't get onto the island we can't use The Destine on Amergin and we can't rescue the islanders and Marnoch Mor. This is hopeless."

"Leave it to me," Montgomery's wife said with a smile. "I'll sort something out for us." Claudine leant forward and said something to the dolphins, who squeaked their understanding, let go of the reins of the shell boat and disappeared under the dark waves. The friends watched in amazement as Claudine stood up and in a calm voice commanded the water to lift them up and push them forward. As they reached two metres above the waves, she pulled a huge gust of wind out of the air and settled it under the shell.

"Hold on tight!" she said as the water subsided and the wind took over. Staggering slightly from the movement, she sat back down next to Morag as the shell took off.

By now, the sky was almost completely dark. Heavy grey clouds were blocking out all but a hint of the full moon: perfect cover for their airborne craft as it hurtled towards the forest side of the castle.

"Can you get it to take us to the cove over there," said Morag, pointing to the little sheltered bay where Kyle the Fisherman had rescued them from the island the last time.

Claudine's hands swirled in the air and the craft turned to the left, swooping over to the island. Soon it was hovering above the clifftop and with a gentle downwards movement of her hands, the wind lowered them to the ground. Morag was the first to clamber off the shell. She stepped down on to the snowy grass and inhaled the familiar damp smell of the black forest. Somewhere deep inside the woods, in a place where only the darkest creatures went, a wolf howled. Morag's heart skipped a beat and she gulped. She fidgeted with her coat, checking the toggles were buttoned and making sure The Destine was still safe inside, before pulling her hood tight over her head. It was freezing cold and a bitter wind whipped at her hair. She faced the direction of the castle and Amergin, and shivered.

"Everything okay, Morag?" Bertie asked. He held a small

Moonstone in his wing. It gave off just enough light for the girl to see the worry in his eyes.

"Yes," she lied. "Where's Aldiss?"

"Here," squeaked the rat, bounding into the Moonstone light.

"And Claudine?"

"Returning the shell to the sea," Aldiss said. "She didn't want it found by the Girallons."

"But that was our only way off the island," wailed Bertie.

"Don't worry, Claudine will be able to get it again," Morag assured him, although she didn't feel confident either. "Besides, once we beat Amergin we'll be able to use one of the island's bat crafts to get home."

***

It didn't take them long to find the path through the forest that would take them directly to the castle. It was a relief to step onto the old worn walkway and out of the forest foliage that was so alive with rustles and squeaks. Every few minutes, they heard the eerie howl of the wolves. One by one the creatures called out to the darkness and were answered by another of their kind. There was a pause and then all of them — Morag guessed there were at least ten — joined together for a loud chorus to the moon. Trying to ignore the vicious creatures, the friends hurried along the path, being careful to keep their light to a minimum so that they would not be noticed from the castle. Bertie led the way, followed by Aldiss, Morag and Claudine. They tripped and stumbled over the rough ground, their feet crunching on the hard winter snow. Ten minutes later, they came to the clearing at the back of the castle. They crouched behind a clump of ferns and studied the fortress before them.

Up on the ramparts, giant guards patrolled. Back and

forth, back and forth; pikes in hands, scowling faces highlighted by the flaming torches around the castle's battlements. The crimson red banners that previously had so proudly flown from the fortress, hung in tatters. The glittering glass windows were dull and broken, and halfway down one of the castle walls there was a large cage in which five figures huddled: captured humans grouped together against the biting wind. The castle, normally so foreboding and strong, had a different air about it now — one of decay and death. It took Morag's breath away.

A loud creaking focused all eyes on the castle's huge gates, which slowly opened to allow a couple of Girallons out. They held torches and harried a group of ragged humans. The humans, who were chained together at the ankles, were carrying two long sack cloths that were the exact shape and size of...

"Are those...bodies?" Aldiss gasped.

"I think so," the girl whispered.

As they watched, the group stopped close to where they were hiding. Morag could now see that a couple of them had shovels in their hands. The Girallons barked some orders and the two humans with the spades began to dig. It was almost impossible work. The ground was hard with ice and even after ten minutes of trying to break into the solid earth they were unable to penetrate it. One of the Girallons roared but was appeased by the other.

"What does it matter," it said. "We will just leave the bodies here for the wolves to eat." Then, turning to the humans, it ordered, "Put them over there," as it pointed at a random spot.

The humans did as they were told and carefully laid the two bodies on the ground. As one of them bent down, her hood fell back and Morag saw with horror that the captured woman was Ivy, the elder from the village of Dragon's End who had helped them before. Morag fought the urge to cry out and watched dismayed as the old woman and her peers were roughly pushed and shoved back towards the castle gates, their chains jangling in the cold winter night.

"This is worse than I thought," Morag whispered.

Aldiss's black eyes glinted in the half light as they watched the gates of the fortress shut with a clunk. "How are we going to get into the castle?" he asked.

"I don't know," said the girl, "but we can't turn back now. We have to help those poor people."

Chapter 13

Whether it was fate or good fortune that the boy giant Arrod snuck out of the castle shortly afterwards, Morag did not know. What she did know was that he was a possible ally. He had been kind to her some months before when she had been captured and given to Mephista as a slave. She had thought then that he had no stomach for cruelty and so hoped he would help now.

She was first aware of him when she spotted someone very tall and thin crawling out of the little door at the back of the castle. She initially feared it was one of the Girallons, but as the figure ran across the open ground, the moon appeared from behind a cloud, allowing her to see clearly the features of her former captor. He seemed afraid, glancing behind him all the time. And the route he was taking suggested he was not leaving the fortress as a free guard, but as an escapee.

He entered the undergrowth as quietly as a giant boy could, discarding pieces of his uniform as he went. Here his gauntlets, there his helmet, then his breastplate. Once unburdened, he stooped and crept forward, heading in the direction of the friends but seemingly unaware of their presence. He was nearly upon them when he suddenly stumbled over the bodies laid out earlier.

"What??" he gasped as he fell. Arrod quickly pushed himself up, feeling as he did what he had fallen over. "Oh my...!" he said in a half whisper as he pulled himself away from the shrouded corpses.

"Arrod, Arrod," Morag called softly.

"Who's there?" the boy giant gasped in the darkness, frozen to the spot.

"It's me, Morag," she replied.

"Morag? Who's Morag?" He crawled towards the sound

of her voice.

"I am the girl MacAndrew took on to your mother's boat a few months ago and sold as a slave to Mephista. You gave me a fur coat before I disembarked — to keep me warm. Remember? We spoke about you doing something different to slaving."

"Morag? Morag? I don't remember...oh yes! Now I do!" he said as he saw her face in the dull glow of a Moonstone. "Are you a ghost?" he hissed, "For if you are I can tell you now I had nothing to do with your death!"

"I'm not a ghost," she replied. "I escaped with my friends. We got the Eye of Lornish. It killed Devlish."

"Yes, I remember now: you killed the master...they told me about it when I started my training, you're famous for it, but what are you doing *here*? Are you *mad*? My Lady has been after you for months and...and...well this is a much more terrible place now, evil. Leave...*now*...before they capture you too."

"We've come to help," she said, putting the Moonstone in her pocket so that its light would not alert the guards on the castle.

"There's more than just you?"

"Yes."

"You've brought an army?" he added, hope in his voice.

"No."

"Then how can you help? Nothing can stop that...thing!"

"Thing?"

"The demon in Devlish's body."

"You *know* about Amergin?"

"He announced it to everyone in the hall a couple of days ago, just after Lady Mephista disappeared. He said he wanted to let us know that all the rumours of a demon in Lord Devlish's body were true and that if we didn't do as he said he'd make fish food out of us. He's brought in more Girallons from the secret jungles of deepest darkest

Africa to make sure we all do what we're told. Three Lords and Ladies managed to escape, but we think the wolves got them. No-one's seen or heard from them."

"Why don't you all take them on together?" Morag wanted to know.

"Everyone is too scared to do anything. The Girallons are strong and vicious. Those beasts killed one of the guards just for sport. And...and...there are terrible stories of people...being eaten," he said with a shudder. "There's evil in that castle, get away while you still can."

"Why did he reveal himself to be Amergin? Why not just keep pretending to be Devlish?" Morag wondered.

"Because for all his evil intentions, Devlish never ate people." Arrod's voice wavered. "There was a story that Amergin was discovered dining on one of the stable boys and...well he was forced to reveal who he was. He's made servants of the Lords and Ladies and the servants are now...well, we don't know what's happening to them. Some of them are in cages, others are missing. The guards are being controlled by the Girallons...We've been biding our time, waiting for a chance to escape, but I managed to get away before everyone else. I thought my mother might help."

"Are you a guard now?"

"Yes," he replied, momentarily proud. "At least, I *was*."

"Great, then you can get us into the castle," Morag said.

"No, I can't. You don't understand, I've just *escaped* from the castle. There's no way I'm going back to work for that demon!" said the boy. "He had the captain of the guards flogged for refusing to round up humans."

"Arrod, if you *don't* help us get into the castle, Amergin will take over not just Murst, but Marnoch Mor and then the rest of the planet. Nowhere will be safe from his clutches. If you leave now and don't help us, it will just be a matter of time before he catches up with you."

"And then you'll really be for it!" added Aldiss, who was getting caught up in it all.

The giant boy paused. They could only just make out the tall strong frame of his body silhouetted against the light from the castle, but could not see his face. He sighed.

"Okay, I'll get you in," he said, "but once you're in you're on your own."

"That's a deal," the girl replied.

"So what's the plan?" he asked as he crouched down beside them and looked at each one in turn.

"Well..." said the girl, "we'll need disguises if we're to walk about the castle without creating suspicions. Arrod, are you able to get Claudine and I some servant's clothing?"

"I could try," he said, sounding depressed. "And then that's it, I can leave?"

"Yes," the girl replied.

"And what are you going to do once you get in?" Arrod asked. "How are you going to stop Amergin?"

"With this!" Morag said, pulling The Destine out from her jacket. She held it up for all to see, but the others weren't reacting as she thought they would. Arrod frowned and the rest gaped. "What?" She looked at the chalice and gasped. There in her hand was not The Destine, but a metal goblet. And not a very nice one at that. It was a gun metal colour and pitted with dents. "Oh no! Where's The Destine?"

With a terrified urgency, Morag groped about inside her jacket but only found Henry and her poetry book within its folds. Henry, who had been sleeping, complained bitterly at being woken, but soon stopped his angry muttering when he learned that The Destine was missing.

"Where is it?" he wanted to know.

"I don't know!" wailed Morag close to tears. "I was so careful with it."

"What are we going to do now?" Aldiss whimpered.

"The Destine was our only hope," sighed Bertie.

They lapsed into silence, unable to take in the enormity of the loss. Without The Destine, Amergin would not be vanquished and would take over the world, enslaving every living creature as he did so. It was too horrible to contemplate.

"Someone must have swapped The Destine for the goblet," Claudine said.

"You're right," said Morag, "but who could have done it? And how?"

She thought back. She had definitely had it in Graar, there was no question about that. And it had definitely been on the train carriage, for she had been forced to move it when Tanktop had shown so much interest in it...

"Tanktop!" she gasped. "*He's* got it! That's why he ran off at the beach!"

"The little sneak!" Aldiss said. He pulled out his wand and brandished it. Little blue sparks fizzed off it and bounced onto nearby ferns. "When I get a hold of him I'm going to turn him into...into...a slug!"

"You'll be turning no-one into anything," Bertie said, gently pushing the wand down so that the rat didn't accidentally magic anyone again. "Put that thing away, you're not helping by getting all agitated."

"Bertie's right," Morag said, pulling her jacket tighter around her body. The wind was getting up. "We need a new plan, but what can we do now?"

***

On the mainland, the dragon was getting ready to pounce. She had followed the increasingly pungent Klapp demon scent for about a mile and at last could see her prey a few metres from her. She crouched in the sand dunes and watched as Tanktop stopped to take a rest. He sat down on a tuft of scratchy grass and pulled something out from nowhere. In the moonlight, Shona could see the shape of a chalice. *That little creep has The Destine,* she thought as she crept closer.

"Hee hee," Tanktop chuckled as he stroked the little wooden cup, "I'll take this to her and she'll be grateful and she'll love old Tanktop, yes she will. My lady will give me lots of nice things to show her gratitude."

Slowly, slowly, Shona crept forward. As Tanktop continued talking to himself, he did not notice the pigmy dragon in the shadows. He did not know she was getting ready to pounce. Too late, he saw her mid-flight as she launched herself at him.

"You thieving little...!" she growled as she caught him in one great claw.

"Eugh, Mistress Dragon," he gasped as she pinned him to the cold sand, "it's so nice to see you again. How can I help you?"

"You can give me *this* for starters!" said Shona, snatching The Destine from his paw with her other claw.

"Er...heh...heh...heh," he said, trying to sound like he was casually laughing. "How did that get *there*?"

"You tell me...and it had better be good," she growled, yellow eyes blazing.

***

Back on Murst, the friends were trying to work out what to do next. Without The Destine, Morag had no idea how they were going to tackle Amergin. They were debating whether it was possible to kill a Mitlock Demon with a silver bullet when they were suddenly aware of a change in the weather. Before any of them could get out of the way a whirlwind appeared before them, spinning and howling. They stared at it in horror, mesmerised by its raw power, unable to move as it alighted on the ground, pulling at the grasses and ferns around them.

"I believe this is yours!" a voice said from within, and as they looked the whirlwind began to subside, leaving before them a large dark shape. Bertie held up his Moonstone and the blue light shone against four large claw-like feet, a long scaly tail and a big tummy. He turned the beam upwards into the toothy smiling face of Shona.

"Shona!" said Morag, scrambling to her feet and hurrying over to her friend. "How did you get here?"

"Shh!" Henry urged. "Or we'll be discovered."

"That's a bit of an unusual story," the dragon replied, whispering now, "but before I tell it I must first return this."

She held out her claw in which Morag could see The Destine. She grasped it to her and hugged it tight.

"How did you get this?" she said in wonder as she clutched it against her torso, relieved. "I thought it was gone forever."

"Well..." the dragon began and she told them how she had pursued Tanktop, and managed to get to him before he had used his whirlwind trick to disappear. "He had switched it for something else when you weren't looking. I knew you couldn't get rid of Amergin without it, so I forced him to use the whirlwind to take me to you."

"And where's the nasty little creature now?" Henry wanted to know.

Shona showed them her other claw, which she'd been holding behind her back. Dangling from it, as meek and mild as a kitten, was a shame-faced Tanktop.

"You nasty horrible thief!" Morag hissed. "You stole from me. How *could* you? You knew The Destine was important to us. What were you thinking? Do you *want* Amergin to take over the world?"

Tanktop shook his head as best he could, his eyes

bulging from being held by the throat.

"*She* made me do it," the Klapp demon gasped. He squirmed and coughed.

"Put him down Shona, you're choking him," Bertie said. "Not that he doesn't deserve it."

The dragon lowered the demon to his feet and loosened her grasp a little.

"*Who* made you do it?" Morag asked.

"*She* made me do it. She wanted The Destine for herself so she could take over," he confessed. "She said she would turn me into a toilet roll tube and give me to a nursery school for the children to paint and crush." He whimpered. "I don't want to be turned into a toilet roll tube," he whined.

It dawned on them all at once to whom he was referring.

"Mephista!" the friends said in unison and were it not for the seriousness of the situation, they would probably have laughed.

"Why am I not surprised?" Claudine added. "She was always in trouble at school."

"*You* went to school with Mephista?" Aldiss gasped.

"I *taught* her at school," the woman corrected. "Anyway that's beside the point," she added hastily, "we've got The Destine back now, so are you all ready to carry out the task ahead? Morag, what was your plan?"

All eyes fell on Morag. She smiled and suddenly felt braver than she had ever felt before. Courage raced through her small body and buoyed her. Destiny had brought her here and it was up to her to fulfil whatever came next.

"What are we going to do with this?" Shona asked, pushing the Klapp demon forward. His eyes were wide with fear.

"Tie him up and gag him," Morag said. "We don't want him giving us away. We can leave him in the bushes and come back for him later."

Somewhere in the forest a lone wolf howled. Tanktop

shuddered and whimpered and cried: "Please don't leave me. The horrible wolfies will eat me up. I don't want to be eaten! And if I'm not eaten I will freeze to death out here in this scary forest. I'm good really. I didn't *mean* to steal. She *made* me, promised me all sorts of goodies that I found hard to resist. Please take me with you. I can help. I can!"

Morag looked at the shivering creature in disgust, but there was also room for pity in her heart.

"Okay," she said, despite the protestations of her friends. "We can put in him a rucksack and hide him in the castle."

"No! No! I don't want to be left alone in the castle to be found by the Girallons!" he squeaked. "Please take me with you as part of your noble gang and I will help."

"*How* will you help?" Shona growled. "So far you've been nothing but a nuisance."

"I helped get you into Graar," he reminded her. "I got you into the city with my rhyme."

"*Morag* worked that one out," snapped the dragon.

Tanktop thought for a moment. He sighed loudly as if some inner conflict was going on in his mind, then he said: "I can get the other Klapp demons on your side. With their help we can raise a rebellion and take over the castle."

Morag glanced at Shona, who was sceptical.

"What do you think?" the girl asked.

"I think we can't trust him," she replied. "I think we should leave him out here for the 'wolfies' to eat!"!

"No! NO!" shrieked the Klapp demon. Morag hastily clamped her hand over his mouth lest he give them away.

"Bertie? Aldiss? Claudine? Any thoughts?"

"I agree with Shona!" replied Bertie smugly. "He can't be trusted. You should know that by now, Morag!"

"I'm with Bertie," squeaked Aldiss, excitedly shadow boxing in the dull light of the Moonstone.

"But what if he *can* help?" Claudine wanted to know.

"I'm thinking that too," agreed Morag.

She looked at Tanktop, who was giving her his best pleading puppydog eyes, then at Shona, who was shaking her head.

"Exactly *how* can the Klapp demons help?" Morag wanted to know.

"I will appeal to the Grand Pappy Meermore for help. He is no friend of those big apes," replied the quivering Tanktop. "He will be pleased to fight against them. I promise. Trust me."

Morag mulled over his proposition, weighing up the pros and cons of having to trust a Klapp demon. Finally she came to her decision.

"I think we should speak to them. There are so few of us. If we *can* get the Klapp demons to help, it will give us a better chance of succeeding," she said.

"But Morag...!" Shona began.

"I don't think we've got any choice," the girl cut in. "We need all the help we can get."

"Morag, I really don't think..." the dragon tried again.

"Shona, what have we got to lose?"

Shona pursed her lips, but she could see that the girl was right.

"Okay, we'll ask them, but please don't be disappointed if they double cross you," she said.

"It's a chance I'm willing to take!" replied the girl.

Chapter 14

"How are we going to get back in?" Morag asked as they got ready to leave.

"The door," the giant boy replied. "I left it open in case...well in case I had to return in a hurry. The woods are not safe at night. The wolves prowl about looking for food and even I'm no match for one of them. I thought that if I needed to, I could go back."

"I'm glad you did," said Morag. "We'll wait here while you go and get our disguises. Be safe!"

"I will," replied the giant.

"I'd rather take my chances with the wolves," muttered Shona as they watched the shadow return to the castle.

"Well, it's good for us that Arrod thought about them!" replied the girl.

Arrod squeezed through the small door and was out of sight. As they waited in the building's shadow, the friends tried to keep their spirits up by talking about what they wanted for Christmas, which was only a few days away. As Aldiss whispered at length about the box of cheeses he desired — describing every type of the ten cheeses in great detail — Morag saw a large shadow emerge from the small doorway. Arrod scuttled across the open space between the castle and the forest and was soon crouching down in the ferns with the rest of them.

"This was the best I could get," he said, handing Morag and Claudine small bundles of foul-smelling clothes.

Morag had never seen such filthy rags before. They had been made of some sort of coarse sacking and smelled of sweat and manure. She held up the tunic. Not even when she had lived with Moira and Jermy had she had to wear such holey, dirty things. They were rough and scratchy. With a sigh, she pulled it over her head and over her own clothes, reluctant to let the horrible thing touch her skin. She then pulled on a pair of loose trousers that were slightly too big for her. She tied the rope belt tight around her waist. Over her head, Arrod placed a short hooded cape. She turned to see Claudine similarly attired.

"Here," Arrod said, handing them three sacks.

"What are these for?" the girl asked.

"To put your friends in," he said. "If you use your rucksacks you'll draw attention to yourselves. They are far too new and modern."

Morag could see he was right, but it took a little gentle coaxing to get Bertie (who was very proud of his lovely clean plumage) and Aldiss (who spent a lot of time every day preening his whiskers) into the greasy smelly sacks. Tanktop, however, jumped in with glee and made himself comfortable. He seemed to relish the stinky dirty bags.

"You know I can't fit inside that narrow doorway," Shona said when things had settled down again.

"I know. I have a job for you!" replied the girl and she whispered something in the dragon's ear. Shona nodded and the two hugged. Then...

"Everyone ready?" Morag asked, closing the neck of her bag, which contained Aldiss, and picking it up. Claudine and Arrod nodded, each picking up their sacks, which hid Bertie and Tanktop respectively.

"Be careful," Shona said, giving Morag a final hug. She seemed reluctant to let her go.

"And you know what to do?" Morag asked her.

"Yes," replied the lizard. "Good luck everyone!"

The dragon stood aside and watched with fear in her heart as her beloved Morag and her friends entered the little door once more. She closed her eyes and prayed for their safe return.

***

Inside, Morag let Bertie, Aldiss and Tanktop out of their bags and the friends stood in the little stone corridor that led up to a passageway next to the Great Hall. The stone walls were freezing to the touch and unlit, so Bertie pulled some Moonstones from his satchel for everyone to use. Arrod took one and led them up into the castle. Claudine brought up the rear. No-one spoke as they carefully made their way inside. The passageway was narrow, and the dirt floor slippery with ice. It was all they could do to keep up with the giant boy who strode purposefully ahead.

Arrod stopped as they reached the wooden doorway at the top of the passageway, the very door that Morag knew would take them into the main public areas of the fortress.

"This is as far as I go," he said.

Morag looked up to him and could see real fear in his eyes. She lunged at him and hugged his legs, which were as long as she was tall.

"Thank you," she said.

"For what?" Arrod looked uncomfortable at the unexpected show of affection.

"For helping," she replied. "I know you're scared…"

"I'm not scared!" he assured her.

"Well, thank you just for helping," she said.

"But I'm not scared!" he said again.

"Of course you're not…"Morag began.

"Well, if you really aren't scared, you'll help us defeat Amergin," Henry's voice sang out from beneath the rags.

"I…well…I need to go and get my mother," Arrod stuttered.

"You could help us get the other giants on side," Claudine suggested.

"And punish the Girallons for what they did to your friend," added Bertie.

"I don't know," he replied, head bowed.

Morag gave him another squeeze.

"Please, Arrod. We could really use your help. The other giants could use your help."

Arrod sighed loudly. Seconds passed and Morag feared he would leave. Then he nodded his head.

"Okay," he said. "I'll stay...if only to give those four-armed monkeys a good hiding!"

"Thank you!" the girl said, releasing him from her hug.

She turned to her friends. Bertie, Aldiss and Tanktop looked at her expectantly.

"This is it!" she said. "You three need to get back into your sacks," she added apologetically. "We can't risk being spotted before we've even begun." Bertie sighed and muttered something as he climbed inside the one the girl proffered. Aldiss hopped into the one Claudine was carrying, but Tanktop refused.

"No-one will think a Klapp demon is out of place at Murst Castle," he said, shaking his head. "I was born here. I don't need to skulk about like a burglar."

"Okay," said Morag uncertainly. She wasn't sure it was such a good idea allowing Tanktop to wander about, he could make a bolt for freedom at any moment, but she needed him, she needed his family and she had to trust him...for now.

She looked at Arrod and nodded to him to open the door, which the giant boy reluctantly did.

Morag gasped when she saw the transformation in the castle as she stepped into the deserted main corridor that ran along one side of the Great Hall. Where once there had been fine wall hangings and tapestries adorning the walls, now there were only rags and tattered bits of cloth. The wooden doors that led into the Great Hall and to other rooms were scratched and some were almost off their hinges. As they went by the Great Hall, Morag paused to peep inside. The wooden thrones, where Mephista and

Devlish had once held court, were smashed. Tables and benches were overturned and wall hangings shredded and discarded. The whole place had an air of violence, of the decay Morag had sensed upon seeing the castle from the outside. She couldn't believe that such destruction had happened in such a short space of time.

A group of Girallons sat against the only table still standing, teasing a group of human slaves as they attempted to clean up. One of the four-armed apes threw pieces of bread at the downtrodden people, shouting: "Here, take this. It's your wages! Haw haw haw!" Morag watched in dismay as the slaves scrabbled for the bits of bread as they hit the dusty floor. Instead of putting them in the bin, she was horrified to see them stuff the bread in their mouths...much to the amusement of their guards. *They're starving*, she realised, watching the slaves fight each other over crumbs. She was about to continue her journey when something about two of the humans caught her eye. There was something oddly familiar about them. One, a female, had rusty red hair. The man was tall and thin.

"Jermy and Moira!" she gasped as she recognised her old guardians. "How did *they* get here?"

"What did you say?" Bertie whispered back.

"Nothing!" she replied as she realised she had caught the attention of one of the Girallons who had turned his eyes to the door and was now staring at her intently. Morag immediately averted her gaze, eyes to the floor, pulled her hood more tightly over her head and walked on. Arrod ran to her side and gave her a shove.

"Come on, slave, get moving," he said gruffly.

"Everything okay over there, boy?" the Girallon called.

"Yes sir. I'm just taking these slaves to the kitchen," Arrod said as he hurried Morag, Claudine and Tanktop away. That seemed to satisfy the Girallon, who shrugged and went back to tormenting the hungry humans.

"That was close," Arrod hissed to Morag. "Be more careful. We don't want to draw attention to ourselves."

"Sorry," she whispered back, "I just got a shock seeing those two there."

"Who are Jermy and Moira?" Claudine asked in a low voice as they hurried towards the stairwell.

"They were my guardians. Queen Flora paid them to look after me when I was smaller," the girl explained. "I don't understand how they got here. Last time I saw them they were in Irvine."

"Amergin has been carrying out raids on the mainland," Arrod explained. "He needs more slaves. He's been taking people from their houses and bringing them here."

"What for?" the girl wanted to know.

"To run the castle, work the land..." he said. Then he hesitated.

"And?" Morag knew from his face there was something he didn't really want to tell her.

"Nothing," said the boy giant, shaking his head.

They were at the stairs now. Morag looked up the familiar stone stairwell, remembering what had happened on the last two occasions she had been here: firstly as a slave to Mephista and then to rescue Montgomery. She shivered and wished she could be elsewhere. She rubbed her eyes, suddenly exhausted from all that she had been through over the past few months.

"Are you all right, Morag?" Henry asked.

"I'm fine," said the girl, rallying. "Let's find the Klapp demons and ask for their help." She turned to Tanktop. "Lead the way."

The Klapp demon gave her a smart, almost mocking salute and turned on his heel. He marched straight to the doorway that led down into the kitchen and opened it. He paused whilst the others caught up.

"This way," he encouraged, leading them inside.

The band of four — plus Bertie and Aldiss in the sacks and Henry around Morag's neck — entered the kitchen, where they found a solitary cook desperately stirring a large cauldron over the huge fire that provided the only light in the dingy room. She jumped as they entered and clutched at her chest.

"Oh you gave me a right turn there you did," she stuttered. "I thought it was them coming for their next meal. It's not ready yet you see and they don't like to be kept waiting. They get very angry, so they do. I mean look what one did to my Grain when he gave them a bowl of soup that was too hot. Grain, show them."

For the first time, the friends became aware that the cook was not alone in the kitchen. In a corner, there was a shuffling and the hunched figure of the cook's son limped into view. Morag recoiled as he came into the firelight. Grain's face was red all down one side and there was a large blister on his cheek.

"They threw a bowl of hot soup at him. Scarred him for life I shouldn't wonder," said the tearful cook. "You must be new here or you would know that no humans are allowed in this kitchen 'cept me and Grain. Now hurry and get out. If they find you here, it won't just be you that gets into trouble, but me and Grain too."

"I'm taking them to the stables," Arrod said, "Kang's orders."

The cook looked at him as if she didn't care if he were taking them to be shot.

"Just get them out," she said, returning to her cauldron.

"I could have helped that boy," Claudine whispered as they hurried across the flagstone kitchen floor to a door in the far corner. "I have some salve in my pocket."

"And I have lotion in my satchel!" piped up a voice from the sack. Bertie was always willing to show off his magic bag's tricks.

"Yes, but she might have given us away!" Morag reminded them as Arrod opened the door.

Morag recognised it as leading to the servants' quarters. Her heart rose. Maybe she would see Chelsea and be able to tell her she had come back for her as promised. She yanked the heavy wooden door open and entered the stairwell. A torch flickered despondently in the draught that was coming from an outside door which opened into the courtyard. As Morag waited for the others to join her she peeked outside and in the light of ten burning braziers saw the silhouetted figures of thirty humans marching up and down on the cobbles outside. They were carrying weapons of various sizes and styles.

"What are they doing?" she whispered to Arrod.

"Training."

"For what?"

He seemed reluctant to tell her.

"For *what*, Arrod?" she insisted.

"To invade...the mainland," he said.

"I don't understand."

"Amergin took the strongest from raids on the mainland for his human army. He's planning to invade the Lowlands on Christmas Day, when the humans will least expect it, then move north to Marnoch Mor."

"And these people agreed to do it?" She was horrified.

"Look at their faces," the boy suggested.

In the dim light Morag could just make out the faces of those marching closest to them. Their eyes were vacant, almost...zombie-like.

"What's wrong with them?" she asked.

"He's using dark magic to control them," replied Arrod. "He's taken away their souls. They can't think for themselves."

"That's terrible!" gasped Aldiss, now out of his bag and

at their feet.

"Yes, it is," replied the girl, all the more determined to put a stop to it. She pursed her lips and was about to lead the friends away when a small cage containing four figures caught her eye. It was pushed up against the wall under a wooden awning a few feet away from where they were hiding in the stairwell. As she peered through the darkness, Morag could see the figures were young men and women. She nudged Arrod.

"Why have they been caged out here in the open?" she asked. "Surely they'll die out here."

Arrod seemed reluctant to comment and didn't say anything until she pushed him. "Well?" she said, waiting for an answer.

"He puts them into cages if they don't do as they are told. Amergin wants to make an example of them."

"How long do they have to stay there?" Morag asked.

"For as long as it takes," he returned.

"For what? For them to die?"

The boy giant nodded. The girl shuddered.

Morag quelled the urge to run over and open the cage there and then, knowing they would be captured as soon as they made a move. She had to concentrate on the main task ahead. She *had* to stop Amergin, no matter the cost. She would free those in the cage later.

"Tanktop, take me to your people now," she said. "We need to stop this monster!"

The Klapp demon nodded and motioned for them to go to the stairs. Morag followed first and was about to ascend when the Klapp demon stopped her.

"No, no," he said, shaking his head. "Not up. Down."

He pointed to where more stairs spiralled into darkness below.

"My fellow Klapp demons are down there," he explained. "We don't get nice rooms like the humans."

"You wouldn't know a nice room if it came up and bit you," muttered Bertie.

Grabbing the only torch, Morag took a deep breath and began her descent, carefully leading the friends down the broken steps. The further they went the colder and damper the stairwell seemed to grow. At one point Morag slipped and was only saved from hurtling into the black by a quick-thinking Claudine grabbing her by the shoulder and yanking her to safety. The torch the girl had been carried didn't fare so well. It slipped out of her hand and bounced off each stair as it fell down and down and down, lighting up the staircase as it went. Some way down, the flame went out, but they could still hear it clattering off the stone stairs — dunk, dunk, dunk. It finally stopped some moments later with a wet squelch. It had hit the bottom.

"Ow!" someone complained. His voice was gruff and strong. "Who's that dropping things on the head of the Grandpappy Meermore? Come down here and show yourself!"

"I'm sorry," Morag called down. "It was an accident."

"An accident?" the voice said. "Hmph! Come down here and apologise in person!"

Behind her Tanktop whined quietly. "Don't get him angry," he whispered as they continued down.

Using Bertie's Moonstone, the friends took their time negotiating the slippery stairs and would not be hurried despite the gruff commands of the bodiless voice.

At last they reached the bottom and came face-to-face with a large Klapp demon. He wasn't alone: an entourage of around 20 more occupied the large cavern with him. The biggest one, whom Morag assumed was Grandpappy Meermore, was sitting on an old whisky barrel that had been cut up to create a seat. It stunk of malt and alcohol. The others squatted on the filthy wet ground. The whole scene was illuminated by one large oil lamp that guttered and flared in the draught that swirled around them. The Klapp demons surveyed them, their eyes glittering in the half light.

"What do you want? Why have you come here?" the big Klapp demon demanded. He took a bite of something in his hand and chewed it thoughtfully.

"We need your help, Grandpappy Meermore," Morag said.

At that the big Klapp demon and the others burst out laughing. Their rough chortles echoed around the cavern, causing the sound to magnify and then die.

"Why would you think that I am the Grandpappy?" the Klapp demon guffawed. "Ha ha, that's funny! I'm not the Grandpappy, no not me." Then he became serious, his eyes narrowing to slits as he said in a deeper voice: "Although I will be soon." Then he noticed someone cowering behind Morag. He stood up and moved towards him. "You there, behind the girl, are you a Klapp demon? You dare to come before me and not show respect? Come here!"

Tanktop, trembling from head to toe, stepped out from behind Morag and, head bowed, walked slowly into the light. Without a word, he threw himself to the ground, arms prostrate, and whimpered: "Forgive me, Skipcap. Forgive me."

A cruel smile played on the lips of the other Klapp demon, who gave the quivering Tanktop a kick. Tanktop yelped.

"That's for disappearing on us!" he snarled as his victim cried out. He kicked Tanktop again. "And that's for...well that's for...just because I felt like it."

"Brother, please forgive me!" Tanktop squealed. "She *made* me leave. She made me promise not to tell you I was going. I had no choice in the matter."

Skipcap was about to give Tanktop another vicious kick when Morag, affronted by what was transpiring, stepped between them.

"That's enough!" she snarled, holding the big Klapp demon back. "Leave him alone!"

Skipcap glared at Morag and shoved her hand from his chest. "Who are you to tell the Grandpappy-in-waiting what to do? You're just a little girl!" he snarled.

Morag stood as tall as she could and matched his stare.

"I am a princess of Marnoch Mor," she said through gritted teeth, "and I'm telling you to leave Tanktop alone." Then she said: "What do you mean Grandpappy-in-waiting? I thought you weren't the Grandpappy?"

"I'm not!" he said in a gruff voice. He continued to stare at the girl, seemingly unwilling to be the first one to blink. "But I will be when Grandpappy dies."

"Then take me to the real Grandpappy," Morag said. "I don't speak to underlings!"

She turned to Tanktop, who was still quivering. "Get up off the floor," she said, exasperated at how spineless the Klapp demon was. He didn't need a second invitation. He scrambled to his feet and stood behind her. Morag turned to Skipcap again.

"I said..."

"I heard what you said," he growled. "But why should I?"

"Because if you don't, that thing — that demon inhabiting Devlish's body..." she pointed to the vaulted ceiling of the room and several Klapp demons looked up fearfully "...will enslave you all. Is that what you want for your people?"

Skipcap snorted.

"We're already enslaved," he sneered.

"We can help to free you."

"Tsk. You can't free us!" he growled. "No-one can free us, least of all a little girl and her pets. There's nothing you can offer us. Go, we want nothing to do with you." He turned away and sat back down on his seat.

"We found Graar!" Tanktop piped up. "And she says we can go back there if we help."

Skipcap's eyes narrowed.

"What about the dragon?"

"We'll sort out the dragon," said Morag as confidently as she could, although she had no idea how they were going to persuade Felix to leave. "I promise you," she added when the lead Klapp demon hesitated.

Skipcap rubbed his matted chin then took another bite of his food.

"She has The Destine," Tanktop added.

A spark lit in Skipcap's eyes and he looked at Morag with added interest.

"We'll let the Grandpappy Meermore decide what's best to do," he said after a moment's thought.

"Fine!" said the girl. Then, after a few seconds during which Skipcap didn't move, she instructed, "Well, take us to him."

Skipcap rose to his feet and with a flick of his head motioned for them to follow him. He took them to the back of the room, where it appeared a pile of rags lay. As Morag drew nearer, she could see by the light of Bertie's Moonstone that it was actually the matted, moulting figure of an elderly Klapp demon. The creature moaned and turned to see who was shining such a light in his tired and unfocussed eyes.

"Go away," he said in a crackling voice. "Leave me in peace."

"Please sir, we've come to ask for your help," Morag said. She knelt beside him. The demon gave her a weak smile.

"Why are you bothering me girl at this time of my life? I'm not going to be here much longer you know, so why do you pester me so?" he whispered. And then he coughed a long and drawn out hacking cough that made Morag fear he was going to bring his insides out. "There's nothing I can do for you. Now, please leave me in peace."

"Daddy! Don't die!" Tanktop pushed past Morag and went to the old demon's side. In his haste, he tripped over Morag's feet and landed with a whump on top of Meermore, who yelped in protest. That didn't stop Tanktop hugging him tightly. "It's me, Tanktop! Speak to me Daddy! Speak to me!"

"Och, get off me, will you!" Grandpappy Meermore snapped, his voice suddenly loud and strong. "You're squashing the life out of me! Get off, you big lump!"

"But Daddy, I just want one more hug before you go to the great Klapp demon Hall of Food in the sky!" Tanktop said, and to Morag's surprise there were genuine tears in his eyes. "Don't die, please don't die, Daddy!"

And then Tanktop began to howl and wail and squeeze his dying father all the more. There was a loud 'Hmph!' from Meermore. He pursed his lips, hauled his hysterical son off of him and sat up. He scowled at Tanktop.

"Who said anything about dying?" he said. "I'm not dying. I was just wanting a bit of peace! It's the only way I can get that lot..." and he motioned towards the other Klapp demons "...to stop pestering me for stuff."

Tanktop's emotions switched instantly from grief to joy. He gave Meermore another hug and was pushed off again for his trouble.

"Oh! I'm so very, very glad!" he said.

Meermore looked up at the assembled friends and frowned.

"Well, now that you have my attention," he said bitterly, "and you are obviously not going to leave me alone, you might as well tell me what you want."

The elderly Klapp demon listened with interest to what Morag had to tell them. He nodded sagely as she spoke of vanquishing Amergin and returning the Klapp demons to Graar. He rubbed the matted fur around his chin as she finished her plea.

"So what do you want us to do?" he asked. "We're spies and thieves, not fighters. We don't have magic, so we're of no use against a demon of Amergin's skills. We'll be massacred."

"I don't need you to fight Amergin," the girl assured him. "I just need you to keep the Girallons busy while I go after him."

Meermore looked at Morag aghast.

"You want us to *what*? Have you any idea how skilled those four-armed monstrosities are at killing people and Klapp demons? They will cut us down and use our bones to make soup!" he squealed.

"She has The Destine, Father," Skipcap said.

Meermore's eyes narrowed as he weighed this up. Then he shook his head.

"No, it's too risky," he said.

Morag could see that pleading with the ruler of the Klapp demons was getting her nowhere, so changed tack.

"Klapp demons are a proud and ancient race, correct?" she said in a loud voice. Grandpappy Meermore nodded. "And you would rather die than remain slaves crushed under the heels of an evil ruler?" Again he nodded, but this time a little hesitantly. The other Klapp demons, who had been listening intently from across the room, began to gather round. "So why won't you help yourselves by helping us? Why do you wish to remain in this squalid state, taking your orders from a terrible creature living in a dead warlock's body?"

Grandpappy Meermore, suddenly aware that all eyes were now on him, could only shrug.

Morag decided to address the room. "Do you want to remain slaves for the rest of your lives? Do you want your children...?"

"Cubs," Tanktop corrected.

"...your cubs to be slaves too? All I'm asking is that you create some kind of diversion to give me enough time to find and conquer Amergin," she said. "I need you. I can't do it without you." Klapp demon heads were nodding all around and some were smiling their wide toothy grins. "So who's with me?"

A couple of the nearest demons gave her a weak cheer.

"I said *who's with me*?"

The rest — along with Bertie, Aldiss, Tanktop and Claudine — cheered loudly. Morag smiled, victorious. She turned to Meermore.

"Well?" she said. "Are you with us or against us?"

Meermore looked round at his tribe and sighed loudly.

"What else will we get for helping you?" he asked, rubbing his stubbly chin thoughtfully.

Morag looked at him as if she couldn't believe what she was hearing. She had promised him Graar and freedom, what more did he want? The ancient Klapp demon answered that unspoken question himself.

"Gold," he said after a moment. "I want gold. Devlish took what little gold we had left when we moved here, we want it back with interest."

Morag looked at Arrod and Claudine. The giant shrugged and the elf nodded to her to accept.

"Mephista's not going to like this!" Henry muttered from around her neck.

"Who cares about that witch?" the girl replied. Then to Meermore she said: "If you can find it, you can have your gold back."

Chapter 15

The plan that had been formulating in Morag's mind over the previous hour was suddenly required as all eyes turned to her for instruction. Thinking quickly, the girl began issuing orders like the princess she had been born to be.

"Make lots of noise, throw things...I don't care what you do, just keep the Girallons away from us. It should be easy, there's only about six of them," she began.

"Thirty," said Arrod. "They brought more in."

"That *many*? I had no idea," Morag frowned, but, on seeing the shocked faces of those gathered round her, composed herself quickly, "I mean...that's manageable. If you stay out of the way of their swords and just create havoc, you should be fine," she added, trying to reassure them. "You're all quick on your feet, it should be easy enough." The Klapp demons suddenly weren't looking so confident. Many were staring at the floor and others began to shuffle off into the shadows. An unlikely hero saved the moment.

"Come on, demons!" shouted Tanktop, who was quivering with excitement. "Let's get our own back on those four-armed monsters! Let's give them a pasting they will never forget! Let's be the Klapp demons we were born to be, like those who once ruled Graar. Let us make our ancestors proud this day!"

That got their attention and there was the sound of muttering around the cavern. Meermore held his hands up for silence. Morag held her breath, wondering what he was going to say now.

"My people," he said, voice wavering slightly, "we can do this. We can be the Klapp demons of legend. No more will we be enslaved by magical folk. Let us go upstairs and play our part in history. Let's go upstairs and fight for our freedom and, most important of all, get our gold back!"

A cheer went up.

"But first we need the others," Meermore added. As Morag watched, the silver-haired Klapp demon threw back his head and howled like a wolf baying at the moon. The sound reverberated off the cavern walls and rose higher and higher and higher. He rounded it off with a couple of barks that were echoed by a few demons in the room.

"Won't that alert the Girallons and Amergin?" Claudine hissed to Morag.

The girl shrugged. "I don't know," she admitted, "but it doesn't matter now...look!"

Above them, a door flew open and around 50 Klapp demons poured down the slippery steps into the cavern below. As the last one entered, Meermore informed them of their plan.

"Skipcap, you take thirty into the public areas and create merry havoc. Tanktop, you lead thirty more and do the same in the guard areas and stables. As you go, keep an eye out for our gold. It's got to be here somewhere. I will lead the rest through the sleeping quarters."

"But Daddy," said Tanktop, "it's too dangerous for you, you are so weak."

The Grandpappy Meermore put a paw on his son's shoulder and smiled.

"When I made a pact with Devlish all those years ago to come to Murst and work for him, I had no idea what I was signing up my people for. I knew he was evil, but we had no homeland and I was tired of us wandering the Earth like the lost tribe we were. If only I had worked harder to find us somewhere we could have called our own, we would not have been forced to live in this way," he said, looking around at the squalid underground room. "By leading you all against Amergin's troops, I can at least do something to help you get out of it. So, let's get up there and create havoc!"

"Wait!" said Morag, running towards the stairwell and placing herself between the first Klapp demon and the exit. "Not yet. We need to get everyone else in place first."

"Claudine, Arrod, Bertie and Aldiss come with me. Klapp demons, give us five minutes to get upstairs and then follow us."

"Good luck!" she added.

***

Trying not to think of the danger ahead, Morag silently led her small band of friends upstairs to the dark kitchen. The cook and Grain were sitting at the table, feet up, drinking a cup of something hot. The cauldron bubbled merrily over the fire. They watched disinterestedly as the group scuttled past them towards the Great Hall. They were rather more interested five minutes later when a stream of eighty Klapp demons passed through their kitchen. The cook gave Grain a quizzical look and Grain raised his eyebrows before they both scrambled to their feet grabbing ladles as weapons as they went. Something was going on and they weren't going to miss it.

Morag left Claudine and Arrod in the hallway that ran alongside the Great Hall. She gave them each a quick hug before setting them off on their way.

"Be careful, Morag," hissed Claudine as the girl, dodo and rat scuttled upstairs to the sleeping quarters. They were going to begin their search in Devlish's room.

The three friends reached the first floor less than a minute later, just as the initial sounds of a battle downstairs filtered up to them. The corridor was still except for a few torn wall-hangings flapping gently on the walls and was dimly lit with Full Moonstones that looked like their energy and light had been sapped. They flickered and fizzled as the friends crept past. There was no other sound save for the drumming of their hearts and the quiet scrape of feet and claws on the wooden floor.

They reached the first door. Mephista's room, Morag mentally noted, as they paused to look inside. The door was lying off its hinges and the witch's room, normally kept so pristine and perfect, had been trashed. By the light of the fire, they could see that the pretty bed clothes had been slashed, the dressing table, with its mirror, smashed on the floor and the diamond panes of the windows broken. Ice-cold wind squealed through the many holes and curled around them in a freezing embrace. Morag shivered and pulled Henry from her rags. His clean round shape in her hand was comforting and she was glad to have him and her other friends with her on this night.

Something moved and whimpered in the corner of the room and the girl froze. Then from the shadows Madam Lewis crawled and stared with frightened eyes at the strange band of possible rescuers standing before her. Unsteadily, she got to her feet and peered at them. Her hair stuck out like straw from a scarecrow and her dress was ripped and missing buttons. A purple bruise had formed under one eye. She stared at them for some moments before recognising the girl and swaying towards her.

"You! This is all your fault," she snarled, pointing a bony finger at Morag. "You brought this on us!" Madame Lewis was now standing before her, eyes crazed with anger.

"No...I...!" Morag protested, trying to back away, but the woman was too quick for her. She grabbed her by the rags and yanked her into the room. Morag felt her feet lift off the ground as Mephista's chief maid held her.

"You did this!" said Madam Lewis, wild with hatred. She gave the girl a shake that was so violent, Morag felt her teeth clatter in her head. "You killed the master and made my lady leave! You've spoiled EVERYTHING!" She pulled a dagger from the folds of her dress and it glinted in the half light as she raised it above her head. "And now I will pay you back!" the woman growled, bringing the knife down.

Morag cried out. Still caught in the woman's vice-like grip, she could only hold her arms up to protect herself and pray for a swift end. She closed her eyes.

She did not see her friends leap into action. As one, Aldiss and Bertie ran at the woman, a blur of feathers and fur. Quick as a flash, Aldiss leapt up her dress and bit her on the arm, neck, face...anywhere he could cause pain. Madam Lewis let go of the girl as she tried to fight off the rat. As Aldiss attacked, Bertie got under her feet, pecking at her legs until he managed to knock her off balance. Screeching like a banshee, the woman flailed, trying to remove the creatures from her person. Giving the dodo a vicious kick that sent him flying across the room, she righted herself and went for Aldiss. She grabbed at her body, trying to catch the rat who at first was too quick for her. Then, with a triumphant grin, Lewis caught him, squeezed him tight and with the skill of a baseball player, threw the terrified rodent against the bed. Aldiss soared across the room, squealing, and landed with a somersault. He quickly scrabbled to his feet ready for another assault, but Bertie was in first. Head down, he ran at the woman, smacking into her legs. She teetered backwards, tripping over the fallen dressing table and fell into the shattered window. The lead that had kept the small diamond panes so beautifully in place for hundreds of years buckled under her weight and dislodged it from its sill.

Madam Lewis screamed as she and the window fell outwards, but her cries were swept away by the wind howling outside. The friends could only watch, horrified, as she sailed into the darkness and was gone. There was a pause and then a distant crash and a tinkling of glass as the woman and window hit the ground outside.

Morag was shocked. She couldn't speak.

"Well, I can't say she didn't deserve that," said Henry smugly. "She was a horrible woman."

"No-one deserves to die like that," said the girl, dazed but finding her voice again. Then a thought suddenly occurred to her and she said to the medallion: "Where were you when this was all happening? Why didn't you just freeze her?"

"It all happened so fast," replied Henry, a little peeved. "Besides, the bird and rat seemed to have everything under control. It was the best fight I've watched in a long while, although I didn't expect the woman to die."

"It was an accident," said the dodo. "She was going to kill Morag. I had to do something. I didn't *mean* for her to die." He looked at Morag. "She would have killed you, I had no choice," he said quietly.

"Yes, I know," she replied, staring at the space that had once contained a window. The wind was now howling through, sending blasts of icy sleet into the room.

A moment's silence passed before Morag recovered herself. "Come on, we've still got to find Amergin."

***

Morag looked ahead to a large wooden door at the end of the corridor. *Devlish's room*, she thought. She gulped and her legs suddenly felt weak. Her heart, which had been drumming ten to the dozen already, beat even harder. She turned to her friends.

"I think you two should stay here," she whispered to Bertie and Aldiss. "I couldn't live with myself if anything happened to you," she added, ignoring their protests. "Henry and I will go on alone. We'll be fine."

"You're not going anywhere," Aldiss whispered back.

"We started this together so we'll end this together."

"He's right," said Bertie.

"Or daft," muttered Henry, but he was secretly impressed by their courage.

Morag smiled at how brave her friends were being. She could see in the determination of their eyes that it was no use arguing with them.

"Okay," she said. "Let's do it."

"Do what?" sneered a voice from behind them. Kang stepped forward, heaving the unconscious body of a slave girl with him. The girl moaned as he dropped her to the ground. She rolled over and Morag gasped. It was Chelsea.

Ignoring the horror on Morag's face, Kang growled. "Well, who have we here? I never thought I'd ever see any of *you* back on Murst," he said. "What are you here for? What do you want?" His eyes narrowed as he leered at her. "Have you come to visit the great Amergin? What a surprise he'll get when I hand Morag, Princess of Marnoch Mor to him. I wonder...what will he want to do with you? He's been saying he needs a new body."

Morag looked at the four-armed creature looming over her and was about to retort when Aldiss stepped in front of her.

"Stand back, Morag," he said, brandishing his tiny wand. "I'll deal with him. There's no way I'm going to let him give you to his master."

At this, Kang leant back his head and laughed heartily.

"He eats creatures like you as a starter!" he told the rat. "Put that thing away before you have someone's eye out with it. You look ridiculous. Everyone knows rats can't do magic!"

"Everyone?" shrieked the rat indignantly. "Who's 'everyone'? I *can* do magic and I'm good at it," he squeaked, "so just you...just you...oh nuts!" he exclaimed. As he had been talking, he had been waving the wand around in an attempt to make it work but had only succeeded in creating a few purple sparks.

Kang chuckled then unsheathed his sword. Its golden handle gleamed as it sliced through the air and cut Aldiss's wand in half. The top clattered to the ground, leaving the stunned rat holding a silver stump.

"That's what I think of vermin with ideas above their station," the four-armed creature scoffed. "Now you three are my prisoners!"

"Not so fast!" Bertie said, scooping Aldiss up and placing him on his feathery back. He withdrew his own wand from his satchel. The silver stick gleamed in the half-darkness but its appearance only made Kang laugh all the more.

"How ridiculous do *you* look?" he sneered between guffaws. "Wait till I tell the boys about this. We'll have a good laugh about it as we roast you both over the fire."

"Not as ridiculous as you're going to look when I've finished with you!" Bertie said a little too calmly, and if he had had teeth to gnash he would have done so right then. He lifted his wand as high as his little wings would allow, said some magic words and flicked the spell towards Kang, who was still laughing heartily. The great ape continued to mock until it suddenly dawned on him that something wasn't right. Horrified, he saw the spell take shape: it was turning him into a harmless white rabbit. Bertie stood firm, wand before him, ready for Kang the rabbit to attack.

"How dare you...!" screamed the rabbit, drumming its feet on the wooden floor. Rabbit Kang attempted to lift the sword again in order to cut the dodo down, but Bertie was too quick for him. He flicked the wand once more and the sword flew out of the creature's grasp, smashing against the stone wall some distance down the corridor.

"Atta boy!" shouted Aldiss as he clung to the feathers on Bertie's back.

"Why you...!" screamed Kang. The dodo flicked the

wand yet again, and before Kang could protest he found himself incarcerated in a blue plastic small animal carrier, the kind Morag had seen people use to take their cats to the vet's.

"Let me out of here!" Kang the rabbit screamed. He tried to gnaw at the chicken wire that held him but succeeded only in damaging his mouth. Blood trickled scarlet red down his lips. "Let me out and I'll only tear you limb from limb!" he rasped.

Bertie ignored him and turned to the girl and medallion.

"Now's your chance!" he hissed to Morag, who was standing open-mouthed nearby. "We'll stay here and guard this one. I don't know how long this spell will last so you'd better hurry and find Amergin. Go!"

"What about Chelsea?" Morag asked, staring down at the girl prostrate on the floor before her. The maid groaned softly as she began to come to her senses.

"Don't worry, we'll see to her."

Morag wasted no more time. With Henry hanging from her neck and The Destine in one hand, she squeezed past her friends and made for Devlish's bedroom. Kang, seeing her intention, tried to shout to warn his master, but was soon silenced by another powerful spell from the dodo. He could only watch with his pink rabbit eyes as the girl pushed open the door.

"How ridiculous do *you* look?" was all she heard Bertie say to Kang as she moved towards the door.

C-R-E-A-K! it went as she gave it a shove. She peeped inside.

The room, beautifully furnished with antique furniture and sumptuous fabrics, was empty.

"Where is he?" Henry wondered, voice hushed.

"I don't know," she whispered.

Morag entered the room, alert and ready to defend herself should the Mitlock demon appear.

"Look under the bed," Henry advised, "he could be hiding."

She did as she was told and knelt by the bed. She threw the heavy covers off and poked her head underneath but found nothing except dust and a pair of slippers. There was no Amergin.

"The wardrobe?" Henry suggested.

Taking a deep breath, Morag went to the wardrobe door and, hand trembling, pulled it open. A heavy velvet robe fell out onto her, causing her to flail about in panic, but once she realised what it was she stopped fighting and let it fall to the floor. A quick search of the wardrobe found only Devlish's clothes, no demon.

"He was supposed to be here," Morag muttered.

"He *was* here," Henry said. "Look over there!"

Morag scanned the room but saw nothing out of the ordinary until her eyes rested on the fireplace. The large marble mantel was ornately carved with flora and fauna, but there was something not quite right about it. It wasn't sitting flush against the wall. A draught could be felt coming from somewhere between the cold stone and mantel. On closer inspection, she discovered a gap between one side of it and the chimney. She slid her fingers into the space and pulled. The mantelpiece swung open to reveal a hidden passageway.

"So this is how he got out," she said as she peered inside. A blast of cold air hit her in the face, causing her to recoil. She looked again. In the gloom, she could just make out a set of steps leading up and a faint hint of light at the top of the staircase. She slipped inside and began to climb.

"Be careful Morag," Henry warned as she ascended.

"I will."

The stairwell consisted of thirty stone steps leading to a little wooden door at the top, which was open and swinging in the wind. She peeked outside at the scene before her.

The door led on to a flat roof parapet that was illuminated by the flickering, faltering flames of seven wooden torches. It was empty save for the gruesome figure of Amergin in Devlish's body being supported by a terrified Jermy as Moira frantically tried to unlock a door at the other side. Over the howl of the wind, Morag heard the demon scream instructions.

"Hurry woman, before I eat you for dinner!" he cried as Moira struggled with the door. "Curses! Kang should have checked this!"

Slowly, so as not to rouse their attention, Morag stepped up on to the parapet. Henry gleamed like a beacon around her neck. So intent were they on escape that Amergin and the others did not see her creep towards him in the darkness, closing the distance across the parapet. The torches guttered and spluttered as the strong gusts of wind blasted them, sending shadows dancing. Mustering every last ounce of courage, and holding The Destine out like an offering, Morag stole forward until she was about a metre from them.

"Amergin!" she cried above the whine of the wind. Her hair whipped around her head, stinging her cheeks, but she ignored it.

The Mitlock Demon turned. So hideous was the creature before her that it was all Morag could do to stand her ground. He was like Devlish, but was clearly not him. The white, white skin of the former warlock's body was now mottled blue and there were black patches in places. His thin white lips were now an ebony colour and his eyes were completely red. Rotted and peeled strips of skin revealed the pale pink of muscle beneath. Morag fought the urge to be sick. Beside him, supporting the demon's borrowed body, a downtrodden Jermy could only stare at her.

Although badly decaying, Amergin was not down and out. He sneered when he saw her.

183

"So you've caught up with me, Morag MacTavish," he shouted over the wind. "And I suppose you're here to stop me."

"Yes and I'm here to send you back to wherever it was you came from," she shouted back. "With this!" she added. She held up The Destine, expecting something to happen, but nothing did. She gave it a shake and tried again. Still nothing. *What's wrong with it?* she thought as Amergin, a cruel smirk on his lips, leaned towards her.

"What's that you've got?" he cried, shaking off Jermy and reaching a skeletal hand towards her. "A cup? Hah hah! What's *that* supposed to do?" He sneered at it.

Morag shook it again, but nothing happened. She fought hard to remember what she had experienced with Toga, but couldn't remember if the hologram had told her anything useful. Nothing. She could remember nothing.

Amergin loomed over her. She took a step back.

"Stop there!" Henry warned suddenly. "I am a magical medallion and I order you to stop," he cried. Then he screwed up his face as he attempted to defend Morag with magic.

The demon, amused, merely waved a hand. Before she could do anything about it, Morag felt a huge tug and Henry was wrenched from around her neck. The last she saw of the medallion was him flying towards the parapet, screaming as he went. A final glimmer in the winter's light and he flew over the ramparts and out of sight.

"Henry!" the girl cried as he vanished. Then she turned to find Amergin was right on her.

"Well, Morag MacTavish," he said. The wind that had been howling now suddenly died and Morag could see or hear nothing but him. "What am I going to do with you?" he said as he gently touched her face.

Morag closed her eyes tightly. She tried not to think of the horror standing before her. She tried hard to calm herself, but sheer terror was threatening to engulf her and she could no longer control her breathing. She gulped for air, panting hard in an effort to regain control. She felt as if she was going to pass out. Her hands were tingling, her chest tight and suddenly she felt herself praying for it all to be over. Amergin grabbed her by the neck and began to squeeze. For someone living in a decaying body, he was remarkably strong. Morag desperately struggled for her life, but could not prise herself from his vice-like grip. Coughing and choking, she tried to gasp a last precious breath and then there was nothing but calm and warmth spreading over her feet.

Chapter 16

Morag opened her eyes and started. *What's going on?* she wondered as she looked down at her bare feet held inches from the warmth of the old stove in the kitchen of Jermy and Moira Stoker's beach guesthouse. She was sitting on the old chair she always sat on, wearing her old pyjamas, living her old life. A huge pile of dishes lay unwashed at the sink. She put her feet down. Yup, still the same old ice-cold linoleum. She frowned. This place was so familiar to her, but she was sure there was something else she was supposed to be doing, *somewhere* else she was supposed to be. She closed her eyes and tried to remember, but... nothing. There were vague memories, faint ghost-like images, but she couldn't focus her mind on them, couldn't make them real.

There was a slight noise behind her and she opened her eyes and turned around. Moira was standing in the doorway in her tatty old white nightdress, holding a slim cigar in one hand. Except it wasn't quite Moira. She looked like her but then didn't. It was as if someone was switching TV channels: one minute Morag was staring at Moira's bloodshot eyes and red hair and the next someone else, someone heart-wrenchingly familiar, only she couldn't think who.

"Why aren't those dishes done, brat?" Moira said. And then in a different, softer voice, and with the other face showing, she said: "Haven't you forgotten something, Morag?"

That voice. She remembered!

"Mum?" she said, staring at Isabella's pretty face.

Moira's sneering face suddenly returned, causing her to recoil.

"That's right, brat. I'm your mother now."

"What's all this noise?" The tall beanpole figure of Jermy appeared at the doorway. He scratched his bottom. "What time is it?"

Morag glanced up at the wall clock and flinched. Instead of the cheap red plastic clock that usually hung there, the face of this one was gold with diamonds and a teeny tiny face. The face winked at her.

"She hasn't done the dishes from last night!" Moira told her. She took a draw on the cigar and blew smoke rings at the puzzled girl.

"Why haven't you done your chores?" Jermy screamed at Morag as he strode towards her, face like thunder. Then he suddenly changed and was someone else, someone broader and better looking.

"Dad?" Morag said, confused.

"You must remember, Morag," her father said. And then the face of Jermy returned. He stooped to her level and with spit flying from his lips, said: "Get those dishes done!"

Giddy with fear and confusion, Morag could only stare at him.

"Didn't you hear me?" Jermy said, raising his fist. Then there was her father's face: "Remember, Morag!"

Bang, bang, bang, bang. Someone was at the door. Jermy froze, hand in mid-air, and stared at Moira, who was watching him from the doorway.

"Post!" a man called through the letterbox. "Don't worry, there's no bills!"

Relief washed over Jermy's face and he nodded for Moira to let the man in. The woman reluctantly opened the back door, revealing a grey bird — a dodo to be precise — in a peaked cap and wearing a little brown leather satchel. A little brown rat was doing star jumps at his side. Morag frowned. They looked like...what were their names? She was sure she had seen them before. The bird, his name was...??

"Morag!" said the rat. "Come back to us! You must remember!"

"Aldiss, leave this to me!" said the dodo, pushing past the surprised Moira and rushing over to Morag. The girl sat back down on the chair and stared at them. "She's under a deep spell," the dodo continued as he examined her eyes. "Yes, it's going to take me a little bit to break it. Have you got your wand with you?"

"Always!" Aldiss replied, brandishing his tiny little wand. *Hadn't that got broken?* Morag wondered and then she thought: *How would I know that?*

"Okay, with me...one...two...three..." said the dodo.

Together they waved their wands and as the bird muttered some magical words, a stream of sparkles shot from both wands and hit Morag in the chest. She screamed and tried to escape, but found herself pinned to the chair.

As the bird and rat were doing this, Jermy and Moira sprang into action and made to grab them. Jermy caught the bird around his ample tummy and Moira tried to stamp on Aldiss, but the rat got out of the way just in time.

"Morag! Wake up! Remember!" squawked Bertie as he struggled to free himself whilst holding the wand on Morag. "Wake up, Morag!"

Jermy's face suddenly morphed back into Nathan's, and Moira's to Isabella's. They both approached the terrified girl. *Remember*, they mouthed. Morag, still caught in the stream of magic, could only watch in horror as they drew closer and closer.

"Remember us, Morag! Remember!" they chanted.

"Remember us, Morag! Remember!" Aldiss and Bertie said.

The girl looked from one pairing to the other and back again. Her mind was whirling. She could feel a headache coming on. She clutched her head and closed her eyes. She felt as if her brain was going to explode.

"Stop it!" she screamed. "Stop it!"

"Remember us!" the four said.

"Stop it, stop it!" she shouted.

"Remember."

"STOP IIIIIIITTTTTTTTT!!!"

And then she suddenly remembered. It all became as clear as crystal. The castle, the demon, the chalice.

She opened her eyes again, expecting to be somewhere else, but found that she was still in the kitchen of Stoker's Guesthouse at Irvine Beach. She smiled anyway.

"You're Bertie and you're Aldiss," she said, pointing first to the bird and then to the rat. "You are my father: Nathan, crown prince of Marnoch Mor. And you are my mother: Isabella. You're trapped in paintings at the Palace."

"Yes!" said Bertie excitedly. "And who are you?"

"I..." said the girl, "am Morag, princess of Marnoch Mor. I don't know how I got back here, but I should be in Murst Castle right now, fighting Amergin with The Destine."

As she said those final words a strange thing happened: it was as if everything was melting, everything except herself, Bertie and Aldiss.

"She's remembered, thank goodness," the rat said with a sigh. "I thought she was a goner there."

As Morag watched, the guesthouse scene swirled away to be replaced by the ramparts of Murst Castle's main building, where it was cold and very windy. The girl shivered as she realised where she was.

"What happened?" she said, clutching her head. Her headache hadn't subsided...in fact it had grown worse.

"Amergin used a distortion spell on you," Bertie explained as he helped her to her feet. "He used it as a way of rendering you motionless while he...well, it looked like he was about to take a bite out of you. If we hadn't come when we did..." And here he shivered.

"If we hadn't come, I think he would have killed you,"

Aldiss continued.

"How did you stop him?" Morag asked, her hand slipping down to her neck.

Bertie puffed his feathers up proudly.

"I used a complicated spell on him," he said a little snootily.

"You shot a bolt of energy at him, you mean," the rat corrected him. "Something trainee wizards learn in first year!"

"It still got him away from Morag!" the bird snapped, angry at his achievement being belittled.

"The fact you singed his rotting body helped," squeaked the rat. "Ew, the smell was *horrible*!"

"It still worked didn't it?" growled Bertie.

"Didn't he fight back?" Morag asked. "He's a Mitlock demon!"

"He did and we thought we were goners at one point, but the wind was so strong he could barely stand to perform a spell, and then when Aldiss bit him on the hand, well…" the dodo began.

"Don't say it," Aldiss said, looking as puce as a hairy-faced rat can.

"Well, what?"

Aldiss closed his eyes in disgust. "I…I…bit off two of his fingers!" he gasped. "It was easy. They just came off… Ugh, I can still taste them!"

"And then what?"

"He screeched in pain and that brought his helpers — those people you used to work for — and there was blood and bits of finger and he tried to get past us again and Bertie blasted him in the face with his wand and then…" the rat said breathlessly.

"…and then he said something about leaving you till next time and his helpers pulled him away!" finished Bertie.

"After that we had to help you. You were bewitched.

The only way we could get you out of the spell was to join you in it and get you to remember who we were," the dodo finished.

"But how did mum and dad get in there?" she wanted to know.

"Yes, that was rather strange," admitted the bird. "I don't know, maybe you projected them on to Jermy and Moira subconsciously. Maybe they were actually helping you. No matter what happened, it helped you to remember who you really are and that is the main thing."

Morag managed a weak smile, quietly grateful that her friends (and possibly her parents) were there to save her.

"What now?" she said, accepting a small drink of water from Bertie's outstretched wing. She shook her head as he pulled a chocolate bar from his satchel and offered it to her.

It was Aldiss who replied.

"We need to get Amergin," he squeaked, "before he escapes."

Morag nodded. "But where did he go? And where's Kang?"

"Oh don't worry about Kang," replied the dodo. "He's quite safe."

Morag rose unsteadily to her feet and brushed down her coat. It was covered in tiny shards of ice. The wind whipped at her hair and she pulled her hood up over her head. On the ground nearby was a small pool of blood and two bony fingers. Stepping past them, she went to retrieve The Destine that was lying nearby. She picked it up and looked at it, wondering why Toga had given it to her when it so obviously didn't work. She told her friends what had happened...or rather what had not happened.

"I don't think I'll bother with it," she said, handing it to the dodo. But he pushed it back to her.

"It must work," Bertie said. "You must take it. You'll

know what to do when the time's right."

"But the time was right earlier and it didn't work," she said.

The bird could only shrug. "Take it anyway," he said.

"You could always brain him with it," suggested Aldiss, who was jogging on the spot to keep warm.

Morag laughed. She could always rely on the rat to lighten the mood.

The door at the other side of the ramparts was now open. As they entered the dark passageway beyond it, Bertie lit a Moonstone and together the three friends used it to negotiate their way down the stone steps. The stairwell clearly hadn't been used for a long time. There were spiders' webs all over the place, the stone steps had cracked and broken in places and a large colony of bats swooped at them as they passed by, squealing their protests. Every now and then they could see tiny drops of blood on the stairs and knew they were on the right track. The stairwell had a musty damp smell interlaced with fresh air. The tall thin windows placed intermittently down it were draughty and some were smashed, allowing icy blasts of winter wind to fill the passageway. Morag shivered and carried on.

The stairs ended at a little wooden door illuminated by one flickering wall torch. From its metal handle, a piece of paper-like skin flapped in the breeze. *Eugh, that must have come off him,* Morag thought as she gingerly flicked it off and turned the handle.

Inside was a disused room full of old furniture that was covered in dust sheets...except for the sofa. Its sheet had been ripped off and thrown aside, and lying on its red velvet was Amergin. His eyes closed, he looked close to death. He was breathing shallowly, his bony chest rising and falling with difficulty. His facial skin had shredded and Morag was sure she could see a cheekbone sticking out. He held his bloody hand to his chest. The borrowed corpse gave off a pungent stench of decay. It filled the room, causing the friends to cover their noses as they stepped closer.

Amergin opened his gleaming red eyes as Morag, Bertie and Aldiss entered the room. A weak smile caused one of his teeth to dislodge and drop on to his rasping chest. Jermy and Moira stood like ghosts behind him, too afraid to do anything but stare at them.

"I give up, you've got me," he said with a rueful smile. "Come closer, Morag, dear," he crooned, "so I might see you better."

"Stay where you are," Bertie warned Morag. "There's a reason why he wants you."

"Back off, bird!" hissed Amergin, eyes blazing. He calmed and said: "Come closer, girl, so I may hold your hand. This body is dying. Kang was supposed to get me a better one, one that lasted, but this one had been lying too long. I had hoped it would last long enough for me to find another replacement, but seems it's not to be." Here he stopped to cough, the sound dry and painful. "I was going to use one of these two," — he nodded towards Jermy and Moira, who whimpered and pulled away — "but I think I've left it too late." The demon continued his lament: "I'm dying, Morag. Come and comfort an old man."

"Don't do it," said Bertie. Then he added in a whisper: "He'll try to take over your body, stay away from him."

"Come here, girl...please!" Amergin pleaded.

"Why should I?" the girl said.

"Because I'm frightened," the demon said. "I don't want to die alone." Morag felt a pang of compassion fill her generous heart and fleetingly considered doing as the demon asked, but that thought was soon discarded when Amergin snapped: "Get over here now, girl!"

"Leave her alone!" Aldiss said, running up to the demon and brandishing his broken wand. "She's not coming anywhere near you!"

"You will come to me, girl, or I'll..." In a flash, Amergin scooped up Aldiss in his good hand. The rat wriggled and squealed. "...I'll tear off his little furry head and gobble the rest of him down!"

Morag couldn't speak and stayed put, but when Amergin took Aldiss's head between his fingers and pressed so hard the rat screamed, she sprang into action. Pulling The Destine out of her jacket pocket and holding it before her, she slowly approached the demon. She didn't take her eyes off him as she carefully moved forward.

"Let him go and I'll come to you," said Morag, stopping just out of reach.

"You're a brave one, Morag MacTavish," said Amergin. His breath was laboured again and he was apparently finding it hard to speak.

"Yes I am brave. I'm also determined to see justice is served. I'm going to send you back to wherever it was you came from," she warned, pointing The Destine at him. "Put the rat down."

Amergin coughed as he tried to laugh.

"I see you still have your little cup," he said. "What do you think you're going to do with it? Fill it with poison and entice me to drink it so this body finally dies? Is that your plan?"

"Let the rat go," Morag continued, "or I'll use this on you."

The demon pulled himself up and stared at her.

"Come closer and I'll release him," he said, eyes glinting in the low light.

Morag took one tentative step closer.

"That's right, on you come," Amergin encouraged.

She stepped forward again. The demon, his borrowed face sagging and his eyes sliding like a bloodhound's, smiled. There was a pause. Then as quick as a flash his hand shot out and he grabbed Morag's arm. The girl let out a yelp. Simultaneously, the demon threw Aldiss from his other hand. The rat sailed into the air, did a forward roll and landed with a flourish on his feet next to Bertie. The dodo, shocked at Morag's capture, didn't even seem to see his friend as he stood beside him.

"Let her go!" he squawked, dancing from claw to claw in his agitation. "Let her go!"

Amergin gave them an evil grin as he dragged the girl closer to him. She tried desperately to pull back as she came a little too close to his peeling face.

"Well, Morag MacTavish, what do you have to say now?" he said.

"Let her go!" cried a voice silent until now.

Morag looked up in surprise to see Moira coming to her rescue.

"C'mon Jermy, let's get him!" Moira yelled as she scuttled around the sofa to take the demon on, but before Jermy could react Amergin fired a bolt of energy at the woman. She squealed as it sent her flying backwards. Moira hit the wall with a crunch and slid into unconsciousness.

"Moira!" Jermy ran to her and received a bolt of his own for his trouble. It hit him square on the back and threw him on top of his wife. "Moira," he said weakly before blacking out.

From his seat, Amergin sniffed. "They were annoying me anyway." He turned his red eyes on Morag and smiled. His teeth, bloody and loose, rattled in his head. "Now for you my pretty!" He pulled her closer, licking his black lips with a white tongue and the girl recoiled from the stench of death that surrounded him.

"No!" squealed Aldiss as he and Bertie ran towards them.

"Oh this is getting tedious!" snapped the demon and he threw a spell at them that froze them mid step. The demon laughed a strange kind of gurgle.

Morag — not one for giving in easily and still gripping The Destine — pushed it towards him. If it didn't work this time she fully intended to hit him with it.

"Take *this,* demon!" she shouted in her best action hero voice, much to the amusement of her captor.

"This *again*!" he said with amusement. "This is getting very boring. That cup obviously does nothing. But I will take it. Give it to me!"

Before Morag could protest the demon had yanked The Destine from her grip and was holding it up to his face so that he might inspect it closer.

"See! I told you it does noth...!"

Before he could finish, Amergin stopped talking. His grip on Morag relaxed and the light went out in his eyes. Devlish's body, rotting and unable to hold itself up any more, tipped forward on to Morag, who screamed and shoved it off. She leapt back and saw the body collapse in on itself until it was completely gone. The Destine clattered onto the dusty floor at her feet.

Then there was silence.

"What happened?" asked Aldiss, coming out of the spell, which had been broken on Amergin's disappearance. He and Bertie were now at her side. Bertie was staring at the scene, his black eyes wide in amazement.

"I-I don't know," the girl stuttered. She stooped down and picked up The Destine. Then, instinctively, Morag held the chalice to her ear.

"What...?" started Bertie.

"Shhhh!" said the girl, listening.

Morag could hear Toga going through his spiel inside The Destine. She looked into the cup, but it seemed empty. She put The Destine back up to her ear.

"Good day," it said, "my name is Toga and I'll be your hologram for today."

"What's going on?" roared Amergin. "Let me out of here!"

There was a whirring sound. The projector, Morag realised.

"You are Amergin, Mitlock Demon," said Toga. "You are an evil demon from another realm who plans to take over the human and magical worlds. You have no friends. You are universally feared and hated."

"All true! Now let me out of here!" screamed the demon.

"Don't interrupt!" Toga scolded. "To be free once more you must give me a memory in which you have been kind."

"Easy!" said the demon.

"Is it?" Toga said.

There was a long pause whilst Morag surmised Toga was searching for kindness. Then: "Amergin, Mitlock Demon, you have failed. For your crimes against humanity and the magical world, as punishment for all the souls you have taken, you will be banished to the deepest darkest place I can find."

There was a fizzing and a long strangled scream that seemed to last for an age. And then there was no sound at all.

"What's happened?" Aldiss asked as Morag lowered The Destine from her ear. She was smiling.

"He's gone! We did it! Amergin is gone for good!" she said.

"Hurray!" shouted the rat, punching the air with one tiny fist.

"Are you sure?" Bertie asked. And when Morag nodded the bird suddenly felt so full of joy he couldn't speak. A nod back was all he could manage.

The girl, exhausted, slid down to the ground and sat for a few moments. They were free of the demon. At last, he was gone. They had scored a momentous victory! No more fear of slavery. She felt so relieved. The three friends hugged each other and for a while no-one said a word. They just savoured the moment.

Then the sounds of fighting and havoc filtered through the tower room door and Morag realised they were the only ones who knew of Amergin's defeat. She hauled herself to her feet, brushed the dust off her coat and turned to her friends.

"Come on, we must tell the others what has happened," she said.

"And capture the Girallons!" Aldiss reminded her.

Chapter 17

A battle was ensuing as Morag (animal carrier in her arms), Bertie and Aldiss entered the hallway that ran alongside the Great Hall. Inside the hall itself several Klapp demons, a giant guard and a handful of humans were holding back five Girallons. The apes were roaring and baring their teeth and their swords were flashing, but the band of resisters, buoyed by the sounds of chaos echoing throughout the castle, held firm. They had the Girallons trapped in one corner of the hall using pikes, battle axes and shields they had wrenched from the walls on which they had been displayed for centuries.

"Amergin has fallen!" Morag shouted, putting down the cage. "Girallons, put down your arms and surrender."

The apes screamed and roared all the louder, and refused to do as they were bid.

"You lie!" they shouted.

"She's telling the truth," said Bertie, pulling out his wand. "Surrender or I'll do to you what I did to Kang." He motioned towards the rabbit in the carrier. The rabbit Kang stared out sullenly.

That got their attention.

"What do you mean?" one demanded. "Kang is strong. Kang is invincible. A mere bird couldn't stop Kang."

"A mere bird didn't," said Bertie, shoving Aldiss forward, "but a rat and a bird did. Your leader is captured and there he will stay until we are ready to deal with him." He waved the wand, causing little blue sparks to fly into the air and crackle around the heads of the apes. "Now, do you want us to turn you into rabbits too or will you come quietly? Are you ready to surrender?"

The Girallon who spoke looked to the others. Then he grinned.

"You lie!" he said, and with a roar the five Girallons rushed forward, scattering the humans and Klapp demons and running towards Morag, Bertie and Aldiss. Before they had time to react, the apes were almost on top of them, swords raised to smite them. The speaker went for Morag, who could only watch open mouthed as he charged towards her.

"No you don't!" growled a familiar voice. There was a roar and a rush of heat as a huge blast of fire enveloped all five Girallons, stopping them in their tracks and making them drop their swords in surprise. Singed, and eyes stinging from the heat, the Girallons backed off and fell to the floor. Morag spun round and saw a green scaly face that was very dear to her.

"Shona!" She ran to hug her friend. "You're here!"

"Arrod and Claudine let me in," the dragon explained as she motioned behind her. Morag looked to see the giant boy and woman standing behind her friend. They were smiling, then Claudine's countenance fell.

"Morag! Shona! Watch out!"

Shona had just enough time to shove Morag out of the way before the Girallon attacked. He brought the sword down on to the dragon and the blade hit her head with a sickening thud. With a roar of pain and anger, the dragon reacted. As blood trickled down her face, she grabbed the Girallon by the neck and shook him. And she continued shaking and squeezing until the Girallon moved no more. Then she let him drop before falling to the ground herself with a weak groan. She closed her eyes.

"Shona!" cried Morag, rushing to her friend. She threw herself on the lifeless body of the dragon. "Shona!" she called again. "Oh please don't die. Please."

Tears rolled down Morag's face and, head on the dragon's still neck, she gave her friend a tight hug.

"Shona!" she said again.

"What? What is it?" the dragon said weakly. "Morag, please can you get off? You're squashing me."

"You're all right," said the girl, relieved. "I thought you were dead."

"No, just tired and a little bit injured," said the dragon opening her great yellow eyes. Morag gave her another hug, but pulled herself off as Shona winced in pain.

"Bertie, I need stuff to clean her up," the girl said.

The dodo sprang into life, pulling a clean handkerchief and a bottle of antiseptic from his satchel. He handed these to Morag who dabbed Shona's head wound. It wasn't a deep cut, but bled all the same. Several minutes later, Morag was able to staunch the bleeding and wrap her beloved friend's head in a bandage also supplied by Bertie.

"Do you think you can stand?" Morag asked.

"I'm fine Morag, stop fussing," said the dragon. She sat up and gingerly touched her bandage. "I'll live," she added with a smile. "It was only a glancing blow. We dragons are very thick skinned you know."

"Thank goodness for that," Morag smiled.

The sounds of fierce fighting echoed throughout the castle and the friends decided to split up to spread the word that Amergin had been defeated and to call on the remaining Girallons to surrender. Within an hour, peace finally reigned in the fortress and the apes had been incarcerated within the dungeons below, including the beleaguered and humiliated Kang, whom Bertie had reluctantly returned to his true shape. The ape roared furiously as they closed the cell door.

"That should keep him safe for a while," Aldiss said as he and Bertie made their way back upstairs.

"Well, if it doesn't I can always turn him back into a rabbit," the dodo sniggered.

***

Morag gathered everyone in the Great Hall: all the former slaves, the giants and the castle's lords and ladies whose fine clothing was tattered and torn from being forced to work as servants. She stood on the platform in front of the two shattered thrones once used by Devlish and Mephista and called on the crowd to quieten.

"People of Murst," the girl began. Out of the corner of her eye, she was aware of Shona wincing at this. Morag knew the dragon still thought of Murst as belonging to her own kind, but there was nothing she could do about that. The pigmy dragons of Murst were gone — with the exception of Shona — and stopping humans living there was not going to bring them back. "I have gathered you here to discuss what happens next. I am Princess Morag of Marnoch Mor and I promise you that I will do everything in my power to help you to rebuild the community that once thrived here. This will be a new start for Murst, a new beginning."

"What about Mephista Devlish?" a familiar voice called from the crowd. "We don't want her back. She's evil and cruel. We want to govern ourselves. We're tired of being slaves."

To the cheers of the many former slaves in the crowd, Chelsea stepped forward. Morag smiled with relief to see the girl safe and well.

"If this is to be a new beginning," Chelsea continued, "we don't want *them* in charge either." She motioned to where a group of alarmed lords and ladies stood.

"What *do* you want, Chelsea?" Morag asked.

"I once asked you to help me be free, you promised me you would and now is your chance to honour that promise," the girl replied. "I want you to help us set up a democratic government here so that *everyone* has a say about what happens on Murst, not just the posh people." She glared at the lords and ladies who huddled closer together.

Morag didn't know what to say. She hadn't bargained on this and didn't know how to proceed. It was Shona who stepped in.

"People of Murst," she calmly began, although Morag knew it must have almost killed her to refer to them like that, "I know you've been repressed and giving you the freedom to make your own rules, your own laws, is something the princess will consider when helping you rebuild Murst. It will be a lot of work and it won't happen overnight, so please be patient. For now, our priority must be to free the people from the cages."

"Then what?" squeaked Aldiss, who was jumping up and down excitedly at her side.

"Then...I vote we work together to find food and hold a celebratory feast to mark the freeing of Murst from the tyrant Amergin!" she replied amongst a whole lot of cheering. She glanced around. "Now, where's the cook?"

The cheers were almost deafening as the cook and her son were shoved forward.

"I'll need help," the cook said, twisting a dishcloth nervously in her hands. "I can't just conjure a feast out of nothing all by myself."

"We'll help!" said Aldiss, pushing Bertie forward. "We know magic!"

"It's settled then," said the dragon. "Now we need volunteers to clean up this mess. You...!" She pointed to the lords and ladies, "...get started on clearing up. Giants, find some tables and chairs. We're celebrating!"

It was about this time that Morag suddenly realised someone was missing — someone heavy and gold and magical.

"Henry!" she gasped, her hand flying to the empty space around her neck where the medallion had once been. "I've lost him. I must find him," she said.

"Where did you last see him?" asked Claudine, who was

busy righting a table.

Morag thought. It was all a haze. Then she remembered.

"I was going after Amergin and he used a spell to take Henry from me. The last time I saw him he was flying over the ramparts. He's somewhere outside!" she said, pulling off the rags that covered her clothes. "I need to go and look for him."

"I'll help," the woman offered.

Outside the weather had worsened. Snow was falling like there was a race on to find which flake could reach the ground first. Morag gathered her coat tighter around her body, glad of its warmth, and pulled her hood up to protect her ears from the biting wind. She and Claudine stepped out of the light of the castle gate and paused. Each had a burning torch to help with the search, but it had become so dark that Morag was beginning to despair that their rescue mission would be over before it had even begun. The falling snow spluttered as it fell on the flames.

"Where did you say he went over?" Claudine asked. Morag wasn't sure. She looked up at the castle ramparts — at the tattered rags that were once magnificent banners and the shattered glass of the multi-paned windows — and frowned.

"We were on the roof of the main building which is towards the rear of the castle, so we need to go round the back," she said, heading that way.

"Hold on a minute, Morag," Claudine said and disappeared inside. She returned moments later holding a broadsword, its blade gleaming in the dull light. "In case there are wolves," the woman explained when she saw the puzzled expression on Morag's face. The girl stared at the heavy battle sword and wondered how the elemental elf could carry it so easily, but decided to keep her questions for later... they had a medallion to find.

The two traipsed through the slushy snow that had

gathered around the square castle walls. They walked past the little secret doorway and scooted around the back. It was dark and gloomy and dank there and Morag hoped they would find Henry quickly, but the snow was getting heavier, making it even more difficult to see and she knew it wouldn't be quite so easy. She called his name. Then she paused to listen for a response. There was nothing.

"Henry! Henry!" she said a little louder. "Where are you?"

"Let's look over there," Claudine suggested, pointing to a patch of grass and ferns a little way away.

"Henry! Where are you?" Morag called, holding her torch up as they walked, but still no response.

The pair pushed through the ferns, ignoring the wet of the curling leaves as they brushed against them. Twice Morag slipped on the snow that was now lying half an inch deep on the ground. Then, as she righted herself for a third time, something glinted in the undergrowth.

"Henry," she said with relief, pushing forwards.

Then she stopped.

The thing that had glinted now blinked and moved towards her. Then a low growl rumbled through the forest and Morag froze. The wolf stepped out of the undergrowth, its great yellow eyes glinting like gold in the torchlight. It bared his teeth, growled again and took a step towards her, licking its lips.

"Morag, don't move!" Claudine hissed from somewhere behind her. "If you move it will pounce."

"What should I do?" the terrified girl asked, eyes darting to one side as if that would help her to see her friend behind her.

"Do nothing," Claudine replied, edging closer and holding the sword before her.

The wolf growled all the more, a low rumble that reminded Morag of the sound of the magical Underground.

And, before she could stop herself, she smiled at the memory.

"What are you so happy about?" the wolf snarled.

Morag and Claudine looked at it in astonishment.

"You can talk?" the girl said.

"Of course I can," replied the wolf, curling its black lips and showing off a set of ferocious incisors.

"But you didn't talk before," the girl said, thinking about her last time on the island, when Shona had blasted a pack of hungry wolves with a torrent of fire, burning the whiskers off them and sending them howling into the forest.

"'Before'...when?" the wolf growled. "What are you talking about?"

"When..." the girl began, but was interrupted by a third voice yelling: "When I barbequed every last one of you stinking matted beasties!"

The wolf, which had indeed been one of the pack to feel the wrath of Shona before, began to whimper and whine at the sight of the furious green pigmy dragon.

"I'm sorry," it said, backing away. Morag could see it was trembling. "I had no idea these were your prey. I'll... um...just go now."

And with that, without the sword even being swung at him, the massive creature turned and, tail between legs, ran hell for leather into the darkness of the Deep Dark Woods. Morag and Claudine breathed out their relief as his frightened cries filled the darkness.

"Thank goodness you were here," Morag said, giving Shona the biggest hug she could muster. "I don't know what I would do without you, you are always coming to my rescue," she added.

"And you mine," the dragon replied, gently nuzzling the girl's snow-laden hair. "So have you found Henry yet?"

The girl shook her head.

"Come on, let's look again," said the dragon kindly.

They searched and searched, but still they could find no sign of the medallion.

"Morag, I think it's time..." Shona started to say.

But just as Morag was about to give up she heard a low groaning coming from the far end of the castle wall.

"Shh!" the girl said placing a finger to her lips. "I heard something."

"Oooooooh!" the moaning grew louder. "Ooooooh my head!"

"Henry?" Morag cried, scouring the snow covered ground. She parted ferns, checked under low-lying branches of bushes and had a good look about, but could see nothing.

"Oooooooooh!" he cried again.

"Where are you?" Shona called. She and Claudine joined Morag on her search.

"Over here," he said. "Follow my voice. I'm over here... That's right...A bit closer...Getting hotter...You're hot, hot, hot...Ooh no, you're getting colder...Yes, yes, there you are. I'm here!"

"Where?" they asked, confused and still searching the ground.

"Here!" snapped the medallion. "Hanging from this tree!"

All eyes looked up and sure enough there was Henry dangling like a Christmas decoration from a high branch of an ancient oak.

"Well stop standing there gawping!" he said. "Get me down!"

It was Shona, who at her standing height was the tallest of the three, who tried to get him first. She stretched up and up, but only succeeded in pawing the dangling medallion. He harrumphed as she tried again.

"Stretch a bit higher," he demanded.

"I'm trying, but I just can't quite reach," said the dragon, puffing from the exertion.

"Useless lizard," the medallion muttered under his breath, but Shona heard him.

"I'm trying my best," she growled, pawing him again and sending him swinging, "but if you're going to be like that I've got a good mind to leave you up there."

Morag, who had been watching all of this thoughtfully, suddenly had an idea. She didn't know why she hadn't thought of it before.

"Henry, can't you free yourself?" she said. "I thought you could move about from person to person. Wasn't that how you came to us in the first place?" she asked. "Remember? On the train? When you left the witch Magma and hid yourself under the seat?"

The medallion was silenced.

"Oh, yes, I forgot," he said sheepishly. There was a faint tinkling and Morag was suddenly aware of something heavy in her jacket pocket. She put her hand in and pulled out the medallion.

"Hello," he said with a cheeky smile.

Now it was Shona's turn to harrumph. "Stupid necklace," she muttered, although she was secretly pleased he was safe.

"So," said the medallion as Morag put him round her neck, "tell me what happened? Did you get him? Nasty horrible creature."

As they walked back to the castle to join the festivities inside, Morag told Henry all about how Amergin had been finally vanquished and Shona filled in what had happened in the rest of the castle.

"Claudine and Arrod let me in, but the battle was in full swing by the time we got there," said the dragon, the excitement of being part of it still lighting her eyes. "I still managed to singe a few Girallons though," she added with a chuckle as she pushed open the castle gates and held them aside for Morag and Claudine.

Inside the castle it was all business. People were hurrying back and forth fetching stools and tables, napkins and cutlery. The Great Hall's transformation was underway. Some of the lords and ladies were sweeping up debris, whilst others were righting the tables that had not been damaged and yet more were setting them up. The giants too were busy helping where they could. Some had removed their heavy armour so that they might move about more easily and had stockpiled it in one corner of the room. The armour shone in the warm light of the fire that the cook and Grain had lit at one end of the room. From somewhere, the cook had rustled up a pig and this was cooking over the fire, the dripping fat causing the flames to crackle and pop. As Morag watched this merry scene, she spotted Bertie and Aldiss working together near the thrones. Bertie was pulling various platters of food from his satchel and Aldiss was helping him to carry them to the table. The little rat, eyes glowing, was struggling with a large plate of chicken drumsticks when Morag joined them.

"Here, let me help you," the girl said, and she lifted the plate, Aldiss and all, on to a table. The rat 'wheeeee-ed' as he rose into the air, causing Morag to laugh heartily. She looked around at all the busy people working together and smiled. This was going to be a celebration to remember.

And oh what a feast there was! There was everything that Morag could think of to eat: succulent roast boar and whole roast potatoes for the giants; great dishes of apples and pears; mashed turnip and potatoes to accompany steaming puddings of haggis; three different flavours of hot soup, including the Marnoch Morian purple carrot soup that was her favourite; seven great mounds of chocolate cakes; barbequed spare ribs with hot sauce; crispy bacon and baked beans; a large cheeseboard with oatcakes and more than fifty types of cheese including Murst Blue; swamp sprouts and festering blowfish for the Klapp demons; six huge barrels of island ale and 20 flagons of berry juice brought up from the castle's stores; a plethora of seafood including lobsters, mussels and shark; home-baked bread straight from the cook's kitchen; porridge cream and sugar; and for Shona, one large bowl of pickled onions.

Someone found a fiddle and someone else a bodhran and together they played and sang old Marnoch Mor and Murst folk songs. It was a merry scene and everyone ate like food was going out of fashion. And they kept on eating until they were stuffed. And everyone agreed it had been the best celebratory meal they had ever had.

Sated and sleepy, one by one the lords and ladies, the former slaves and servants, the Klapp demons and the giants went off to bed. Tomorrow would be a new day, a new beginning for them and they each wanted to get as much rest as possible. Morag watched them go.

"We'll need to help them," Bertie said to her. "They'll need assistance to rebuild their society, getting the farms up and running, setting up some sort of government. They'll need to elect a leader and they need proper food. Goodness, there's a lot to do!"

"Yes," she replied, "but don't worry, I'll arrange for help from Marnoch Mor. I'm sure the townspeople will be happy to help."

"What are you going to do about the prisoners?"

"I'll have the Witches, Wizards and Warlocks Convention deal with them."

"And Mephista?"

"She's still to keep her end of the bargain," she answered, thinking about her parents trapped in their pictures.

"But she's not going to get Murst back," he reminded her.

"I know," she replied. *Which means she won't undo the spell that trapped my parents,* she thought unhappily.

Chapter 18

"No," said Mephista as she lazily draped herself over her prison bed.

"What do you mean 'no'?" Morag demanded. "You promised!"

"I said I would break the spell *only* if you returned Murst to me. And you haven't done that," snapped the witch.

"I got rid of Amergin," said the girl, tears pricking the back of her eyes.

"Yes, you did," the witch agreed, "but you haven't returned Murst to *me*...I am no longer its ruler."

"They don't want you back," said Bertie. "They voted and they want to govern themselves."

"Stupid islanders!" Mephista growled. "I was a magnificent ruler, even better than my father, and now they repay me for all my kindnesses by banning me from my own homeland."

"Kindnesses? You were *never* kind!" Aldiss said. He clamped a paw over his mouth as the witch turned her steely gaze on him.

"Who asked for *your* opinion?" she hissed.

They were in Mephista's cell underneath the palace in Marnoch Mor. Despite it being a prison, Morag had ordered that the witch be kept in comfort. The small secure room was packed with cosy chairs, a large bed and a small dressing table at which Mephista took her meals and admired herself in the little mirror that sat on top. The dressing table was heaving under beauty products and hairbrushes, and on it the witch had placed a golden goblet of wine. She reached for it and her delicate white hand closed around the heavy cup. She pulled it to her and lifted it to her lips. She took a sip before speaking again.

"So what's it to be, Morag? Restore Murst to me — and

ensure my place as its ruler — and I will free your parents. Leave things as they are...and poor old Isabella and Nathan remain as oil paintings forever," she said.

"You know I can't give you Murst," Morag sighed as she sat down heavily on a chair. She pursed her lips before she replied, giving herself a little more time to think out her answer. "And I don't think you are in any position to make demands," said the girl.

Mephista smirked.

"If I were you," Morag continued, "and I was about to go before the WWWC for crimes against humans, for the attempted murder of myself and Montgomery and for unleashing into this world a terrifying demon..."

"That last bit was a mistake," said the witch.

"...then I would be doing everything I could to show that I was mending my ways and doing some good."

"For a change," muttered the dodo.

"That is why you should keep your promise to me and release my parents," Morag finished. "If you do, I will speak up on your behalf at your trial."

Mephista snorted derisively.

"Are you threatening me? *Me*? Daughter of Devlish and the greatest witch this world has ever seen?" she said. Although her words were strong, Morag thought she detected a little fear in her voice.

"Call it what you want, Mephista," said Morag, "but the facts are: if you don't free my parents, there will be no-one to defend you in front of the Witches, Wizards and Warlocks Convention and you will be severely punished for what you have done."

"No-one? Don't be silly, I have lots of friends," replied the witch, her voice wavering slightly. "I have lots of powerful, good friends who will speak up for me."

"You have no-one," said the girl. She stood up. "We'll leave now and let you think it over."

Morag was sure she could see a flicker of concern on the witch's face, so she turned and led Bertie and Aldiss to the cell door. She knocked a couple of times and the guard let them out. Without saying another word, and without looking back, the girl, bird and rat left Mephista to her own dark thoughts.

"Do you think she believed you?" Bertie asked as they climbed the stairs to the main part of the palace.

"She'd better," replied the girl, "because everything I said was true and she knows it!"

"What do you want to do now? The trials don't begin for another two hours," the bird asked.

"How about some tea and cakes in the library?" she suggested.

Aldiss squeaked in delight. "Yes please!" he shouted before Bertie could even get a word out.

***

Morag expected Mephista to send for her before the trial began, but no word came from the witch. In front of the blazing library fire, the dodo and rat at her side, Morag ate the fruit scones and tea without any of her normal relish and prayed Mephista would see sense.

An hour passed, then two. And so it was time to go to the court. Heart heavy with the knowledge that her parents might never be free, the girl — a key witness — Bertie and Aldiss pulled on their winter coats and boots and walked out of the palace and across the town square to the town hall.

Shona stood at the huge town hall doors to escort them inside. She gave Morag a wink to reassure her, but Morag did not feel okay. Nervous about standing up in court in front of all the Marnoch Mor inhabitants, devastated that Mephista had gone back on her word and scared of seeing

Kang again, she felt sick and tired and anxious all at once. Her mouth was dry and it felt like a million butterflies were all trying to get out of her gurgling stomach at the same time. She followed the dragon inside.

Montgomery and the Witches, Wizards and Warlocks Convention — the WWWC as it was more commonly referred to — had set up the main committee room as a court. The large oval table they normally sat around in the centre of the room had been moved to one end. There sat the judges: the witch Magma, Arklet the wizard and Zenna the dryad. To their left, seats had been set out for a 12-strong jury and already Morag could see several of the jury members — Marnoch Morians of all shapes and sizes — were taking their seats. There was a witch, two wizards, a satyr, two gnomes, a dodo, three fairies, a unicorn and an elf. They were chatting amiably to each other as they settled down. To the right of the judges was a large metal cage surrounded by giant guards from Murst. Directly in front were a large comfortable-looking armchair and a small vintage table on which sat a little metal tray with a bottle of water and a glass. Rows of seats had been set out in a theatre style about three metres behind the armchair and scores of townspeople were filing in to watch the proceedings.

"What happens now?" Morag asked in a strained voice as the metaphorical butterflies now tried to push their way right up out of her throat.

"You just need to tell the truth," the dragon replied. "Come on, we need to go into the witness-room down the hall and wait to be called."

As Morag turned to walk from the room a dark shape loomed in the corner of her eye and something large swiped down at her. But for the quick thinking of the dragon who yanked her out of the way, Kang's punch would have caught Morag on the head. The dragon growled at the prisoner as his guards, two giants, seized him.

"How could you let that happen?" Shona snarled. "He should be restrained!"

"He was, my lady," said one of the guards, "but he got loose momentarily."

"Don't let it happen again!" she snapped. Then, turning to Morag, she asked, "Are you all right?"

The girl was white-faced.

"Yes," she replied, watching the growling, spitting Girallon being forcibly led into the courtroom.

"I'll get you for what you've done, girl!" he shouted as he was shoved away from her. "You murdered my master! I'll get you!"

"Just ignore him, Morag," said Bertie, putting a protective wing around her. "There's no way he can hurt you now."

"Yeah!" agreed the rat, turning and sticking his tongue out at the now closed door of the courtroom. "And if he tries we're here to protect you."

"Thanks guys," the girl said and forced a smile.

Shona led them down the wooden-panelled corridor to a softly lit room that reminded Morag of pictures she had seen of old-fashioned gentlemen's clubs. The room was filled with leather chairs and little tables; the walls were lined with floor-to-ceiling bookcases full of leather-bound classics; and a log fire roared beneath a beautifully carved wooden mantel, on which sat a little wooden clock.

"There you are!" a voice behind a newspaper said. Montgomery folded the paper neatly and placed it on a nearby table. He smiled. "Come and sit with me and have some hot chocolate. You all look a bit pasty-faced, if you don't mind me saying so!"

As they gathered around him, he continued cheerfully: "I've got marshmallows to toast too. Fancy one?"

Before anyone could answer, the door opened behind Shona and one of the WWWC members entered. Nell, a blue-haired elf, nodded to everyone before saying: "You're being called, Montgomery. You're on first."

For the first time, Morag saw the worry in the wizard's eyes. *He's nervous too*, she thought and suddenly forgot her own fears as she empathised with her friend.

"Good luck," they called as the wizard departed, closing the door behind him.

"Well, it looks like we've got the hot chocolate all to ourselves," said the dragon passing round the cups.

***

It seemed to Morag like Montgomery had been away for hours and hours, but really only an hour-and-a-half passed before Nell stuck her head around the door again and called for *her*. The girl jumped when she heard her name and looked in alarm at her friends.

"You'll be fine," Bertie said kindly. He stuck his beak into his satchel and pulled out a little white handkerchief with the initials MM embroidered in deep pink. "In case you feel the need to sneeze or...or...cry," he explained as he handed Morag the gift.

"Thank you."

"Off you go," Shona said, "the court is waiting. Remember: just tell the truth and you will be all right."

"Yes," replied the girl, steeling herself. She gave them each a hug before following Nell out of the room. The pesky stomach butterflies seemed to have been plaguing her of late and returned once again as she entered the courtroom behind the tall elegant elf. The place was in uproar as she moved towards the witness-chair, but as soon it was realised she was there, the noise quickly died down and the audience watched her with greedy interest. Morag, legs like jelly, stood before the judges and waited to hear what would happen next.

"Are you Morag MacTavish, Son of Nathan, Crown Prince, and are you a princess of Marnoch Mor?" Arklet asked.

"Yes," she replied in a small voice.

"We can't hear you!" someone shouted from the back of the court.

"Order in court!" Arklet said, banging the gavel in his hand. "Please speak up."

"I said 'yes'," said the girl.

"Please be seated," Arklet said. The girl sat.

"Now Miss MacTavish," Magma said, taking over, "you know why you are here today? You've come to give evidence in the trial of Mephista Devlish and Kang, is that correct?"

"Yes." Morag turned towards the cage and saw the evil dark eyes of Kang piercing into her. Beside him, Mephista, red hair gleaming in the light, was smirking.

"Miss MacTavish, can you tell the court what happened on the day of November thirtieth this year?" the judge asked.

And so Morag went through the disappearance of Montgomery and of going after him. She spoke about being captured by the Klapp demon Tanktop and being taken to the dungeon room. She told them about seeing the figure lying there under a blanket and realising that Montgomery was lying nearby, injured and unconscious.

"Then Kang..." she continued.

"For the purposes of the court, can you please point out who you mean?" Zenna said.

"Kang, that's him there!" she replied, pointing to the furious ape gripping the bars of the cage with all four hands. He growled menacingly at her and rattled his cage. "Kang brought a trolley into the room and it was laden with all sorts of things that Mephista...that's the lady there...was going to use for a spell to bring Devlish back."

"She lies! The girl lies!" shouted the ape. "I wasn't even

there!"

"I'm not lying!" Morag retorted.

"Could the defendant please quieten down and stop trying to damage the cage?"

"But she's lying!" roared Kang.

The judge ignored the ape and said: "Please continue."

"Well Mephista used the spell to bring Devlish back, but we found out later that it wasn't Devlish, it was a Mitlock Demon called Amergin using Devlish's body. Kang had meddled with the spell and helped Amergin, not Devlish, to come from wherever he had been imprisoned."

"You're LYING!!" roared Kang and he rattled the bars some more.

"Guards, quieten that creature!" ordered one of the other judges.

But, as the guards leapt into action, Kang suddenly roared angrily and, as he did so, used all four arms to force apart the bars that had been restraining him. He squeezed through the space and rushed at Morag.

Everything seemed to happen in slow motion. As he leapt to rugby-tackle the terrified girl, a bolt of light shot out from somewhere and hit him square on the back. He fell to the ground short of Morag's chair, eyes unblinking, an evil snarl still on his lips and the smell of singed fur rising from him. There was a collective cry of fear in the courtroom and everyone stood to get a better look. Amidst shouting and sobbing and a general cacophony, the three judges banged their gavels furiously, calling for order. Morag stared at the dead four-armed Girallon and then glanced up at the red witch. Mephista was standing in the cage looking very pleased with herself and waving a long thin silver wand at the girl. It was smoking. The witch then slipped through the hole in the cage's bars. She surveyed the chaotic scene, raised her wand and sent a bolt of lightning to the ceiling. It banged loudly as it hit, causing everyone to stop what they were doing.

"That's better," the witch said, having drawn their attention. "I couldn't hear myself think."

"You...*you* did this," Morag said, pointing at the dead ape.

"Yes," she replied with a smile. "He would have killed you if I hadn't." Then she said: "I suppose that makes *me* a heroine!"

"Give me the wand, Mephista," the girl demanded, holding out a hand. The witch hesitated and looked around the courtroom. Three guards were moving towards her. She quickly handed over the wand then folded her arms tightly across her chest. Morag took the wand to the judges.

"Morag, are you all right?" Montgomery, Shona, Bertie and Aldiss were at the open door of the courtroom looking extremely worried.

"Yes," she replied with a shaky smile. "Kang attacked and Mephista stopped him."

Mephista smirked again. Montgomery frowned, opened his mouth to say something else, but was stopped by the witch holding up a slender hand.

"Save your lectures for later, James Montgomery," she said. "Allow me to talk. I think you'll like what I've got to say. I've decided to change my plea," she said, looking directly at Morag, "if the *princess* here will allow it."

To Morag she whispered: "I've decided to accept your offer. Having heard all the evidence, you lot have clearly got it in for me. I'm sure I've not done half the things you said I did. So, if I free your parents and plead guilty, what will happen to me?"

"I don't know," the girl replied truthfully. "It's not for me to say, it's for the court. What do you *want* to happen?"

"Let me go and I will bother you no more," hissed the witch.

"But you did unspeakable things."

"Yes, but under the influence of my father. If you had had such a rotten upbringing as mine, you would have turned out like me as well," Mephista said.

"I *did* have a rotten upbringing," replied the girl crossly, "but *I* turned out all right. Having rubbish parents or guardians is no excuse for being evil. You make your own decisions in life. You could have been good, but you *chose* to be bad."

Mephista pursed her lips and said no more.

Morag had an idea. "Stay here," she said. "I need to talk to the judges and Montgomery."

Chapter 19

Morag, Montgomery and the judges went back to the witness-room to discuss Mephista's future and it was there that she put forward her idea. Montgomery and the others were horrified at the prospect of letting the witch go without — as they saw it — any real punishment, but the girl assured them that Mephista would be punished enough.

"Please say yes," she pleaded, "I promised my parents I'd free them and this is my only chance of keeping that promise."

"I think it could work," said Arklet.

"It would certainly prevent her harming anyone else in the future," said Magma.

"It just doesn't seem a *big enough* punishment," mused Zenna. "She murdered people after all, including that ape half an hour ago. What sort of message will we be sending out if we let her off?"

"But you *won't* be letting her off," said Morag. "She will have to serve a sentence and she'll hate every minute of it, I promise you! Plus it sorts out what should happen to my former guardians, Jermy and Moira. They might have tried to save me from Amergin, but they still need to be punished for everything they did before."

"What do you think, Montgomery?" Magma asked.

The wizard, who up until then had barely said a word, took a deep breath and thought about his answer before speaking.

"I think that if we want to free Nathan and Isabella we really have no choice but to do as Morag suggests," he said. "I know Mephista has done some terrible things, but knowing her as I do I think this is a punishment that she will really feel. I think we should do it."

Morag smiled and before she could stop herself she burst into tears. Montgomery gave her a hug.

"I'm sorry," she said, "I just feel so relieved that this is all nearly over. It's been a terrible few months and all I want now is to get to know my parents properly and live a real family life. Thank you all so much for agreeing to this."

Montgomery gave her a squeeze.

"C'mon," he said, "let's go and break the good news to Mephista."

***

The witch was sitting in the witness-chair scowling at the four guards watching over her. As the doors of the courtroom opened, she sat up and considered the five people walking down the aisle towards her.

"Well?" she demanded. "Have you agreed to my offer?"

Morag looked up at Montgomery and he smiled at her. *You tell her,* he mouthed. So, walking as proudly as she could, Morag approached the witch and gave her a large smile. She nodded.

"Yes..." she said.

Mephista clapped her hands.

"...but there are conditions."

"What conditions?" the witch snarled.

"You will be allowed to go into exile *where* we say and *how* we say on condition that you free my parents from their paintings," said the girl.

Mephista clasped her hands and raised them to her lips as she thought about it.

Come on, accept it, Morag thought, *you don't really have a choice.*

"And where will this exile be? Somewhere without comfort...somewhere like the North Pole?" she asked.

"No, no, you'll still be on mainland Scotland, living in a house with running water and heating," Morag replied.

Mephista pursed her lips. The audience held their collective breaths, waiting for her decision. The witch stood, brushed down her long velvet dress and gave her perfectly shiny hair a flick.

"Okay, I accept," she said dramatically, as if expecting to be cheered for conceding.

There was a huge round of applause, but it wasn't for Mephista. Morag allowed herself a small chuckle of delight.

"Bring me the paintings now, before I change my mind," said the witch, sitting down again and trying to keep her composure. "Might as well get it over with," she muttered.

The paintings of Isabella and Nathan were duly fetched from their room. Morag explained to them what was going to happen as she helped prop them up against the desk behind which the judges had earlier sat. Mephista held out her hand, causing Morag to draw a quizzical expression.

"I need my wand," the witch said patronisingly.

Morag glanced at Montgomery.

"Give it to her," he said. "But Mephista, I must warn you that if you try anything I'll..."

"Oh pooh, Montgomery!" Mephista retorted. "I know the score. I know what will happen. However, I need my wand to undo the spell. I won't try anything." Then seeing the look on Montgomery's face that told her he did not trust her, she added with a sneer: "I promise."

Morag fetched the wand from Bertie — who had been keeping it safe in his satchel — and handed it to the witch. Mephista stroked it as if it were a pet and then with a disgruntled frown got down to work. She closed her eyes and took a deep breath. Muttering as she exhaled, she swooshed the wand through the air, making the shape of an eight lying on its side. The muttering grew louder and black and gold sparks flew from the wand. They hit the two paintings, bathing them in an oddly changing and swirling light. Morag cried out but the witch ignored her and continued with her spell. Her words grew to a loud cry.

"...creatures of darkness, creatures of night, release these two from their prisons...NOW!" cried the witch. With her wand, she threw a ball of white light at the paintings that was so bright everyone watching was forced to shield their eyes. When the light abated, there was a loud gasp. Morag blinked. She couldn't believe her eyes. Standing — unsteadily — before her were two exhausted figures.

"Mum...? Dad...?" the girl said uncertainly.

The light completely cleared and Morag ran into their arms just in time to catch them both as they swooned.

"Help me!" the girl yelled, buckling under their weight. Shona leapt to her rescue, while Mephista just stood and smirked. Montgomery also stepped in to help and together the three placed Isabella on the chair and perched Nathan on the edge of the table.

"What's wrong with them?" Morag asked desperately.

"They've been trapped in those paintings for a decade," Montgomery said. "They're not used to standing up for themselves. Come on, let's get them to the Palace for some rest."

Morag nodded and moved to help her mother stand again.

"What about me?" Mephista wanted to know.

"Oh I'll deal with you soon enough," promised Montgomery as he hoisted Nathan up.

***

It took several days of rest and care for Nathan and Isabella to regain their strength. Morag was on tenterhooks for the whole time. She was almost constantly at their side, fetching drinks, helping them eat and worrying over them.

Four days after Mephista's spell freed them, Nathan and Isabella were finally able to get up and go downstairs to sit in the Palace's winter garden and enjoy the heat of the tropical glasshouse. Morag, overjoyed to have her parents back, sat between them, happy to be part of a real family at last. They were visited that day by Shona, Bertie and Aldiss who were keen to spend some time with their friend. Montgomery also popped in to let them know the latest news.

"James, what *did* happen to Mephista?" Nathan asked his old friend. "We never did get to hear the full story. How was she punished?"

Montgomery smiled and helped himself to a piece of shortbread from a plate proffered by Morag. He winked at the girl before beginning his story.

"Do you want to tell them or shall I?" he asked the girl.

"You tell them," she said, "I only know part of it."

And so the wizard, surrounded by the royal family and their dearest friends, told the astonished gathering of the witch of Murst's fate.

Nathan chuckled as Montgomery finished his explanation. "She'll hate it."

"What a clever idea," said Isabella, giving her daughter another hug.

"Yes it was," replied Montgomery, giving Morag a look of pride. "So what are your plans for tonight Morag? Are you going carolling with the rest of us?"

"Carolling?" Morag asked.

"Yes, we always go carolling on Christmas Eve," replied the wizard.

"Christmas Eve! I had forgotten! Oh no! I've been so busy I haven't bought any presents!" wailed Morag.

"Don't you worry about a thing," Isabella said. "You've already given us the best present we could possibly ask for: being out of those paintings and being with you."

Chapter 20

The woman stood nervously in the hallway of the Palace. She twisted a lock of long dark hair in one hand and glanced up at a picture of her estranged husband.

"You wanted to see me?" the girl said.

The woman smiled. "I've come to say goodbye, Morag," said Claudine. "It's time I went home."

"But...you can't go. What about me? What about Montgomery? I'd hoped you two would make up and..." the girl started.

"Get back together?" the woman suggested. Then she smiled. "No, that's not going to happen."

"Oh!"

Silence descended. Then the woman inhaled loudly.

"Okay, time for me to go. I've been away from home too long," she said, still smiling. "Goodbye Morag. It's been fun."

"Oh Claudine! Please don't go! Please stay and live at the Palace!" the girl said, running up to her and giving her a big hug.

"I can't, Morag. I am an Elemental Elf. I need to be in the countryside. But I *will* come and visit. I promise. And you must visit me."

"Thank you so much for all your help," said the girl through sobs. "We couldn't have done it without you."

Claudine gave the girl a squeeze before releasing her and turning towards the door.

"Claudine, wait!" Montgomery was in the hallway running towards them. "Were you going to leave without saying goodbye?" he asked, hurt.

"I thought it was best," replied the woman, with a hint of sadness.

"No," said Montgomery, "we have some things to talk about."

"But I need to get home. My animals..."

"Then let me accompany you," he suggested, taking hold of one of Claudine's hands. "Marnoch Mor can survive without me for a day or two." He winked at Morag. "We have our royal family back, after all. Morag, will you let everyone know where I've gone?"

"Of course," said the girl happily.

"That's settled then."

"James, are you sure?" Claudine wanted to know.

"Yes, I think it's time we made up, don't you?" He took her hand, brought it to his lips and kissed it. "I've missed you, Claud."

"And I you," she replied.

"We should never have left it so long. I'm sorry."

"Me too."

"Let's go then. We have a lot to talk about."

With a final hug for Morag, the estranged husband and wife walked hand in hand out of the Palace. Morag watched them go, grinning broadly, before rejoining her family and friends in the library where a lively game of Snap was taking place.

***

On the west coast of Scotland, in a small guesthouse overlooking the cold wintry water at the seaside town of Irvine, a red-haired former witch stared out at the dark brooding storm on the horizon. Up to her elbows in soap suds, a dish-scrubber in one hand, she scowled as she remembered her life on an island a day's journey away.

I had servants to do this, she thought as she scrubbed at an oven dish's particularly tough cooked-on morsel. *My hands are going to be ruined! I shouldn't be doing this! I'm Mephista Devlish, daughter of Devlish. My father would be furious if he could see me now. This is all that Morag*

MacTavish's fault! This was her idea!

There was the sound of heavy footsteps on the stairwell in the hallway. Quickly she resumed scrubbing, knowing full well that the witch Tingly — the all-too-clever-no-nonsense new manager of the inn — would be in any minute to check she was working. *I can't believe I've ended up like this...me! Mephista Devlish! This is so humiliating! I just hope no-one I know comes here. That would be too embarrassing.*

The shrill voice of Tingly filtered through from the hallway. "Mephista! Have you not finished those dishes yet?"

Tingly had overseen a makeover the guesthouse. It had been turned into an inn for magical people.

"Nearly done!" Mephista shouted back.

Just then Jermy and Moira came in carrying yet more dirty dishes for the former witch to wash. Both seemed transformed under the watchful eye of Tingly, who had them cleaning the rooms, doing the ironing and washing up, serving the guests' meals, cleaning the toilets...everything staff might be expected to do. Jermy had actually had a proper bath and had shaved. He was wearing a fresh white shirt, black waistcoat, smart trousers and shiny black shoes. His normally greasy hair was clean and had been cut into a neat style. Moira too had been smartened up. She was wearing a black long-sleeved dress with a white frilly apron and a little frilly waitress cap. Her normally mottled legs were swathed in dark tights and on her feet she wore flat black shoes. Her unruly dyed hair had also been tamed, returned to its natural brown and cut into a smart bob. Despite the change to their physical appearances, their nasty characters remained and surfaced as soon as they saw the witch.

"Here's more. And Tingly says you've to hurry up," Moira sneered.

"Yeah, then you can get me and Moira our tea," Jermy added.

Mephista flinched and threw down her dish-scrubber. The suds flew into the air, coating her front, but she didn't seem to notice as she rounded on them. Eyes blazing, she curled her lips and through gritted teeth said: "Let's get one thing straight. I call the shots round here, not you two snivelling little grubs. I'll be finished the dishes when I'm finished and you'll get your own tea. Understand?"

At that moment, Tingly appeared at the door. She was a tall, matronly witch who worked hard and expected the same from everyone else. Her black eyes seemed to glow in the dull light of the kitchen and she drew her wand from her sleeve.

"Is there a reason why you three are standing talking and not working?" She made sure they all saw the wand in her hand.

Moira slid behind Jermy who answered: "No, Miss Tingly."

"Mephista? Are you causing trouble again?"

"No," replied the former witch, returning to her station at the sink.

"No, *Miss Tingly*," the witch corrected.

"No, Miss Tingly," muttered Mephista.

"I can't hear you. Speak up."

"No, Miss Tingly," said a reluctant Mephista. She scowled as the bitter words left her lips.

"Good, well get on with it!" snapped Tingly. To Jermy and Moira, she added: "Well don't just stand there gawping, get working!"

Morag's former guardians scuttled out of the kitchen, closely followed by their new manager. Once she was sure they had gone, Mephista threw the dish-scrubber down again in fury. The splash soaked her as it had before, but she didn't care. *I'll get you for this, Morag MacTavish, you see if I don't. I don't know how I'll do it, but if it takes me till the day I die, I will get you for this!*

She stared out of the window again, anger rising still further in her stomach. As she did so, something matted and dark caught her attention out of the corner of her eye. When she looked properly there was nothing there. She went to the back door, opened it and stared out. There it was again. *No, it couldn't be!* As she stood waiting, something furry, something stinky, something sneaky flew out of the sand dunes and launched itself at her feet. It wrapped its long arms and legs around her as it hugged. The smell of rotting fish wafted up to Mephista's delicate nose, causing it to wrinkle in disgust.

"Mistress, mistress, I've found you at last! They wouldn't tell me where you were and I've searched for days, but now I've found you!"

"How are you, Tanktop?" Mephista asked as she carefully peeled the Klapp demon off.

"I'm very good," he said with a grin that showed off a set of yellowing teeth.

"Well I'm not," said the former witch, her lips twisting into a grimace. "They have me doing menial work here. It's humiliating. I feel so...so...horrible. I'll never smile again."

"Not even when I show you this?" the Klapp demon replied. He presented her with a long silver wand...*her* wand. She grasped it joyfully.

"Where did you get this?" she asked breathlessly. "*How* did you get this? I thought it was locked up in the Palace?

Tanktop shrugged and grinned all the more.

Mephista beamed "Oh who cares where or how you got it! The thing is that you *did* get it and you've brought it to me. Clever, clever Tanktop!" she said. "Oh Morag MacTavish, you'd better watch out because I'm coming to get you!"

Jubilant, Mephista pointed her wand at the mountain

of dishes. "This lot can go for a start," she said, then cast a spell.

Nothing happened.

"What...?" And so she tried again. Still nothing. And so she tried a simple, reliable spell to make the water bubble.

The smirk on Tanktop's face was replaced by a look of horror as the water remained still. He backed into the corner, quivering.

"It doesn't work here!" Mephista shrieked at him, hurling the wand against a large, dirty pan.

Beyond the kitchen door, Tingly rolled her eyes and shook her head. And then chortled quietly to herself. Had Mephista really thought Morag and Montgomery were that stupid?

The End